TH[illegible] WIFE

ASHLEY TAYLOR JACKSON

BLACK SWAN
DIGITAL

First published in 2025
Concept created by Black Swan Digital. Developed by Annie Kenyon.

"We understand how dangerous a mask can be.
We all become what we pretend to be."
Patrick Rothfuss, *The Name of the Wind*

"I almost wish I hadn't gone down that rabbit-hole—and yet
—and
yet—it's rather curious, you know, this sort of life!"_
Lewis Caroll, *Alice's Adventures in Wonderland*

PROLOGUE

They always say fire purifies, but as I stand here, watching this perfect house turn to ash, I feel no closer to clean. The flames rip through the glass walls, spreading like greedy fingers, devouring everything they touch. Heat pulses against my skin, even from this distance. I wish it could burn me too, scrape me raw, strip me down until there's nothing left but something else.

The sun is relentless, its spring warmth thick on my shoulders, pressing down like a weight. It shouldn't be this bright, not today, not now. The sky is a brilliant, cloudless blue, a cruel contrast to the black smoke rising into the air, curling and twisting like it's alive. I can smell the fire from here—sharp, acrid, suffocating—but beneath it, there's the tang of salt from the ocean. The breeze carries it up the hill, teasing me, soft and cool, as if to mock the inferno below.

The sea stretches endlessly beyond the cliff, calm, indifferent. Its surface gleams under the sunlight, the waves rolling in gentle, predictable rhythms. The sight should be soothing, but it only makes the flames more vivid, more violent. The ocean doesn't care about this moment, about what I've done. It doesn't care about him, or the lies, or the damage he left behind. It just keeps moving, endless and eternal, while I stand here, choking on smoke and bitterness.

The house was a masterpiece. All those sharp, clean lines, the endless walls of glass that made it feel like you were always on display. A monument to brilliance, ambition, and control. I used to hate the way it loomed on the cliff, daring the world to challenge it. Now I hate the way it burns, like it's still trying to defy me even as it falls apart.

I press my hands into the rough bark of a tree beside me, grounding myself against my dizziness. My palms sting, raw from the alcohol, my fingers still sticky with the residue. I can feel the matchstick between them, even now. The phantom weight of it, the sharp snap as I struck it, lingers in my mind. I wonder if anyone ever thought I had it in me. If, even for a second, they realised I'd do this.

Probably not. They always thought I was weak. Easy to manipulate. Easy to break. They were wrong.

But I thought this through. Every second of it. Every crack of wood, every shattering pane of glass, every choking breath of smoke—this is mine. My plan. My fire. My story. My script.

The flames surge higher, swallowing what's left of us all, and burying the truth, the deep, dark secrets that were trapped within those walls. A place where I never quite belonged. A place where I was welcome, only as a tourist. A visitor.

That is what people do though, isn't it? Build walls. Walls of glass so thin you'd think you could break through, until you tried and found yourself bleeding.

The fire doesn't care about secrets or walls. It licks at the edges of the structure, consuming it all the same. I watch as the supports give way, the entire east side collapsing in a cascade of sparks and embers. It should feel satisfying, but all I feel is anger —hot, bitter, suffocating.

The sirens are coming now, distant but getting closer.

They're rushing to save something that's already gone. Something that never really existed.

The breeze shifts, carrying smoke up the hill toward me. It stings my eyes and burns my throat, but I don't move. My hair clings to my damp skin, and the heat feels alive, like it's crawling over me. I want to run but I stay because I also want to see it fall. I want to see the last of it crumble into nothing.

The ocean glimmers beyond the smoke, steady and endless and I love the view from here. It reminds you of your place in the world. Small. Insignificant, like just another piece of furniture in a carefully curated life.

My pulse pounds in my ears, and for a moment, I feel lightheaded. The sirens are louder now, the wail cutting through the roar of the flames. I should run, but my legs won't move. The bitterness holds me here, tethered to the destruction, to this moment that I've waited for, that I've constructed.

And then, finally, the house collapses in on itself, a groan of metal and timber giving way. The fire surges one last time, a victorious scream, before it begins to settle.

It's over.

But the weight in my chest doesn't lift. The smoke clings to me, seeps into my skin. The fire may be dying, but I can feel it burning inside me still, devouring the edges of who I used to be. I turn toward the trees, the taste of ash on my tongue, and take a step into the shadows.

I don't look back. I don't need to.

By morning, there will be nothing left of this place. And I will have vanished.

1

Alice Harper glanced at the clock on the gallery wall, her heart sinking at how slowly the hands crept forward. It was only 3:17pm. Still hours to go before she could escape this pristine white cage, a space that felt more like a museum for people than for art. The gallery was eerily silent except for the occasional sound of her boss's designer heels on the polished floor.

She was crouched near the corner of the room, unpacking a shipment of sculptures. Her hands moved mechanically, slicing through layers of bubble wrap with a box cutter. A delicate ceramic dove emerged from the packaging, its pure white glaze catching the gallery's cold, artificial lighting. She knew better than to feel any connection to the pieces—they weren't hers.

Alice shifted uncomfortably, the seams of her polyester black trousers digging into her knees. "Careful with that," a sharp voice called from behind her.

Alice flinched, turning to see her boss looming over her. Naomi Grant was tall and commanding, with perfectly coiffed dark hair and a wardrobe that oozed power and sophistication. She didn't look at Alice—she looked through her, like she was just another piece of gallery furniture.

"Yes, of course," Alice murmured, her voice barely audible. She hated how quiet she sounded, how she always seemed to shrink under Naomi's gaze.

Naomi let out a disapproving hum and crossed her arms. "That's a $10,000 piece. If you drop it, you're paying for it."

Alice's cheeks flushed. "I won't drop it."

"Well, let's hope not," Naomi said with a tight, humourless smile. "By the way, I'll need you to stay late tonight. The client wants the private viewing room set up for tomorrow evening."

Alice's stomach sank. She'd already stayed late twice this week, and she hadn't been paid for the overtime. "I—uh, I had plans tonight," she said hesitantly, though the plans were a quick drink with a friend before heading home to put on an oversized sweatshirt and work on her sketchbook until she fell asleep.

Naomi raised a perfectly arched eyebrow and waved a dismissive hand. "Cancel them. This is more important."

And just like that, Alice's attempt at standing up for herself dissolved into nothing. She turned back to the sculpture, her hands tightening around it. She knew better than to argue. Naomi had a way of making her feel like a child caught doing something wrong, her words slicing through Alice's paper-thin armour with precision.

There had been a time when Alice's life had been painted in bright, hopeful strokes, when the world had seemed like a canvas waiting to be brought to life. Back in her senior year at art school, she had been the kind of person people noticed. Professors had praised her for the raw emotion in her work. She won the department's Rising Star award and had been interviewed for a local arts magazine, her face smiling nervously on the cover alongside one of her abstract paintings.

"You're going to do big things," her favourite professor, Mr Garland, had said during her final critique. "Just don't let the world dull you down."

At the time, Alice had laughed and brushed off the comment, too focused on what lay ahead. She'd been bursting with ideas and ambition, ready to conquer the Seattle art scene. Her first solo show had been small but promising—a few sales, enough to convince her that she could make it work. That she belonged.

But the years after graduation hadn't been as kind as she'd hoped. The jobs she thought would sustain her art—gallery assistant, art teaching assistant, freelance designer—were harder to come by than she'd anticipated.

When her father had passed away unexpectedly, her mother's grief had swallowed the family whole, and Alice had returned home to help pick up the pieces. By the time she came back to Seattle a year later, the momentum she'd built in her career had vanished. Galleries didn't remember her name, her savings had been drained, and she was left scrambling, taking any work she could.

That was how she'd ended up here, in Naomi's gallery, unpacking other people's successes while her own dreams gathered dust in the corners of her small apartment.

When Alice finally left the gallery that evening, the sun was already sinking behind the skyline, casting the streets of Seattle in shades of gold and purple and illuminating the skyline. The weight of the day clung to her like a second skin, her body aching from hours of standing, bending, unpacking. She slung her bag over her shoulder and stepped into the cool air, the faint hum of the city filling her ears.

Her phone buzzed. Clara.

Where are you? I'm at B Bar. You owe me a drink.

Alice smiled faintly and typed back. *On my way.*

Clara had been her friend since college, back when Alice had been full of ambition. Clara had always believed in her more than Alice believed in herself, and lately, Alice had started to wonder if even Clara's faith was running thin. Every time Clara asked about her portfolio Alice would dodge the question, mumbling something about being too busy with work.

The truth was, she hadn't painted anything in months. She tried to draw still, but nothing she produced ever felt good enough.

Her tiny studio apartment was littered with unfinished canvases, each one a reminder of her failure. She'd start something—a streak of bold red, a textured swirl of blue—but before long, the doubt would creep in, whispering. And then the brushes would go down, and she'd find herself paralysed by the weight of her own expectations.

By the time she reached B Bar, Clara was already waiting at a small table near the window, a half-empty glass of wine in front of her. Her blonde hair was pulled into a messy bun, and she waved enthusiastically as Alice walked in.

Clara was cool, unpredictable and if Alice ever admitted it, a bit flaky. Months went by when they didn't speak, despite living in the same city. Alice never knew which version of Clara she was going to get, but she liked her and for some reason, she thought that Clara liked her too.

"About time," Clara said as Alice slid into the seat across from her. "I was starting to think you'd bailed."

"Sorry. Naomi made me stay late again" Alice said, signalling to the bartender to order a glass of whatever was the cheapest wine on the menu.

Clara rolled her eyes and fiddled with her nose piercing. "I don't know why you let her walk all over you. You're way too talented to be stuck in that place."

Alice laughed dryly. "Talented? I haven't painted anything worth looking at in over a year."

"That's because you're too busy working yourself to death for a woman who doesn't appreciate you," Clara shot back. "You need to quit. Get out of there. Focus on your art. She's a bitch. You know it. I know it."

Alice shook her head, lowering her gaze to the scratched tabletop. "It's not that simple. Rent doesn't pay itself, and I don't exactly have a line of buyers waiting for my work."

Clara leaned forward, her voice softening. "You'll never make it if you don't give yourself the opportunity to try. When's the last time you even submitted to a show?"

Alice stared into the distance; her mind drifting before she could stop it. "The last time I really tried, my dad told me I was making the biggest mistake of my life. Maybe he was right."

Clara frowned, setting her glass down with a soft clink. "What are you talking about? Your dad loved you."

"Sure, he loved me," Alice said, her voice tinged with bitterness and lacking the certainty Clara exuded. "But he never understood me. When I got into art school he spent all his time trying to talk me out of it. Kept saying I should just do something practical. Follow in his footsteps."

Clara raised a pierced eyebrow. "You? An accountant?"

Alice laughed, though there was no humour in it. "Can you imagine? Dad thought it was the perfect job. Secure, respectable, reliable. Boring. He said I'd thank him someday if I went into numbers instead of paint. 'A steady paycheck will always love you more than passion ever will'."

"I don't think I've ever heard you talk about this," Clara said with an eyebrow raised. "Did you ever consider it?"

Alice took a sip of her wine, letting the fruity taste linger on her tongue. She didn't know why but tonight she felt she could open up. Sitting in the trendy bar in her cheap work trousers, Alice realised she felt just as out of place as she did at work. "Not really. But he tried so hard to convince me. He even dragged me to his office once to show me what my 'future' could look like. I sat at his desk while he handed me a calculator and one of his spreadsheets, beaming like he'd just handed me the key to the kingdom."

Clara snorted. "That sounds like a nightmare."

"It was." Alice smiled faintly, the memory bittersweet. "But it wasn't just about accounting. Dad grew up with nothing, you know? He worked his ass off to build a stable life for us. He thought being an artist was throwing all that away."

"And you didn't agree." Clara waved at someone on the other side of the bar who she recognised.

Alice shook her head. "I thought he was wrong. I thought if I just worked hard enough, I could prove to him that art wasn't a waste of time. That I could make it. But when he died..." Her voice caught, and she looked down, blinking rapidly. "When he died, I couldn't stop wondering if he'd been right all along."

Clara reached across the table and placed her hand over Alice's, focusing on their conversation properly for the first time. "He wasn't. And you've got nothing to prove, Alice. Not to him, not to anyone. You don't have to live in his shadow forever you know."

Alice forced a smile. "I just wish I could have shown him something, you know? Something that would have made him proud."

"He *was* proud," Clara said firmly. "He just didn't know how to show it. Parents don't always get it right, but that doesn't mean they don't see you, Alice. He saw you."

The words hung between them, fragile and heavy all at once.

Alice swirled the wine in her glass, the liquid catching the dim light of the bar. "Maybe. But it's hard not to think about everything I didn't do. The chances I didn't take."

Clara sat back, her gaze unwavering. "You still have time, Alice. You don't have to let his doubts—or your own—define you."

Alice looked up, meeting Clara's dark eyes. For a moment, she wanted to believe her friend, to cling to the idea that she could still rewrite the story she'd been living. But doubt had a way of sinking its claws into her, telling her that she'd already failed.

"Maybe," Alice said at last, her voice quiet. "But sometimes it feels like I've already missed my chance."

Clara sighed, her frustration visible in the set of her jaw. "You haven't. And I'm going to keep reminding you of that until you believe it. Okay?"

Alice couldn't help but smile, even if it was small. "Okay."

Clara raised her glass, and Alice lifted hers in response. The clink of their glasses was soft, but the sound felt like a tiny spark in Alice's mind. It was something.

And for now, something was enough. Anything was something.

2

The gallery was silent that morning, its sterile white walls absorbing the hum of the city outside. Alice had been alone for hours, her world reduced to the muted sound of the rhythmic tear of bubble wrap as she unpacked artwork. Naomi's orders had been clear: the private viewing room needed to be flawless by tonight. "The client wants everything to be perfect. No mistakes, Alice," she had snapped before disappearing for a meeting. "People like this don't tolerate incompetence."

Now, as Alice carefully adjusted the lighting over the centrepiece sculpture, she couldn't help but feel a familiar knot of tension. It wasn't the work itself that unsettled her—it was the nagging thought that no matter how hard she tried, it would never be enough. Not for Naomi, and certainly not for herself.

The sculpture she was positioning was striking in its simplicity—a polished bronze piece depicting a pair of interlocked hands, their fingers twisting together as if caught between connection and separation. It glowed under the soft lighting, casting intricate patterns on the white pedestal below. Around it, other pieces dotted the room: a sprawling abstract painting alive with fiery reds and blacks, a delicate installation of glass shards suspended from the ceiling like frozen raindrops, and a series of charcoal sketches framed in minimalistic black borders.

The soft chime of the gallery door opening broke her focus. She glanced up, expecting one of the caterers, but instead she saw Aiden Chandler.

He moved into the room with an effortless grace, his tailored navy suit impeccable against the gallery's minimalism. The cut of his jacket emphasized his broad shoulders, and the crisp white shirt beneath complemented the salt-and-pepper streaks in his hair. His angular face was clean-shaven, his jawline sharp enough to carve stone. His dark eyes swept across the space with quiet intensity. There was a magnetic quality about him—a man who didn't just enter a room but claimed it.

Alice's heart stuttered as recognition hit her. She knew his name, his face—practically everyone in Seattle did. Hell, everyone in the country did. Aiden Chandler, tech innovator, billionaire, and philanthropist, had become a near-mythic figure in the city's social circles. But that wasn't why her pulse quickened. It was the shadows behind the headlines that came rushing to the surface, the ones that lingered long after the glossy interviews faded.

His wife, Lydia Chandler, the woman who had vanished a year ago, leaving behind a flurry of unanswered questions and relentless tabloid speculation. No body. No note. Just whispers of foul play and a man who had emerged from the ordeal stoic, untouchable, and—for some—too composed.

Alice swallowed hard as Aiden's gaze landed on her. His presence filled the room.

"You've done a remarkable job with the space," he said, his voice deep, smooth, and disarming.

Alice blinked, startled that he was addressing her directly. "Oh, um, thank you," she said, tucking a stray strand of hair behind her ear. She suddenly became acutely aware of how she must look. Her loose blouse—a faded pale blue colour—was crumpled from hours of moving sculptures, and the black slacks she wore were too snug, cutting into her waist uncomfortably. Even her scuffed suede flats seemed painfully out of place in his presence.

"We're still getting everything ready for tonight," she added, her tone apologetic.

His lips curved into a faint smile, but there was something about it that didn't reach his eyes. "Thoughtful placement," he continued, his gaze drifting to the centrepiece sculpture. "It draws the eye without overwhelming the room."

"You notice details," Alice said before she could stop herself.

Aiden turned back to her, his smile widening ever so slightly. "I've always had an eye for beautiful things."

Electricity hung in the air between them, weighty and ambiguous. Alice wasn't sure if he meant it as a compliment, but the intensity of his attention made her cheeks flush. She glanced down at the clipboard in her hands, suddenly self-conscious. Her fingers toyed with the edge of the paper.

"Are you an artist?" he asked, his tone softening as his eyes examined her from head to toe.

Alice hesitated. It wasn't the first time she'd been asked that question, but something about the way Aiden phrased it—like it wasn't just small talk—made her uncomfortable. "I... used to paint," she admitted, her voice quiet. "But now I work here."

"Why'd you stop?" His question was direct, cutting through the silence like a blade as he moved closer to a piece on the wall, inspecting it with his head at a slight angle.

She opened her mouth to answer but faltered. How could she explain the years of self-doubt, the crushing weight of rejection? Instead, she shrugged, trying to appear indifferent. "Life got in the way."

"Or you let it," Aiden said, his tone neutral but uncomfortably accurate.

Alice's gaze snapped to his, her cheeks still burning. He held her stare, unflinching, as if daring her to argue. But she couldn't. He wasn't wrong.

For a moment, neither of them spoke. The air between them crackled with something unspoken. She felt exposed, as though Aiden could see straight through her to the insecurities she tried so hard to hide.

A sudden burst of laughter from the caterers in the adjoining room shattered the moment. She cleared her throat and focused her attention on the sculpture. "I should... probably finish setting up."

Aiden didn't move. He stood with his hands in his pockets, "It's rare," he said after a pause, "to meet someone who feels out of place in their own life."

Alice fingers paused, hovering over the sculpture. She turned to him slowly, "What makes you think that about me?"

His smile returned. "Just a hunch."

For a moment, she forgot where she was, the gallery around her fading into the background. There was something about him—an intensity, a quiet force—that drew her in. And yet, beneath that polished exterior, she thought she glimpsed something raw, something fractured, something vulnerable.

"I should let you get back to work," Aiden said finally, his tone lighter. "But I'll see you tonight."

As he turned to leave, Alice asked, "You're coming to the viewing?"

He paused, glancing over his shoulder. "Of course. Art is one of the few things worth showing up for. And besides, I am hosting this event."

Alice watched as he disappeared into the main gallery, her

mind racing. Aiden Chandler was magnetic, no question. But there was something else, behind his flawless appearance?

Her thoughts drifted back to the stories about Lydia, the beautiful socialite who had vanished without a trace. The tabloids had painted a sordid picture—accusations, rumours, conspiracy theories—but none of it had stuck. Aiden had emerged from the ordeal unscathed, his empire intact, his reputation untouchable. And yet...

She glanced at the sculpture, its metallic curves gleaming under the gallery lights, and tried to refocus her mind. The day wasn't over, and she still had hours of work ahead of her. But no matter how hard she tried, she couldn't stop thinking about Aiden's eyes on her—sharp, knowing, and just a little too familiar.

3

Alice sat cross-legged on the worn rug in her small, rented apartment, her laptop balanced precariously on the edge of the coffee table. The glow of the screen lit up her pale face as she scrolled through page after page of search results, her curiosity consuming her.

Lydia Chandler.

The name carried a weight, even in the impersonal confines of a search engine. Image after image flooded Alice's screen: Lydia at charity galas, Lydia lounging on impossibly luxurious yachts, Lydia posing effortlessly on cobblestone streets in Europe, all while clad in designer clothes that somehow looked casual. She was beautiful—strikingly so—with sun-kissed skin, honey-blonde waist length hair, and a smile that felt both warm and unattainable. She was the kind of woman other women wanted to be.

Lydia had been a media influencer turned lifestyle mogul. She'd amassed millions of followers who hung on her every word, eager to emulate her "perfect life." Her Instagram feed was a meticulously curated blend of aspirational content: sunrise yoga on tropical beaches, candid laughter over champagne with friends, and thoughtful reflections in captions about "living your truth." But beneath the gloss, something about it felt... hollow. Manufactured.

Alice clicked on an old blog post titled *"Five Steps to the Life You Deserve"* and scanned the text. Lydia was everything Alice wasn't—confident, and wise, all tied up with a beautiful bow. Lydia had been adored, envied, worshipped even. Alice felt like a shadow in comparison, the pale echo of a woman who had set an impossible standard.

Her fingers hovered over the keyboard as she hesitated, then typed a new search: *Lydia Chandler disappearance.*

The details unfurled like a noir thriller. A year ago, Lydia had boarded her yacht and disappeared. Aiden wasn't with her, and the details of why were murky. The yacht had never returned, and neither had Lydia. No distress signal. No wreckage. No body. It was as though the sea had swallowed her whole.

Theories online were endless. Some believed Lydia had been the victim of an accident—rough waters or a faulty engine. Others suggested she had staged her own disappearance, tired of the life she'd created. And then there were the darker corners of the internet, the ones that whispered of foul play, pointing to Aiden as the prime suspect. He had been questioned, of course, but no evidence tied him to her disappearance.

There was something unsettling about a man who seemed so composed in the face of tragedy, whose grief—if it existed—never spilled out in public.

Alice leaned back against the couch. She thought of the man she'd met a few days ago—charming, enigmatic, with eyes that seemed to see straight through her. Was the charm just a mask, hiding something far more malevolent beneath?

Her gaze fell to the corner of the laptop screen. A small ad for a local art fair flickered there, a reminder of the world she'd once been a part of. She'd told herself it was because she didn't have time, but the truth was she'd given up. Her paints sat untouched in the corner of her apartment, the brushes stiff with dried pigment. Now, even picking up a brush felt like a battle she couldn't win.

With her thoughts still entrenched in the mystery of Lydia Chandler's disappearance, she flinched when her phone buzzed. It was a notification from her gallery app. She sighed, closing the laptop with a snap and letting her thoughts drift back to that evening.

The exhibition had been a whirlwind. Alice had spent weeks preparing for it, curating pieces, working overtime to ensure every detail was perfect. She hadn't expected Aiden to walk into her life—his reputation didn't exactly align with the modest charm of the local art scene.

"Alice," he'd said warmly, approaching her after the final guests had filtered out and the gallery lights had dimmed. He'd been standing in the entryway, holding a glass of red wine, a faint smile on his face, the wine staining his lips. "You did an incredible job tonight."

Alice had been too tired to deflect the compliment, merely thanking him with a nod. Her nerves had been jangling from the long evening.

"I'd like to thank you properly," he'd continued, his voice low but smooth. "You've clearly poured your heart into this. How about a drink? My treat."

Aiden had a way of speaking that made her feel as though she were the only person in the room.

Alice had hesitated, unsure if it was appropriate. Aiden was a client of the gallery, after all, someone she was supposed to impress. But then he'd added, almost casually, "I'd also love to hear more about your work. It's clear you're not just a curator—you're an artist."

She felt a rush of blood to her cheeks and the familiar pang of self-doubt twisting in her chest. But there had been something about the way he'd said it, with a sincerity that felt entirely natural.

So, she'd agreed.

They'd walked to a small bar a few blocks away; the kind of place Alice had passed a dozen times but never thought to enter. It was quiet, intimate—just the faint hum of jazz in the background and the occasional clink of glasses. Aiden had ordered a whiskey neat, while Alice, still unsure how to act in his presence, had stuck to a glass of white wine.

As they talked, Aiden had surprised her. He wasn't just the polished, enigmatic man she'd expected; there was an ease to him, a quiet intelligence that made her feel oddly comfortable. He'd asked thoughtful questions about her inspirations, and the struggles of finding her voice as an artist. It was the first time in years that anyone had shown genuine interest in her, and it had left her both exhilarated and unnerved.

She'd bravely shown him some photographs of her work. At one point, Aiden had leaned forward, his elbows resting on the table, his eyes fixed on hers. "You shouldn't let fear hold you back, Alice. Talent like yours—it deserves to be seen."

His words had stayed with her, lingering like an echo long after they'd parted ways that night. And now, as she sat alone in her apartment, her paints still untouched.

Her phone buzzed again, pulling her from her thoughts. It was a message from Aiden.

Aiden: *I have a feeling you have more stories to tell. See you soon.*

Alice stared at the message, her heart racing. She couldn't tell if the unease in her chest was excitement or dread.

She glanced at the clock. It was nearly seven. Aiden would be here in less than two hours.

Alice moved to her closet and stared at the meagre selection of clothes hanging inside. Most of them were variations of the same thing: neutral blouses and plain trousers—gallery-appropriate but far from exciting. She pulled out a navy dress she hadn't worn in over a year and held it up to the mirror. It was simple but flattering, with a cinched waist and a flowing skirt that hit just above the knee. Not exactly glamorous, but it would have to do.

She slipped into the dress and stood before the mirror, smoothing out the fabric. Her reflection stared back at her, and she couldn't help but notice every flaw. Her hair, though freshly washed, refused to sit the way she wanted. Her makeup felt too subtle, too safe. She pressed her hands to her stomach, anxiety knotting tighter with every passing second.

How could she possibly be a match for Aiden Chandler?

Lydia had been luminous, larger than life. She'd moved through the world with the kind of confidence that made people stop and stare. And Alice… well, Alice was quiet, unsure, a woman who had spent years blending into the background.

The thought hung in her mind, bitter and unsettling. She didn't even know Aiden. Not really. And yet, she already felt the weight of expectation. It wasn't fair, but life rarely was.

Alice shook her head, trying to push the thoughts away. Tonight wasn't about Lydia—it was about her. About the strange pull she'd felt toward Aiden, the way his presence had sparked something in her she hadn't felt in years. She wasn't sure if it was excitement or danger, but either way, she couldn't ignore it.

She checked her reflection one last time, adjusting the delicate gold necklace she'd almost forgotten she owned. It had been a gift from her grandmother, a tiny charm shaped like a paintbrush. She'd worn it often during her college days, back when she still believed in herself. Tonight, it felt like a reminder of the person she used to be—and maybe, the person she still could be.

A knock at the door startled her, and her heart leapt into her throat. She glanced at the clock. He was early.

Alice took a deep breath, smoothing her dress one last time before crossing the room. She hesitated for a moment, her hand hovering over the doorknob. Then, with a steadying exhale, she opened it.

Aiden stood in the hallway. His frame backlit by the warm glow of the corridor light. He held a single white rose in his hand. His eyes met hers, and the chemistry she felt was undeniable.

"You look stunning," he said, his voice low and velvety. The sincerity in his tone caught her off guard.

"Thank you," Alice replied, her voice barely above a whisper. She stepped aside, allowing him to enter. As he moved past her, she caught a faint hint of his cologne—warm, rich, with a subtle edge.

Aiden handed her the rose, his fingers brushing hers briefly, and the contact sent a jolt of warmth through her. "I thought this might suit you," he said softly, his gaze lingering on her face.

Alice looked down at the rose. "It's beautiful. Thank you."

He smiled, and for a moment, the world outside her apartment seemed to fade away. "You're nervous," he said.

"A little," Alice admitted, biting her lip.

"Don't be," Aiden said, his voice soothing.

She nodded, meeting his gaze, and allowed herself to

believe, if only for a moment, that maybe, just maybe, she could step into this world.

"Shall we?" he asked, offering her his arm.

Alice hesitated only briefly before taking it. As they stepped out into the night, the cool air brushing against her skin, she couldn't help but feel that this was the start of something exhilarating.

4

The Caribbean sun dipped below the horizon, painting the sky in streaks of peach and crimson as Alice stepped out onto the terrace. The warm breeze carried the faint scent of salt and jasmine, ruffling her hair as she gazed out at the infinity pool, its edge blending seamlessly into the vast expanse of ocean beyond.

Alice still couldn't quite believe she was here, on Moskito in the British Virgin Islands, with Aiden. It had been only two months since their first date, yet her life had transformed. Aiden had pulled her into a romance so intense, so all-consuming, that she sometimes wondered if she was living someone else's life. There was something almost dizzying about the speed of it all.

"Miss Harper," a voice interrupted her thoughts. She turned to see the villa's butler, Ricco, standing at a respectful distance. "Mr. Chandler is ready for you."

She followed Ricco, a large Caribbean man in a tropical shirt, through the villa, her sandals tapping softly against the tiled floor as she walked. The soft glow of lanterns lit the path through the lush grounds, and the sound of waves crashing against the cliffs below created a soothing rhythm.

The past two months raced through her mind as she walked.

Their second date had been surreal. He'd arranged for a private viewing at the most prestigious art gallery in Seattle. Champagne was laid on as well as a violinist. At first, she had been overwhelmed by the gesture. It wasn't at all what she was used to.

They had wandered through the gallery together, discussing the pieces on display and she'd found her comfort zone, a place where she could hold her own and felt at ease. Aiden had surprised her with his keen eye and thoughtful commentary, but it was the way he listened to her that had truly caught her off guard.

Most men she had dated before had only pretended to care about what she thought, offering polite nods while their attention and hands wandered. But Aiden had focused on her, his gaze steady and his responses genuine. When she'd hesitantly mentioned her own struggles with art, he hadn't brushed it aside or offered empty platitudes. Instead, he had asked her questions that dug deeper, making her feel seen in a way she never had.

By the end of the night, she had been terrified. Aiden was different. He had the power to upend the quiet, predictable life she had built for herself. And he had.

In the weeks that followed, Aiden had wasted no time drawing her into his world. Their dates had been a whirlwind of private dinners, romantic, luxury trips, and moments that felt almost cinematic in their perfection. Yet, despite the extravagance of it all, Aiden had a way of making her feel like the most important part of it. He paid attention to the smallest details—what kind of wine she liked, how she preferred her coffee, the way she would instinctively tuck her dark hair behind her ear when she was nervous. And the passion between them... that was unlike anything Alice had ever experienced.

She could still remember the first time they had kissed, the way his hand had cradled her face as though she were something precious. The kiss had started slow, a tentative exploration, but it hadn't stayed that way for long. The fire between them had ignited so quickly, so fiercely, that it had left her breathless. Aiden had a way of touching her that made her feel desired in every sense of the word, his intensity both thrilling and overwhelming.

As Alice stepped into the garden, she stopped in her tracks, her breath catching at the sight before her. A small table was set under a canopy of twinkling string lights, its surface flickering with candles and decorated with a cascade of red roses. She breathed in the scent of the flowers mingled with the fragrant Caribbean air. In the distance, the ocean shimmered under the rising moon, a backdrop so stunning Alice thought she felt the floor move beneath her feet, like a tidal wave had lifted her up into the air and she was floating among the stars.

Aiden stood next to the table, his dark linen shirt ironed to perfection as always, his salt-and-pepper hair catching the soft light. When their eyes met, his lips curved into a smile that sent a rush of heat through Alice's body. He always had that effect on her, no matter how many times she told herself to stay grounded.

"You look beautiful," he said as she approached, his voice low and warm, his dark eyes sweeping over her body with an intensity that made her tingle.

Alice could find no words.

He stepped closer, taking her hand in his. His touch was firm yet gentle. "You inspire me," he said, his eyes locking onto hers. "I want tonight to reflect that."

The dinner unfolded like something out of a dream. The chef, flown in from New York, presented course after course of exquisite dishes that looked more like art than food. But as always, Alice found herself paying more attention to Aiden than to what was on her plate. She had no other choice, when he looked that good.

They talked about everything and nothing, the conversation flowing easily. As the evening wore on.

"Does it ever scare you?" Alice asked softly, swirling the wine in her glass. "How fast this has all happened?"

Aiden leaned back in his chair, studying her with that same penetrating gaze that always made her feel like he could see into her soul. "I think it would scare me more if it didn't feel so... right," he said. "You're not someone I want to take my time with, Alice. You're someone I want to dive into."

His words sent a flush of heat through her, and she looked away. "But what if we're moving too fast?" she murmured. "What if we—"

"Crash?" Aiden finished for her. He leaned forward, his hand covering hers on the table. "Then we crash. But I'd rather do that than play it safe."

Alice's breath hitched as she met his gaze, the intensity in his eyes making her heart race. "You make it sound so simple," she said.

"It is simple," Aiden replied, his voice soft but firm. "When I'm with you, I'm not thinking about the past or the future. I'm just... here."

The vulnerability in his words took her by surprise, and she felt a lump rise in her throat. "I feel the same," she admitted, her voice barely above a whisper.

Aiden smiled, his hand tightening around hers. "Then let's not waste another second."

As the dessert was cleared away, Aiden rose from his seat and moved to her side, pulling a small red velvet box from his pocket. Alice's breath hitched as he knelt before her, his eyes fixed on hers with an intensity that left her dizzy.

"Alice Harper," he said, opening the box to reveal a breathtaking diamond ring, the enormous centre stone reflecting the thousands of stars in the sky above. "Will you marry me?"

The world seemed to stand still. The sound of the waves faded, the flicker of the candles blurred, and all Alice could see was him. Aiden. The man who had swept into her life like a hurricane, turning everything upside down.

Tears welled in her eyes as she nodded, a smile breaking across her face. "Yes," she whispered, her voice and hands trembling. "Yes, I'll marry you."

Aiden's face lit up with rare, genuine joy as he slipped the ring onto her finger before he pulled her into his arms, and the rest of the world seemed to fade away.

Later, as they walked hand in hand through the grounds, the cool breeze brushing against their skin, Alice stopped and turned to him. "Aiden, why me?" she asked, her voice barely audible over the sound of the waves.

Aiden cupped her face in his hands, his thumbs brushing lightly over her cheeks. "Because you make me feel alive, Alice. You see me—not the man everyone else sees, but the man I am. And you make me want to be better."

Alice's heart swelled at his words, and for the first time, she allowed herself to believe that maybe, just maybe, this whirlwind romance was exactly what she deserved. She leaned into him, her lips finding his in a hungry kiss, the passion between them igniting once again under the Caribbean night sky.

. . .

The world had fallen away. There was no sound but the gentle crash of waves against the cliffs below, no light but the soft glow of the moon reflecting off the ocean, and no sensation but the warmth of Aiden's hands as they slid to the small of her back, pulling her closer. Alice melted into him, her hands tangling in the fabric of his shirt as the kiss deepened. It was intoxicating—slow at first, teasing, then consuming, as if he couldn't get enough of her.

Aiden broke away just long enough to look into her eyes, his breath mingling with hers. "You have no idea what you do to me," he murmured, his voice low and rough, sending a shiver through her.

Alice felt her knees weaken. She had never felt this way before—like every inch of her body was alive, humming with electricity, attuned to his every touch. "I think I might have an idea," she replied, her voice trembling with desire.

Aiden chuckled softly, his fingers tracing the line of her mouth. "You're incredible, Alice Harper," he said, his tone reverent. "And I'm not just saying that because you're driving me absolutely crazy right now."

Her cheeks flushed, but she couldn't help the smile that spread across her face. "Good," she whispered.

"Come with me," he said softly, his voice filled with a quiet urgency.

He led her back into the villa, the lanterns casting a warm, golden glow over the polished wood floors. The open-plan space was expansive, yet somehow felt intimate with him by her side. Aiden didn't say a word as he guided her up the spiral staircase to the bedroom.

The suite was as breathtaking as the rest of the villa, with floor-to-ceiling windows that offered an unobstructed view of the ocean. The bed was draped in crisp white linens, and the room was softly illuminated by the moonlight streaming through the glass. But Alice barely noticed any of it; her attention was entirely on Aiden.

The look in his eyes said it all. It was a mix of longing and restraint, a battle between wanting to savour every moment and giving in to the fire that burned between them.

He turned to face her, his hands coming to rest on her hips as he studied her expression. "I'm going to make you feel so special." His lips pressed against her neck as she groaned, his voice gentle but laced with a vulnerability that made her groin ache.

Alice shook her head, her fingers brushing against the stubble on his jaw. "Don't stop," she said, her voice steady.

Aiden's lips curved into a small, almost relieved smile before he leaned down to kiss her again. This time, there was nothing tentative about it. His hands roamed her back, tracing the curves of her body, while hers explored the broad planes of his chest and shoulders. The space between them disappeared as they moved together, each touch igniting a spark.

When his hands found the zipper of her dress, he paused, his eyes searching hers for permission. Alice nodded, her breath hitching as the fabric slid from her shoulders and pooled at her feet. She felt exposed but not self-conscious, not with the way Aiden was looking at her—as if she were a masterpiece he couldn't take his eyes off of.

"You're so beautiful," he murmured, his fingers trailing down her arms. The sincerity in his voice made her chest tighten, and she reached up to pull him closer, her lips finding his in a kiss that was a demand for more.

Time seemed to blur as they came together, the passion between them consuming and overwhelming. Every touch, every whispered word, felt like a promise, a declaration. Aiden was unrelenting in his desire for her, and Alice found herself letting go of every doubt, every insecurity.

As his hand slid between her legs, parting them, Alice held onto his hair, her breath quivering.

Later, they lay tangled together on the bed, the sheets twisted around their bodies as the sound of the waves drifted through the open windows. Alice rested her head on Aiden's chest, listening to the steady rhythm of his heartbeat as his fingers traced lazy circles on her bare shoulder.

"From the moment I met you, I knew I had to have you."

She cupped his face in her hands, her thumbs brushing lightly over his cheeks. "That's because it's right," she said, her voice steady and sure.

"Sometimes, life doesn't wait for you to catch up. Sometimes, it forces you to take a leap, I guess."

Alice's eyes filled with tears, but she didn't try to blink them away. Instead, she leaned in to kiss him, pouring everything she felt into that one simple act. When she pulled back, she rested her forehead against his, her voice barely above a whisper. "You make me feel brave."

Aiden smiled, his arms tightening around her. "That's because you are brave," he said. "And sexy, and clever. I promise, I'll do everything I can to make sure you never forget that."

They stayed like that for what felt like hours, wrapped up in their private intimacy. For the first time in a long time, Alice felt like she was exactly where she was meant to be—not just in Aiden's arms, but in her own life. And as she drifted off to sleep, her fears silenced, she couldn't help but think that maybe, just maybe, she had found something real. Something worth holding on to.

5

The hotel suite buzzed with a frenzied energy, but Alice felt entirely removed from it. Hairdryers roared, makeup brushes clicked against palettes, and assistants zipped around like bees, arranging and rearranging every detail of her bridal look. The air smelled like hairspray and roses, heavy and sweet, and Alice felt suffocated by it all.

She sat in front of the massive mirror, staring at the woman looking back at her. She wondered if the hair cut Aiden had suggested really did suit her after all.

Her reflection was flawless—a porcelain complexion, delicately shadowed eyes, and lips painted a soft, muted pink. Her hair, swept into an elegant updo, shimmered under the golden light of the vanity. She looked every bit the part of the princess bride she was supposed to be. But she didn't feel like one. She felt like a fraud.

The dress, a masterpiece of lace and beadwork, hugged her body in all the right places. The cathedral-length veil draped behind her, spilling across the plush carpet like liquid light. Every detail was perfect—too perfect. It didn't feel like her wedding. It felt like she was playing a role. A role she wasn't sure she could carry off.

In the chaos of the preparations, a hollow ache pulsed in her stomach. It came in waves, every time she glanced toward the door and remembered that her father wouldn't be walking through it.

He had been gone for years now, taken by a sudden heart attack that had left Alice and her family reeling. On days like today, his absence felt like a wound that would never heal.

Alice's mother, Marjorie, of course, had found ways to cope —ways that involved ignoring the loss altogether and redirecting her energy into social manoeuvring. Today, she was in her element, flitting about the suite with a glass of champagne in hand, as she inspected every detail of Alice's look.

"Oh, Alice, this wedding is beyond anything I could have dreamed of," Marjorie gushed, her voice filled with unrestrained excitement. "The Chandlers certainly know how to do things properly. Did you see the floral arrangements? Orchids flown in from Thailand! And the guest list—my goodness, the President is here! Can you imagine? The President!"

Alice forced a smile, though it felt like a grimace. Her mother's enthusiasm was boundless, and entirely focused on the wrong things. "That's... great, Mom," she said quietly.

"Great?" Marjorie spun toward her, her eyes widening in mock horror. "Sweetheart, this is monumental. This wedding is going to be in every magazine. Vogue, Harper's Bazaar—you name it. Can you imagine the photos? You, standing next to Aiden Chandler, the golden couple of the year! You'll be the talk of the town for months!"

Alice's stomach churned at the thought. The idea of being in the spotlight, scrutinized by strangers, made her want to disappear. But her mother didn't notice—she never did.

Marjorie had spent the last few months basking in the glow of Alice's engagement, revelling in the prestige of becoming part of the Chandler family. It was all she could talk about. The grandeur of the wedding, the status it afforded her, the doors it would open.

"You're marrying one of the wealthiest men in the country, darling," Marjorie continued, her voice dripping with awe. "Do you realise what that means? You'll never have to worry about anything ever again. And, oh, the charities we'll be able to support. I've already been networking with some of Aiden's connections—"

"Mom, please stop," Alice said, her voice firmer than she intended. She set her bouquet down on the vanity, her hands trembling slightly. "This isn't your wedding. It's mine."

Marjorie blinked, momentarily thrown off by Alice's tone, before quickly recovering. "Of course, sweetheart," she said, her smile tight. "I just want you to understand how important this is. For both of us."

For both of us. The words struck Alice like a blow. She knew her mother meant well—in her own way—but it was hard not to feel like a pawn in Marjorie's endless pursuit of social validation.

Ever since Alice had brought Aiden home to meet her family, Marjorie had been practically delirious with joy, her eyes lighting up at every mention of his name. She had spent hours bragging to her friends about her future son-in-law, dropping casual hints about his private jet and sprawling estate. And now, on the morning of the wedding, it was clear that Marjorie was far more interested in the spectacle than the significance.

Beth, on the other hand, had been quiet. She sat on the sofa, her phone in hand, watching Alice carefully between swipes on her screen. Alice had always appreciated her sister's steady presence. But today, Beth's watchful gaze made her feel exposed, like a fragile object about to crack.

"This is a lot," Beth murmured, more to herself than anyone else, as she looked around the lavish suite.

Alice glanced at her sister in the mirror, her throat tightening. "It's fine," she said quickly, hoping to shut down the conversation before it started.

Beth leaned forward, her elbows resting on her knees. "No, Alice, it's a lot. Are you sure you're okay? This isn't very you."

"I said I'm fine," Alice snapped, the words sharper than she intended.

Beth leaned back, crossing her arms. "You know you don't have to do this," she said softly. "Not if you're not ready."

Alice let out a shaky breath, her fingers twisting in her lap. She glanced down at the diamond on her left hand, its brilliance almost blinding under the light. Aiden had chosen it himself—a custom design, just like everything else in their life together. And yet, as she stared at the ring, she couldn't help but feel the weight of it pressing against her skin.

"It's not about being ready," Alice said finally, her voice subdued. "It's about stepping up. This is what I agreed to when I said yes."

Beth's expression softened, but her concern didn't fade. "You don't have to be anyone but yourself, you know. And you're sure the age gap isn't a problem?"

"It's only 16 years. It's not like he's over the hill."

"But you're not even thirty yet. You've got your life ahead of you."

Alice smiled faintly, though it didn't reach her eyes. "I wish it were that simple."

As the stylists resumed their work, Alice's mind wandered back to her father. He would have hated this wedding; she thought with a pang of sadness. He had always valued simplicity over spectacle, sincerity over showmanship. When she was younger, he used to tease her about her dreams of a fairytale wedding, telling her that it wasn't the flowers or the dress that mattered—it was the person waiting at the end of the aisle.

He would have liked Aiden, she thought. Aiden's charm, his confidence, his quiet strength—they were all qualities her father would have admired. But it wasn't just admiration that drew Alice to Aiden.

In so many ways, Aiden reminded her of her father: his protectiveness, his ability to make her feel safe, his unwavering certainty about the future.

And maybe that was why she had fallen for him so quickly—because he filled a void she hadn't realised was still there. Aiden wasn't just her partner; he was her anchor. A part of her clung to him, not just out of love, but out of a desperate need to feel grounded in a world that often felt overwhelming.

She thought about the hundreds of guests waiting for her arrival and felt saddened that Clara wouldn't be there.

"Babe, thanks for the invite, this really isn't my scene," she'd said holding out her arms covered with tattoos. "I'm not exactly establishment," she snorted, "and well, fuck it," her tone became serious for a moment, "I'm not exactly sure it suits you either."

When Alice descended the staircase, her heart was heavy with the weight of her doubts. The grand foyer was filled with the quiet hum of activity as guests began to take their seats. The scent of roses lingered in the air, mingling with the faint aroma of polished wood and candle wax.

Aiden stood at the end of the aisle; his gaze fixed on her with an intensity that made her breath catch

As their eyes met, Alice felt a flicker of hope. Maybe, just maybe, this could work. Maybe, with Aiden by her side, she could learn to navigate this world, to embrace the life she had chosen. And maybe, one day, she would feel like she truly belonged in it.

6

The car rolled smoothly up the winding driveway of the Evermere estate, the tyres crunching over the gravel as the house came into view. Alice caught her breath, her eyes widening at the sight of it. She had seen the house before, of course—in photographs—but somehow, it seemed even more imposing now. The sleek, ultra-modern mansion perched on the cliff like a glass-and-steel sentinel, its sharp angles catching the pale morning light. Below, the ocean stretched endlessly, crashing against the jagged rocks with a muted roar.

As the car came to a stop, Alice smoothed the fabric of her dress trying to calm her nerves. She told herself it was just the residual fatigue from their long flight back from the Italian Riviera. The honeymoon had been exquisite, a blur of turquoise waters and sun-drenched villages. But now, returning to reality—or, more accurately, *his* reality—felt like stepping into a foreign world.

The driver opened the door, and Aiden stepped out first, offering Alice his hand. "Welcome home, Mrs. Chandler," he said with a smile.

Alice hesitated for just a second before taking his hand. The title felt strange, like a jacket that didn't fit.

The massive front doors opened, and a tall, severe-looking woman stepped out to greet them. Karen Rivers. Alice recognised her immediately, though the woman's crisp black suit and impeccable posture made her seem even more formidable in person than Alice remembered. Karen had been Aiden's personal assistant for years, and from what Alice understood, she had been deeply involved in every aspect of Lydia's life as well.

Karen a woman in her early sixties, carried herself with grace and a sense of authority that came from years of experience and self-assurance. Her hair, now a soft silver with traces of her original dark blonde, is styled in a sleek chin-length bob that frames her face elegantly. Her skin, though marked with fine lines and deeper wrinkles around her eyes and mouth, has a healthy glow, maintained with care and a subtle application of makeup. Her piercing gray-blue eyes remain sharp and discerning, a defining feature that had only grown more striking with age.

Karen's slender figure shows no signs of frailty, a testament to an active life in service. She wears her age proudly, dressing in a way that is both sophisticated and age-appropriate, favoring timeless, tailored clothing. That day, she wore a sweater in a soft dove gray, layered under a tailored, double-breasted blazer in a charcoal. Her slim trousers are immaculately pressed. On her feet she wore partical, low-heeled black leather ankle boots.

Despite her polished appearance, there's a hint of something unsettling in her demeanor, an air of quiet confidence that makes her presence commanding.

"Welcome back, Mr. Chandler," Karen said, her voice cool and professional as she stepped forward. She glanced briefly at Alice, her expression unreadable. "Mrs. Chandler."

"Thank you, Karen," Aiden replied, his tone easy and familiar. He gestured toward Evermere. "How are things here?"

"Everything is as you left it," Karen said, her gaze flickering to Alice for the briefest moment. "The staff is prepared for Mrs. Chandler's arrival."

Alice smiled politely, though Karen's tone made her feel uncomfortable. It wasn't outright hostile, but there was a sharpness to it, an edge that made Alice feel as though she were being measured—and found wanting.

Aiden didn't seem to notice. He placed a hand on Alice's back and guided her toward the entrance. The doors swung open as they approached, revealing the sprawling interior. It was everything Alice remembered: sleek, minimalist, and impossibly modern. The walls were made of glass, offering uninterrupted views of the grounds and the ocean in the distance, while the floors were a polished concrete so pristine it seemed to gleam. The furniture was sparse but impossibly expensive, each piece a statement in and of itself. It didn't feel like home.

As Alice stepped inside, she couldn't shake the feeling of coldness. Evermere was breathtaking, certainly, but it felt more like a museum than a home. There was no warmth here, no sense of comfort. And as her eyes wandered over the carefully curated decor, she realised why.

Alice glanced at him, forcing a smile. "It's incredible," she said, her voice soft. And it was. The soaring ceilings, the clean lines, the seamless blend of indoor and outdoor spaces—it was an architectural masterpiece. But as her gaze returned to the room, she couldn't help but feel that it wasn't made for someone like her. It was too perfect, too polished, too... Aiden. Too Lydia.

"It should be," Aiden said with a slight smile, gesturing for her to follow him further into the house. "This place has been my project for years. He hesitated for the briefest moment before continuing, "...after I took over the company. I wanted something that reflected the future, something bold and forward-thinking. That is why I called it Evermere."

"It took three years to complete," Aiden continued as they walked. "I worked with some of the best architects in the world. Everything here was custom-designed, down to the smallest detail. The glass was imported from Germany. The furniture is mostly Scandinavian. Even the lighting was designed to mimic the natural progression of the sun throughout the day."

His voice was animated now, his eyes bright with enthusiasm. He spoke of clean energy systems, innovative materials, and seamless integration with the landscape. Alice listened carefully, nodding at the right moments, but the more he spoke, the more out of place she felt.

This house wasn't a home; it was a statement, a symbol of Aiden's power and vision. It reflected everything he had achieved and everything he wanted to represent. And standing there, in the middle of it all, Alice realised how out of place she was.

"It's incredible," she said again, quietly missing the comfort of her small apartment, while wondering if she would ever feel settled in a place like this.

Aiden stopped walking and turned to face her, his brow furrowing. "What's wrong?" he asked, his tone softening.

Alice hesitated, her fingers twisting together. "It's just..." She trailed off, searching for the right words. "It's so much."

Aiden reached out to take her hands in his. "It is," he admitted. "But you'll get used to it. This is your home now, Alice. Evermere is our home."

Our home. The words hung in the air, heavy with expectation. Alice wanted to believe him, wanted to feel like she could make this place hers. But as she glanced around the room again, taking in the sharp angles and pristine surfaces, she couldn't help but feel like a guest in someone else's life.

Lydia's.

Her presence lingered in every corner of the house. The art on the walls, the books on the shelves, the subtle details that spoke to her impeccable taste and meticulous planning. Even the faint scent in the air—something floral and sophisticated—felt like a remnant of her. Alice's chest tightened as she noticed a perfectly arranged stack of coffee table books on the low, glass-topped table. On top of the pile was a hardcover book with Lydia's face on the cover: *Living Beautifully: The Lydia Chandler Guide to Perfection.*

Karen's voice broke through Alice's thoughts. "I've taken the liberty of arranging a tour for Mrs. Chandler later this week, she said, her tone clipped. "So she can familiarise herself with Evermere and the household staff."

Alice took note of how everyone always referred to the house by its name, as it were a person. As it were alive.

"That's thoughtful, Karen," Aiden said, glancing at Alice. "Would you like that?"

Alice nodded quickly, forcing a smile. "Yes, of course. That would be... helpful."

Karen gave a curt nod but said nothing more. She turned to Aiden, her demeanour softening slightly.

"Shall I have the staff bring your luggage to your room?"

"Yes, thank you," Aiden said, his hand still resting lightly on Alice's back. "That'll be all for now."

Karen hesitated, her eyes flicking back to Alice once more before she left. The moment she was gone, Alice exhaled slowly, realising she'd been holding her breath. Aiden turned to her, his expression warm and reassuring.

"Don't mind Karen," he said, as if reading her thoughts. "She can be a bit... intense, but she means well. She's been with me for years. She's practically family."

Alice nodded, though her chest still felt tight. *Family,* she thought.

Aiden led her further into the house, pointing out various features as they went—the state-of-the-art kitchen, the expansive library, the indoor pool. But Alice barely registered his words. Her eyes kept snagging on the traces of Lydia that seemed woven into the very fabric of the building. A collection of perfectly framed photographs hung in one hallway, most of them featuring Lydia at glamorous events, her smile dazzling and confident. In the living room, a sleek console table held a vase of fresh white roses—the same flowers Lydia had been known for always keeping in the house. She same flower Aiden had given her on their second date.

When they reached the master bedroom, Alice's unease deepened. The room was as immaculate as the rest of the building, with floor-to-ceiling windows offering breathtaking views of the ocean. But it was the details that unsettled her—the soft cream throw draped across the foot of the bed, the collection of antique perfume bottles arranged on the vanity, the silk dressing gown hanging in the closet. It was all Lydia. She wondered why these things hadn't been cleared away. Lydia had been gone for nearly eighteen months.

Alice felt a pang of inadequacy as she stepped inside, her fingers brushing the edge of the cream throw. She knew it wasn't fair to compare herself to Lydia, but it was impossible not to. Lydia had been a presence, larger than life, a woman who had cultivated perfection in every aspect of her existence. And now, Alice felt like an intruder, a stand-in for someone that Evermere —and perhaps even the people in it—weren't ready to let go of.

Aiden turned to her. "What do you think?"

Alice hesitated, her eyes darting around the room. She wanted to tell him the truth—that the house felt cold and unwelcoming, that she felt like a ghost wandering through

Lydia's life. But she didn't want to seem ungrateful. He had brought her here, into his life, and she owed it to him to try.

"It's beautiful," she said finally, forcing a smile. "It's... a lot to take in."

Aiden chuckled, pressing a kiss to her forehead. "You'll get used to it. This is your home now, Alice. You can make it your own."

Alice nodded, though deep down, she wasn't sure she believed him. How could she make this place her own when every corner of it seemed to whisper Lydia's name?

As Aiden pulled her into his arms, she rested her head against his chest, letting his warmth wash over her. But even as she closed her eyes, the coldness of Evermere lingered, settling into her bones.

Karen returned a moment later, her low heels echoing on the polished floor as she approached. "The staff has prepared everything for your return," she said crisply. "Mrs. Chandler's wardrobe has been moved into the master suite, and the chef has prepared a welcome dinner for this evening."

"Excellent," Aiden said, his tone brisk as he glanced at Alice. "Chef Laurent is one of the best."

Alice nodded politely, though the mention of a personal chef only added to her sense of unease. This life of luxury and perfection was so far removed from anything she had ever known. Growing up, her family's home had been small and cluttered, filled with mismatched furniture and the scent of her father's cooking. It had been messy and imperfect, but it had felt real. This house, for all its beauty, felt like a carefully constructed illusion.

As Karen disappeared down the hallway, Aiden turned back to Alice, his hand finding the small of her back once more. "Come on," he said, his smile warm. "Let me show you the view from the roof terrace."

Alice followed him without a word, her steps slow and hesitant as they moved through Evermere. The ocean stretched out before them, endless and unyielding, its waves lapping against the cliffs below. It was breathtaking, certainly, but as Alice stared out at the horizon, she felt that she was standing on the edge of something vast and unfamiliar.

Aiden slipped an arm around her shoulders, pulling her close. "It's going to be amazing, Alice," he said softly. "You'll see. You're part of this now."

She nodded, leaning into his embrace, but her thoughts were far away. For Aiden, Evermere was a testament to his vision, his power, his ability to shape the world around him. For Alice, it was a reminder of how much she had to learn, to adapt, to become and Alice couldn't help but wonder if she would ever become the wife he needed her to be. And for a moment she wondered if she even wanted to become that person.

7

The house was silent. Too silent.

Alice wandered the cavernous halls of Evermere, her footsteps muffled by the pristine silk rugs that lined the floors. The endless expanse of glass walls framed a breathtaking view of the ocean, but the building's cold, modern elegance only deepened the ache of loneliness that had settled in her chest since Aiden left for Europe two days ago.

He'd promised it wouldn't be long—a week, perhaps two—but every single day felt like an eternity. Without his steady presence, Evermere felt vast and unwelcoming, each empty room echoing with the weight of its history.

Alice paused in the main living area; her gaze drawn to the sleek, minimalistic furniture arranged with magazine-perfect precision. A low coffee table of smoked glass sat in the centre of the room, its surface holding a few carefully curated books. At first glance, it looked like an ordinary setup, but Alice knew better. These weren't just books—they were *Lydia's* books.

She reached out hesitantly, picking up one of the volumes. The title gleamed in gold: *Living Beautifully: The Lydia Evermere Guide to Perfection.* Lydia's face stared back at Alice from the cover, her smile dazzling, her beautiful honey-blonde hair cascading over her shoulders in soft waves. Alice had seen this image a hundred times before—in the house, online, even in Aiden's office—but it still struck her like a blow.

The book was one of many pieces of Lydia's curated legacy scattered throughout the estate. It wasn't just her books—every room bore her imprint. The art on the walls, the neutral-toned furniture, even the arrangement of fresh white roses in glass vases. It was as if Evermere was a shrine to her, a living monument to her life and accomplishments that only reminded Alice of her own inadequacies.

Alice set the book down and moved to the mantelpiece, where a series of framed photographs caught her eye. She'd noticed them before but had never lingered. Now, she couldn't help herself. One photo showed Lydia and Aiden at a film premiere as Aiden stood beside her in a crisp tuxedo. Another showed them on holiday, Lydia laughing as she leaned against Aiden, her sun-kissed skin glowing against the turquoise sea. They looked impossibly happy, impossibly perfect.

Alice's throat tightened as she stared at the photos. She wanted to look away, but she couldn't.

With a sigh, she turned away and climbed the sweeping staircase to the second floor, her hands trailing along the cool metal railing. The house seemed to grow colder as she ascended, the silence closing in around her. On the landing, she hesitated, her gaze drawn to a door at the end of the hallway.

Lydia's closet.

Something about it felt too personal, too invasive, as if opening that door would be crossing a line. But now, alone in the house, her curiosity got the better of her. She approached slowly, her heart pounding in her chest as she turned the knob and pushed the door open.

The air inside was still. The room was immaculate, just like everything else in Evermere. Rows of designer clothes hung neatly in colour-coordinated order, their soft fabrics shimmering under the overhead lighting. Shelves lined the walls, displaying an array of expensive accessories: handbags, shoes, sunglasses, all perfectly arranged. A glass case in the centre of the room held Lydia's jewellery, each piece glittering like it had been plucked from a fairy tale.

Alice stepped inside, her fingers brushing the edge of a silk blouse. Even the labels on the shelves were handwritten in Lydia's elegant script. It was as if time had frozen here, preserving a piece of her that refused to fade.

Alice's eyes landed on a leather-bound journal resting on one of the shelves. She hesitated, her fingers hovering over it. She knew she shouldn't. It wasn't hers. But something about it called to her. Slowly, she picked it up and flipped through the pages. It wasn't a journal, exactly—it was more of a planner, filled with Lydia's notes and to-do lists. Her handwriting was as flawless as the rest of her, each word written with precision.

Photoshoot 2 PM. Call Karen re: brand sponsorship.

Confirm dinner with Vogue editor.

Order fresh roses for the house.

The notes were mundane, yet they painted a picture of a life meticulously managed, every moment accounted for. Alice set the planner down, a strange mixture of envy and resentment rising in her chest. How could she ever hope to carve out her own space in a house—and a life—so was completely dominated by Lydia's memory?

She left the closet and made her way back downstairs. In the kitchen, she poured herself a glass of water, hoping to sooth her dry throat. She leaned against the counter, her gaze drifting out the window to the cliffside beyond. The ocean was calm today, its surface glinting under the sunlight. It should have been comforting, but it only made her feel more isolated.

Her phone buzzed on the counter, and she picked it up, her heart sinking as she opened Instagram. Another post about Lydia. This one was from a fan account, a throwback photo of Lydia at some glamorous gala. The caption read: *"Lydia Chandler was truly one of a kind. No one could ever replace her. #icon #perfection."*

Alice scrolled through the comments, her stomach twisting as she read the familiar criticisms.

Her replacement is so plain.

Aiden downgraded, let's be real.

Lydia had class. This new wife is just a plain bitch.

Her hand tightened around the phone as she closed the app, her breath coming in shallow gasps. She told herself it didn't matter, that these were just strangers on the internet who knew nothing about her. But the words still cut deep, feeding into the doubts that had been growing inside her since the wedding.

She thought of Aiden, of his promises to help her open her own gallery, to give her the space to pursue her passions. But as she stood here, surrounded by Lydia's lingering presence, she wondered if that space would ever truly be hers—or if she would always be living in someone else's shadow.

The sound of footsteps made her jump, and she turned to see Karen standing in the doorway, her expression as cold and unreadable as ever.

"Is everything all right, Mrs. Chandler?" Karen asked, her tone polite but distant.

Alice nodded quickly, forcing a smile. "Yes, everything's fine. Thank you."

Karen lingered for a moment, her gaze sharp and appraising, before nodding curtly. Alice exhaled slowly, the knot in her chest tightening further.

As she stared out at the ocean once more, a single thought echoed in her mind: *I don't belong here.*

Alice stayed staring out at the ocean as if its vastness could swallow her doubts. But no matter how hard she tried to remain centred, the silence of Evermere seemed to press against her, amplifying every insecure thought.

She moved to the sink, rinsing out her glass, when Karen spoke again, her presence as sharp and deliberate as ever. Alice tensed. Karen didn't rush; she moved like someone who knew she belonged, her every step purposeful, her every glance assessing.

"It must be quite a change for you, adjusting to Evermere." Karen said, her tone clipped but polite.

Alice set the glass down and turned to face her. "It's... different to what I'm used to."

Karen smiled thinly, the kind of smile that didn't reach her eyes. "Yes, it's quite a house. Lydia had such a gift for creating a home that felt..." She paused, searching for the word. "Timeless."

Alice bristled. "It is beautiful. She had excellent taste."

"She did," Karen agreed, her tone softening slightly. She stepped closer, her gaze drifting around the room. "Everything you see here—the decor, the art, even the layout—it's all Lydia. She had such a vision. She never left anything to chance."

Alice didn't respond, unsure of how to navigate this conversation. She shifted awkwardly, her fingers curling around the edge of the counter.

Karen's gaze flicked back to her, sharp and calculating. "It must be... daunting, stepping into her shoes."

Alice felt the words like a slap, though Karen's tone remained even. "I'm not trying to replace her," she said softly. "I just want to build a life with Aiden."

"Of course," Karen said smoothly, though her expression betrayed a hint of scepticism. "But it's not easy, is it? Lydia was..." She sighed, as though the memory of Lydia was too much to put into words. "She was extraordinary. She had this... presence about her, this way of making everything seem effortless."

Alice swallowed hard; her throat tight. "She sounds remarkable."

"Oh, she was," Karen said, her voice taking on a reverent tone. "She was so much more than what people saw online. She was brilliant, ambitious, generous. She gave so much of herself —to her followers, to the people she loved. She wanted everything to be perfect, not for herself, but for others. That's why her disappearance was such a tragedy. A woman like that, gone too soon..." She trailed off, shaking her head as if the thought was too painful to bear.

Alice hesitated, her heart pounding. "It must have been difficult for everyone. Losing her like that."

Karen's eyes darkened slightly, and she leaned against the counter, her posture deceptively casual. "Difficult doesn't even begin to cover it. For Aiden especially. He was devastated, of course. Losing Lydia broke something in him, though he hides it well. He'll never get over it." She paused, her gaze locking onto Alice's.

A chill ran down Alice's spine. "I thought it was an accident," she said carefully. "The yacht went missing, didn't it?"

Karen tilted her head, her expression unreadable. "That's what the reports say. But no wreckage was ever found. No distress signal, no debris. It's as if she and the yacht just vanished into thin air and Lydia with it." She straightened, brushing a non-existent speck of dust from her sleeve. "And Lydia wasn't the type to leave things to chance. She always had a plan. It didn't make sense."

Alice's pulse quickened, a mix of curiosity and unease tightening in her chest. "Do you think... she could still be out there? Somewhere?" The thought horrified her.

Karen's smile returned, faint and knowing. "I think Lydia was far more complicated than most people realise. She had layers, secrets. We all do, after all, don't we?"

Alice didn't know how to respond. She wanted to ask more, to press Karen for details, but the older woman's expression had already shifted, closing off like a door being quietly locked.

Karen glanced at the clock on the wall. "Well, I should get back to work. Evermere requires constant attention." She turned to leave but paused in the doorway, glancing over her shoulder. "I'm sure you'll settle in eventually, Mrs. Chandler. It just takes time. But remember, Lydia set a very high standard." Her eyes gleamed with something Alice couldn't quite place—was it pity? Or something more sinister? "People expect you to live up to it."

With that, Karen disappeared down the hall, leaving Alice alone in the kitchen. The silence returned, heavier than before, and Alice felt the chill of it seep into her bones.

She leaned against the counter, her mind racing. Karen's words echoed in her head, the subtle barbs and insinuations cutting deep.

For the first time, Evermere didn't just feel cold and unwelcoming. It felt haunted—not by ghosts, but by secrets.

8

Aiden's return brought a strange kind of relief. His presence filled the empty spaces, his voice cutting through the heavy silence that had settled over the estate while he was away. Yet, for Alice, it also brought a renewed sense of tension.

She watched him from the corner of the sprawling living room as he spoke with David Steinberg, the estate manager. David was a steadying presence in the household, a man in his late forties with silver hair and a calm, measured way of speaking. He had been kind to Alice from the start, offering her quiet reassurances when she seemed overwhelmed.

"Everything's in order," David said, handing Aiden a leather-bound folder. "The landscaping team has been briefed, and the security upgrades you requested have been completed."

Aiden nodded, flipping through the pages without really looking at them. "Good. "And the gallery?" Alice asked.

"Still under discussion," David replied, glancing briefly at Alice before looking back at Aiden. "The architects are waiting for your final approval on the designs."

Alice's stomach twisted. The gallery—the one Aiden had

promised to help her open—was still nothing more than an idea on paper. She had tried to bring it up a few times, but Aiden always waved it off, saying there were more pressing matters to handle first. She didn't want to push him, but the delay was beginning to irritate her.

Once David left the room, Alice approached cautiously. "Did David say anything?" she asked, trying to sound casual.

Aiden looked up from the folder, his brow furrowing slightly. "Why? About what?"

"About my discussion with him. About Lydia. I was just... curious," Alice mumbled.

Aiden's expression darkened, and he closed the folder with a sharp snap. "Alice, I've told you before—Lydia's life isn't something you need to concern yourself with. Don't go asking questions."

His tone was firm, but there was something else beneath it, something that made Alice feel like a dog being scolded. She bristled, her cheeks flushing. "I wasn't trying to pry. David didn't say anything. In fact he refused to discuss it which is why"

"Enough!" Aiden interrupted, his voice colder now. "David is a good man, but it's not his place—or yours—to dig into the past. Lydia is gone. Let her rest."

The words stung, and Alice took a step back, her throat tightening. She hadn't meant to upset him, but now she felt like she'd crossed an invisible line. "I'm sorry," she murmured.

Aiden sighed, pinching the bridge of his nose. "I don't want to argue about this. You're my wife, Alice. I need you to trust me."

"I do trust you," Alice said quickly, desperate to mend whatever rift she'd inadvertently created.

"Good," he said, his tone softening. "Then let's put this behind us. We have an event to attend tonight, and I need you to focus on that."

Alice nodded, though her chest still felt tight. "What kind of event?"

"A charity gala," Aiden said, releasing her hand. "It's important. There will be people there I need you to meet."

Alice's stomach twisted. She hated these events—the scrutiny, the whispers. But she nodded anyway, forcing a smile. "I'll get ready."

"I've already taken care of that," Aiden said, gesturing toward the staircase. "There's a dress on the bed for you. I think you'll look stunning in it."

His words were meant to be reassuring, but Alice couldn't help feeling a flicker of unease. She climbed the stairs slowly, her footsteps echoing in the uneasy quiet of Evermere. When she reached the master bedroom, she found the dress laid out carefully on the bed, its silk fabric shimmering beneath the soft light. It was breathtaking—a deep crimson gown with a fitted bodice and a flowing skirt that rippled like water. But it wasn't the dress she would have chosen for herself. It was bold, commanding, and completely at odds with her usual more subtle style.

She picked it up, running her fingers over the fabric. It was beautiful. But yet again it didn't feel like her. She glanced at the mirror, imagining herself in the dress, standing beside Aiden as the world watched. Would they see her, or would they only see Lydia's replacement?

Pushing the thought aside, Alice slipped into the dress and stood before the mirror. The gown fit perfectly, its deep colour bringing warmth to her pale skin. She adjusted the straps, pulling the fabric down over her hips, and forced herself to smile. This was what Aiden wanted, and she would do it for him.

As she picked up the stiletto heels he'd left beside the bed, a wave of determination washed over her. She would go to the gala. She would smile and charm the guests. And she would prove—to Aiden, to the world, and to herself—that she could do this.

But Evermere was strange place to settle into. It felt haunted, not by ghosts, but by secrets.

The gala was a spectacle.

The grand ballroom, with its glittering chandeliers and walls of mirrored panels, was packed with influential people. The soft hum of conversation mingled with the gentle strains of a live string quartet, creating an atmosphere of effortless sophistication. Yet to Alice, it felt anything but effortless.

The moment she and Aiden stepped out of the car, they had been met by a barrage of flashing lights and shouting voices. Paparazzi lined the carpeted walkway, their cameras snapping frantically as they called out Aiden's name—and hers, though with far less enthusiasm. Alice clung to Aiden's arm, her smile frozen in place as he led her forward, waving politely to the crowd. She could tell he felt at home in front of the press. She didn't.

Inside, the attention was no less overwhelming. Guests swarmed around Aiden, eager to shake his hand or catch his attention. CEOs, politicians, and celebrities drifted in and out of their orbit, their eyes flicking to Alice with varying degrees of curiosity. Some smiled warmly, but most offered her a thin, assessing look she had come to dread—polite, but loaded with judgment.

"You're doing great," Aiden murmured in her ear as they paused near the bar. His tone was reassuring. She nodded, forcing another smile as she sipped from the champagne flute he had handed her.

The dress he'd chosen clung to her body in all the right ways, its colour drawing more attention than she liked. She caught more than a few people staring at her, their eyes flicking over her as if trying to determine how she measured up. Her nerves buzzed under her skin.

"Alice," Aiden said, pulling her gently toward a cluster of guests near the edge of the room. "There's someone I'd like you to meet."

She followed him, conscious of each step she took in her stilettos, as they approached a tall man with sharp features and a slick suit. His dark hair was thinning, and his plump mouth curled into a practiced smile as they drew near.

"Alice, this is Ian Carlisle," Aiden said, his tone cool but cordial. "He was Lydia's business partner."

Ian's smile widened as he extended a hand to Alice. "Ah, the *new* Mrs. Chandler. It's a pleasure to finally meet you. I've heard so much about you."

Alice took his hand, his grip firm and lingering just a second too long. "It's nice to meet you too, Mr. Carlisle."

"Please, call me Ian," he said smoothly. His gaze flicked to Aiden. "You've done well, Aiden. She's lovely."

Aiden's expression didn't change, but Alice felt the tension in his posture. "Thank you," he said evenly.

Ian turned back to Alice; his eyes gleaming with interest. "It must be quite an adjustment, stepping into this world. Lydia always said it took a strong constitution to navigate it."

Alice's smile faltered, and she glanced at Aiden, hoping for some kind of rescue. But he was already scanning the room, his attention elsewhere. "It's definitely... a challenge," she said, her voice hesitant.

Ian chuckled, the sound low and knowing. "I imagine it is. Lydia, of course, was a natural. She had a way of commanding a room, didn't she, Aiden?"

"She was special," Aiden said curtly, his tone leaving no room for elaboration.

Ian didn't seem to notice—or perhaps he didn't care. He leaned slightly closer to Alice, his voice dropping to a conspiratorial tone. "You know, Lydia and I built something incredible together. She had such vision, such drive. But even she struggled sometimes. It's not all fun and games."

Alice's pulse quickened. "What do you mean?"

Ian's eyes sparkled with something sly, and he glanced at Aiden before continuing. "Oh, just that life in the spotlight comes with its challenges. Relationships, especially, can be... complicated."

Aiden's mouth tightened. "That's enough, Ian."

Ian raised his hands in mock surrender, his smile never wavering. "Of course, of course. I didn't mean to overstep." He turned back to Alice, his gaze lingering a beat too long. "I'm sure you'll settle into it, Mrs. Chandler. You seem... adaptable."

Alice didn't know how to respond, her mind buzzing with his implication. She forced a polite smile as Ian excused himself, his presence leaving a chill behind.

As Ian disappeared into the crowd, Alice's fingers tightened around the stem of the glass flute as she tried to process the conversation. The man had a presence that felt almost predatory, like a shark circling in calm waters. There was something about his smile that made her skin crawl.

"Who the hell does he think he is?" She watched as he brushed his hand against the backside of a famous model standing meters away.

"Don't pay any attention to him," Aiden said quietly, his hand brushing against the small of her back, making her flinch. His voice was steady, but there was an edge to it, a tension that hadn't been there before. "Ian thrives on stirring up drama. He's always been that way."

Alice nodded, but her thoughts were far from settled.

"It doesn't fucking matter what he implies," Aiden continued, his tone sharp. "You don't need to concern yourself with any of that. Let's just focus on tonight."

She nodded again, though the knot in her stomach didn't loosen. Aiden's attitude only strengthened her unease. Ian's comments had been deliberate—of that, she was certain. He had wanted to unsettle her.

Her gaze drifted across the room, searching for Ian. He stood near the edge of the dance floor, a drink in hand as he spoke to a woman in an orange gown. His posture was relaxed, his smile charming, but Alice couldn't shake the feeling that he was watching her even as he laughed at something the woman said.

"Who *is* he, really?" Alice asked, her voice low.

Aiden followed her gaze, his lips tightening again. "Ian was one of Lydia's closest collaborators. He helped her launch her brand, secure partnerships, expand her reach. He was... indispensable to her success."

There was something in Aiden's tone that made Alice pause. "You don't like him," she said, more a statement than a question. "Do you?"

Aiden hesitated. "It's not about liking him. Ian is—was—a necessary part of Lydia's life. He's clever, and he knows how to get under people's skin."

Alice frowned, her unease growing. "Why would Lydia work with someone like that?"

"Because she thought she needed him," Aiden said, his voice tight. "And maybe she did. But Ian always had his own agenda."

As the evening wore on, Alice couldn't shake the feeling of being watched. Even as she and Aiden moved through the crowd, exchanging pleasantries and making polite conversation, she felt the weight of Ian's gaze lingering on her. It wasn't overt—he was too skilled for that—but she caught him glancing her way more than once, his expression unsettling.

Alice glanced at Aiden, his profile calm and composed as he greeted another guest. He was so good at this—at navigating these events, at maintaining the sculptured image. But beneath the surface, she knew that there were cracks in the foundation. And she was beginning to wonder how deep they went.

Later in the evening, Alice found herself alone for the first time since they had arrived. Aiden had been pulled into a conversation with a group of investors, and she had excused herself to get some air. She stood near the edge of the ballroom as she watched the crowd.

"Feeling like a duck out of water?"

Alice stiffened at the sound of Ian's voice. She turned to find him standing beside her, his smile as smooth as ever. "A little," she admitted, though she immediately regretted the honesty.

"It's a lot to take in, isn't it?" he said, his tone almost sympathetic. "This world can be... unforgiving."

Alice met his gaze, her nerves buzzing. "I'll manage."

Ian chuckled, the sound low and knowing. "I'm sure you will. But if you ever need advice—someone who understands what you're going through—I hope you'll consider me a friend. I'm very good to my friends." He said looking her up and down, undressing her with his eyes.

Alice forced a polite smile. "Thank you, Ian. That's kind of you, but Aiden takes care of all my... needs."

His smile widened, but there was something menacing about it, something that made Alice want to run away. "The pleasure is mine, Mrs. Chandler," he said, his tone laced with something she couldn't quite place.

And with that, he disappeared back into the crowd, leaving Alice standing alone. As the music swelled and the room spun around her, she couldn't help but wonder what kind of life she had stepped into and whether she really had the stomach for people like Ian Carlisle.

9

The first rays of morning light streamed through the glass walls of the bedroom, painting the room in hues of soft gold and pale pink. Alice stirred beneath the silk sheets; the warmth of Aiden's body pressed against her back. She felt his arm draped over her waist, his fingers brushing the bare skin of her hip where her nightgown had ridden up in the night.

For a moment, she stayed still, letting herself savour the quiet intimacy of the moment. The steady rhythm of his breathing, the faint scent of his cologne lingering on the pillow—these were the moments she treasured most, the ones that reminded her why she was there.

Aiden stirred behind her, his arm tightening slightly around her waist. "Morning," he murmured, his voice low and rough with sleep.

Alice smiled faintly; her eyes still closed. "Morning."

He shifted, pressing a lazy kiss to her shoulder. His lips were warm, and the gentle scrape of his stubble sent a shiver through her. "You were restless last night," he said softly, his hand trailing up her side, his fingers grazing the curve of her ribs.

"Was I?" She turned onto her back to face him, his hair

slightly tousled. In the morning light, he looked less like the polished, commanding man who moved through the world with such authority and more like the vulnerable one she wanted him to be.

"You were," he said, a small smile playing on his lips. "Something on your mind?"

Alice hesitated, her fingers brushing against his lips playfully. Her insecurities felt too heavy to put into words. "I'm fine."

Aiden studied her for a moment. "You worry too much," he said, his hand slipping beneath the sheets to rest on her thigh.

Alice nodded, her breath catching as his hand began to move, tracing slow, deliberate circles against her skin. He leaned down, capturing her lips in a kiss that was soft at first, then deeper, more insistent. His weight shifted, and she let herself sink into the mattress, her hands tangling in his hair as his body pressed against hers.

His mouth trailed from her lips to her neck, his breath hot against her skin. Alice arched beneath him, her hands sliding over the smooth expanse of his back, pulling him into her.

"You're beautiful," he murmured against her collarbone, his voice thick with something she couldn't quite name. "So fucking beautiful."

Alice closed her eyes, letting herself get lost in him. The feel of his hands, his lips, the way he murmured her name, intoxicating. In moments like these, she could almost forget the ever-present shadow of Lydia, and the doubts that circled like vultures.

When it was over, Aiden rolled onto his side, pulling her against his chest. Alice rested her head on his shoulder, her fingers tracing lazy patterns over his skin. For a while, they lay in comfortable silence, the only sound the distant waves.

Eventually, Aiden stirred, pressing a kiss to the top of her head. "I have to get going," his voice breaking the spell of the morning.

Alice sighed, the warmth of his body already beginning to fade as he sat up and swung his legs over the edge of the bed. She watched as he reached for his clothes, his movements quick and efficient. He had a way of switching gears so seamlessly, slipping from the role of her lover to the commanding businessman the world knew him as.

Aiden buttoned his shirt, glancing at her over his shoulder. "We have a dinner with Ian tonight," he said, his tone casual. "I'll be back late, but don't worry about anything. Just be ready."

Alice nodded, sitting up as she clutched the sheet to her chest. "I'll see you tonight, then."

He crossed the room and leaned down, brushing a final kiss against her lips. "You'll be perfect," he said with a small smile. And then he was gone, leaving her alone in the vast, echoing silence of a house that still didn't feel like home.

~

By the time evening arrived, Alice was on edge. She had changed into a sleek black dress Aiden has asked her to wear, the fabric clinging to her figure that made her feel both exposed and unsteady. She stood in front of the mirror, adjusting the delicate diamond necklace Aiden had given her as a gift on their wedding day, and tried to summon some semblance of confidence.

The sound of the doorbell echoed through Evermere. Alice descended the staircase to find Ian already making himself at home in the living room. He was holding a glass of whiskey, his posture relaxed as he surveyed the room with an air of practiced ease.

"Ah, Alice," he said smoothly, standing as she approached.

"You look lovely, as always." His familiarly made her feel instantly uncomfortable.

"Thank you," Alice said, her voice tight. "Make yourself at home."

"I will," Ian replied, his eyes glinting with something unreadable.

Alice's smile faltered, but before she could respond, Karen appeared in the doorway, her expression as composed as ever. She carried a tray with a bottle of wine and two glasses, which she set down on the coffee table with precision.

"Mrs. Chandler," Karen said, her tone polite but cool. "I trust everything is to your liking?"

"Yes, thank you," Alice replied pouring herself a glass of wine.

Karen lingered, her gaze flicking between Alice and Ian. "Lydia always loved hosting dinners like this," she said, her voice tinged with nostalgia as she served the food and drinks.

Ian chuckled, swirling his whiskey. "Indeed. Lydia was one of a kind. But Aiden has always had a way of picking women with... potential."

The words were a knife, their edges dulled only slightly by the false smile on Ian's face.

"Thank you, Ian. That's very kind of you."

Aiden entered the room, his presence commanding as always. He moved to Alice's side, placing a reassuring hand on her back as he often did. "Ian, Karen," he said, his tone firm. "Let's keep tonight focused on the future, shall we?"

Karen inclined her head, though her expression remained impassive. "Of course, Mr. Chandler."

Ian smirked, raising his glass in a mock toast. "To the future, then."

. . .

Dinner was a strained affair. The dining room, with its floor-to-ceiling windows overlooking the view. The table, set with crystal glasses and silver chargers, reminded her of the show she was expected to put on.

The conversation started politely enough—discussions of recent business ventures, charitable events, and the state of the economy. But it didn't take long for the subtle barbs to begin.

"So, Alice," Ian said, setting his wine glass down and fixing her with a smile that didn't quite reach his eyes. "How are you finding married life? Adjusting well, I hope?"

Alice nodded, her fingers tightening around her fork. "It's been wonderful, thank you."

"Wonderful," Ian repeated, drawing the word out as though testing its weight. "That's good to hear. Of course, it must be quite a change for you. Lydia always said it was... an acquired taste."

Alice's stomach twisted. "I'm sure it's an adjustment for anyone," she said carefully, glancing at Aiden for support. But he was focused on his plate, his expression unreadable. "Not everyone craves the finer things in life." She instantly regretted the comment as Aiden glared at her.

Karen, who had been quiet until now, waiting for further requests or instructions, stepped forward slightly. "It is an adjustment," she said, her tone smooth but pointed. "It demands a certain level of poise, of confidence. Mrs Chandler understood that. She had a way of putting people at ease, of making everything seem effortless. It's not something you can teach." A look Alice couldn't decipher passed between Ian and Karen, but Aiden didn't seem to notice.

"Lydia was extraordinary, a one off." Ian agreed, his gaze flicking back to Alice. "But I'm sure you'll find your own way, Alice. In time."

The words felt like a backhanded compliment, and Alice

struggled to keep her composure. "Thank you," she said quietly hoping Aiden would step in.

Karen smiled thinly. "Aiden has always had a gift for recognising potential. He must see something in you, Alice. Something... special."

The implication hung heavy in the air, and Alice felt her cheeks burn. Before she could respond, Aiden spoke, his voice firm but calm. "Alice is exactly where she belongs."

Karen inclined her head, her expression unreadable. "Of course." She excused herself and left the dining room.

The conversation shifted then, but the tension remained. Ian launched into a story about a recent business deal, his voice dripping with self-satisfaction as he detailed the negotiations. Ian and Aiden spoke with the ease of people who had been part of this world for years, their words laced with an unspoken code that Alice struggled to follow.

At one point, Ian turned back to Alice, his eyes gleaming with curiosity. "Do you have any plans to get involved with Aiden's work?" he asked. "Lydia was always so hands-on. She had such a brilliant mind for strategy."

Alice hesitated, unsure how to respond. "I'm still figuring out where I can contribute," she said. "Aiden's work is... impressive but technology isn't really my area."

Ian chuckled, his smile widening. "That's an understatement." His cutting remark was shameless. "But don't worry—Aiden's a patient man."

Alice's grip on her fork tightened, but she forced herself to smile. "I'm sure I'll find my footing."

"I have no doubt," Ian said smoothly, though there was a glint of amusement in his eyes that made her want to punch him.

. . .

By the time dessert was served—a delicate parfait accompanied by vintage port—Alice's nerves were frayed. The pressure of the evening weighed heavy on her, every comment and glance reinforcing the feeling that she was out of her depth. Aiden, sensing her discomfort, placed a hand over hers beneath the table.

"You're doing fine," he whispered, his voice low enough that only she could hear.

But fine wasn't enough. As the evening wore on, Alice felt like she was being tested—and failing. She didn't understand why Aiden tolerated this man and why he was allowed to speak to her like she was dirt.

When the dinner finally ended and their guest left, Alice retreated to the bedroom, her chest tight with frustration and hurt. Aiden joined her a few minutes later, his expression unreadable as he loosened his tie.

"Alice," he said softly, sitting beside her on the edge of the bed. "You can't let people get to you. I need you to be strong."

Alice nodded, though the knot in her chest didn't loosen. "I just... I don't know how to compete with her, Aiden. Everyone loved her so much. I feel like a guest in my own life."

"You're not competing with her," Aiden said firmly. He tilted her chin up, forcing her to meet his gaze. "You are my wife now."

But as he kissed her, his lips insistent against hers, Alice couldn't help but wonder if it was really that simple—or if Lydia would always be there between them.

10

The quiet hum of Aiden's voice filtered through the thick wooden door of his office. It had been like this for days— him retreating into his work, spending hours in meetings and on calls while Alice drifted aimlessly through the sprawling grounds of Evermere. The warmth that had defined their early days together was slipping away, replaced by a cold professionalism.

She stood outside the door, hesitating, her hand hovering just above the brass handle. They hadn't spoken properly in days, their conversations reduced to passing comments about schedules and dinner plans. It wasn't the life she had imagined when they got engaged. The promise of starting a gallery, of pursuing her passion for art, had been her anchor through the whirlwind of their relationship. But now, that promise felt like a distant memory.

Taking a deep breath, Alice pushed the door open and stepped inside. Aiden was at his desk, surrounded by sleek monitors and piles of documents. He barely glanced up as she entered, his fingers flying over the keyboard.

"Aiden," she began softly, her voice almost hesitant. "Can we talk?"

He sighed, leaning back in his chair as he removed his glasses. "I'm in the middle of something, Alice. Can it wait?"

"No, it can't," she said, surprising herself with the firmness in her tone. She crossed the room and sat in one of the chairs opposite his desk, her hands clasped tightly in her lap. "We need to talk about the gallery."

Aiden rubbed his temples, his expression weary. "Alice, we've discussed this—"

"No, we haven't," she interrupted, her voice sharper now. "You keep brushing it off, but you promised me, Aiden. You said you'd help me open my own gallery. You said it would be my project, my chance to build something."

He looked at her then, his gaze sharp but unreadable. "And I meant it. But things have changed."

"Changed how?" Alice asked, her voice rising slightly. "You haven't even explained—"

"Alice," he said, cutting her off, his tone firm. "Do you know how much fucking scrutiny we're under? Every decision we make, every move *you* make, is watched and analysed. The press is already circling, and if you open a gallery, it's only going to invite more attention."

Alice's face twisted. "Why are we letting them dictate how we live? This is about me, Aiden. About what I need. I can't just sit around here all day, feeling like a guest in *your* house. I need this. I need something that's mine. I need a life of my own."

Aiden's jaw tightened, and his voice turned colder. "Being my wife *is* something, Alice. That should be enough."

The words hit her like a physical blow, and for a moment, she couldn't speak, her nails digging into her palms. "Enough for who?" she whispered, her throat tightening. "For you? For the press? For those vile social media vultures? What about me, Aiden? What about what I want?"

Aiden leaned forward, his elbows resting on the desk. "Alice, this life isn't easy. There are expectations, pressures you don't fully understand yet. I'm trying to protect you from that."

"Protect me?" she said, her voice trembling with anger. "Or control me?"

Aiden's face hardened, and he stood, towering over her. "You're blowing this out of proportion. We'll revisit the gallery later. Trust me. I know what's best for you."

"Trust you?" Alice's voice cracked, a mix of disbelief and frustration spilling out. "I trusted you when you said we'd build something together. When you said you believed in me. But now it feels like all you care about is how I look in the tabloids or whether I'm smiling enough at your parties. I'm not your child. I'm your fucking wife."

"That's not fair," Aiden snapped, his voice rising and his fists clenching. "Don't you think I have enough on my plate already? Do you think I don't want you to be fucking happy? This isn't about just you, Alice. It's about me too. It's about *us*."

Alice recoiled, her breath catching in her throat. "Us?" she repeated, her voice barely above a whisper. "That's what this is about, isn't it? It's not about protecting me. It's about making sure I don't tarnish your perfect image."

Aiden's closed his eyes and for a moment, he didn't respond. When he finally spoke, his tone was cold and measured. "You're overreacting."

"No, I'm not," Alice said, standing now, her heart pounding in her chest. "I gave up everything for you, Aiden. My life, my independence, my dreams. And all I've asked for is this one thing—a chance to have something that's mine. But instead, you keep shutting me out, making decisions for me like I'm some kind of accessory. I'm not a doll you can dress up and parade. I'm not Lydia."

Aiden's eyes narrowed, and the tension in the room became almost unbearable. "No," he said through gritted teeth, "you're not." The words felt like a slap across her face. "This is what you signed up for, Alice," he said evenly. "And if you're struggling to keep up, maybe you need to take a hard look at yourself."

Alice felt tears prick at the corners of her eyes. She swallowed hard, refusing to let him see her cry. "Maybe I do," she said quietly, her voice trembling. "Because this... this isn't what I thought it would be and I'm not sure you're the man I thought you were."

Aiden's expression flickered for a moment, a brief flash of something that might have been regret. But it was gone as quickly as it had appeared, replaced by the same cool detachment he had been wearing for days. "Grow up," he said, turning back to his desk. "Right now, I have work to do."

Alice stood there for a moment, her chest tight with anger and hurt. She wanted to scream, to swear, to throw something, to demand that he look at her and really *see* her. But instead, she turned and walked out of the office, the door slamming shut behind her.

As she made her way down the hall, Alice felt a crushing weight settle over her. She had always known that marrying Aiden would come with some pressure, but she had never expected to feel so small, so powerless.

She wondered if the future Aiden had promised her was nothing more than an illusion, a gilded cage built to keep her exactly where he wanted her.

Alice went into the kitchen where Karen was overseeing the staff.

The older woman glanced up; her ice blue eyes unreadable.

"Mrs. Chandler," she said, her tone as crisp as ever. "Is everything all right?"

"No," Alice admitted, sinking into one of the chairs at the breakfast bar. "I don't think it is."

Karen waved at the staff dismissively, folding her hands neatly in front of her. "What seems to be the problem?"

Alice hesitated, unsure how much she should say. But the words spilled out anyway, in a rush of infuriation. "It's Aiden. He doesn't want me to open the gallery. He thinks... he thinks being his wife should be enough."

Karen tilted her head slightly. "And it isn't?"

Alice looked away, her voice barely above a whisper. "I don't know. I feel so... trapped here."

Karen sighed softly, as though Alice's words were both predictable and tiresome. "Mrs. Chandler," she said, her voice carrying an edge of condescension. "You're married to one of the most powerful men in the country. Do you realise what people would give to be in your position? You have a beautiful home, wealth, influence. Perhaps it's time to focus on appreciating what you have."

Alice's cheeks flushed, a mix of embarrassment and anger rising within her. "That's not the point. I'm not ungrateful, Karen. I just... I want to feel like I matter."

Karen's eyes sharpened, her tone turning cold. "Your role, Mrs. Chandler, is to support Aiden. To make his life easier. Lydia understood that. She knew how to play her part."

Alice flinched at the mention of Lydia, the name cutting through her like a blade. "I am not Lydia," she said feeling deflated.

"No," Karen agreed, her voice soft but laced with something Alice couldn't quite place. "You're not."

The words hung in the air, heavy with implication. Karen

turned away, leaving Alice alone in the kitchen with a hollow ache in her chest.

For a moment, she just sat there, staring at the empty room around her. Then, slowly, she rose and made her way back to the bedroom. She paused by the window, staring out at the vast expanse of ocean.

She didn't know how long she stood there, but when she finally turned away, her resolve hardened. The honeymoon was well and truly over and now she had the rest of her marriage to navigate.

If Aiden wanted her to stay quiet and play the perfect wife, she would—for now.

11

Evermere was too quiet. Too vast. Too alive.

Alice sat curled on the cream-colored sofa in the living room, staring at the wide expanse of glass that revealed the ocean beyond. The waves rolled in steadily, rhythmic crashes against the cliffs below, their constancy doing little to soothe her nerves. She had planned to spend the day reading and sketching—anything to distract herself—but she couldn't shake the feeling that she wasn't alone.

It wasn't just the emptiness of the house or the absence of Aiden, who had spent more and more time locked away in his office or away on business. It was the glitches. At least, that's what Aiden called them.

The first had been small—lights flickering on and off, the smart thermostat suddenly switching the temperature from comfortable to freezing. But then the screens started behaving oddly. It had begun a few days ago when Alice passed the main hallway, and one of the screens embedded in the wall flickered to life, showing a slideshow of photos she hadn't activated.

At first, she had thought they were Aiden's—memories of

vacations or business trips. But the images weren't Aiden's. They were Lydia's.

The screen had shown Lydia laughing on a yacht, her blonde hair blowing in the wind. Lydia on a red carpet, her hand resting on Aiden's arm as they posed for the cameras. Lydia in the kitchen of Evermere, looking radiant as she pulled a tray of cookies from the oven. Lydia at a photoshoot.

Lydia. Lydia. Lydia.

"Stop," Alice had said, her voice shaking.

The screen had gone dark immediately, the smart system reacting to her order. She'd laughed nervously, brushing it off as some strange technical hiccup. But the incidents didn't stop. If anything, they grew worse.

This morning, she had woken to find the bedroom mirror projecting one of Lydia's old videos—a cheery vlog about curating the perfect wardrobe. Lydia's voice had filled the room, too loud, too real, as if she were still there. The mirror had ignored Alice's commands to turn off until she unplugged the device entirely.

Now, as she sat on the sofa, her unease deepened. She set her book down and glanced around the room, her gaze snagging on the built-in bookshelf across from her. Something was off. She stood and walked over, her fingers brushing the spines of the books. Her sketchbook, which she had left on the coffee table the night before, was now tucked neatly onto the shelf.

"Did I put this here?"

Her phone buzzed on the coffee table, and she snatched it up, grateful for the distraction. It was an email notification—from her own account. Frowning, she opened it. The subject line read: *Event Proposal: Honouring Lydia Chandler.*

Her stomach dropped as she skimmed the email. It was addressed to a list of contacts she didn't recognise—journalists, socialites, even a few of Lydia's former business partners. The email outlined plans for a gala to celebrate Lydia's legacy, complete with suggested dates, venues, and themes.

Alice's hands trembled as she scrolled to the bottom. The signature was hers. It was written as if she had sent it, but she hadn't.

"What the hell..." she whispered.

Her heart pounded as she called Aiden, but the call went straight to voicemail. She considered leaving a message but thought better of it. What would she say? That the house was conspiring against her? That she was beginning to doubt her own grip on reality?

Evermere felt colder now, the chill seeping into Alice's skin despite the thermostat reading a comfortable 72 degrees. She stood in the living room, clutching her phone like a lifeline, her mind racing. She thought about calling someone—maybe Beth, or Clara. Instead, she paced the room, her bare feet silent against the plush rug.

"Okay," she muttered to herself. "It's just a glitch. A stupid, tech glitch."

But even as she said it, she didn't believe it. Evermere was too high spec for something like this to happen accidentally. Aiden had spared no expense when he'd had it built. Every system, every device, was state-of-the-art. It was designed to make life easy, and yet now if felt like it was playing tricks on her.

She walked to the kitchen, her fingers drumming nervously against the marble countertop. The room was immaculate, every surface gleaming, every appliance in its place. It was the kind of kitchen that looked like it belonged in a magazine spread, not a real home. Alice rarely used it. She preferred simpler spaces, places where she didn't have to worry that she might break something.

As she reached for a glass of water, the fridge door opened on its own with a soft hiss. Alice froze, her pulse quickening as she stared at the open door. Slowly, she stepped forward and peered inside. The shelves were neatly stocked, everything arranged with obsessive precision. Just like always. Nothing seemed out of place.

She closed the door, her hand trembling slightly, and turned back to the counter. But when she looked at the glass she had set down, her blood ran cold.

There was a lipstick mark on the side of it. Bright red lipstick. Like Lydia used to wear.

Alice staggered back, her breath hitching in her throat. "No," she whispered.

She wiped the glass with her sleeve, erasing the mark, but the feeling of dread didn't fade. She turned and hurried out of the kitchen, her bare feet slapping against the cool tiles as she made her way back to the living room.

The lights flickered as she entered, plunging her into momentary darkness before flaring back to life. Her gaze darted to the wall screen, which had come alive again. This time, it displayed a single image—a photo of Lydia standing in front of the house, her smile wide and radiant with bright red lipstick. The words beneath the photo made Alice's stomach twist:

Welcome Home.

"No," Alice said aloud, shaking her head. "Stop it! Turn off!"

The screen went dark, but the silence that followed felt oppressive. She sank onto the sofa, her head in her hands, trying to steady her breathing. It wasn't real, she told herself. It couldn't be real. The house was just... malfunctioning.

But deep down, she didn't believe that. Deep down, she felt like the house was watching her. Plaguing her. Haunting her.

By the time Karen arrived in the late afternoon, Alice was desperate for company. She met her in the kitchen, where Karen was directing the staff in her usual brisk, no-nonsense manner.

"Karen," Alice said, her voice tight. "Can we talk?"

Karen glanced up from the list in her hands, her expression unreadable. "Of course, Mrs. Chandler. What's on your mind?"

Alice hesitated, the weight of her unease pressing down on her. "It's...Evermere. The smart system. It's been acting strangely."

"Strangely how?" Karen asked, arching an eyebrow.

"It keeps showing me things. Lydia's things—photos, videos. And now there's an email that I didn't send, but it looks like it came from me. I don't understand what's happening."

Karen's lips pressed into a thin line, and she set the list down. "The smart system is state-of-the-art," she said calmly. "It's unlikely to malfunction without reason."

"Then what's causing it?" Alice pressed. "Because it feels like..." She trailed off, unsure how to finish the sentence without sounding paranoid.

Karen stepped closer, her gaze sharp. "Like what, Mrs. Chandler?"

"Like ... it's trying to mess with me. Make me feel..." Alice stopped, swallowing hard. She didn't want to say the word *crazy*.

Karen's expression softened slightly, though her tone remained cool. "Evermere was designed with Lydia in mind. Many of its settings and preferences were hers. It's possible the system hasn't fully transitioned to your preferences yet."

"That doesn't explain the email." Alice bit her lip.

Karen tilted her head, her eyes narrowing. "Perhaps you forgot sending it."

"I didn't send it," Alice snapped.

Karen didn't flinch. Instead, she leaned slightly closer, her voice lowering. "Mrs. Chandler, you're under a lot of pressure.

It's understandable to feel overwhelmed. But perhaps it would help to focus on something positive—like hosting an event to honour Lydia's legacy."

Alice froze. "You want me to host an event... for Lydia?"

Karen nodded, her expression brightening. "It would be a wonderful way to show your appreciation for her contributions. The press would adore it, and it would help establish you as a gracious and thoughtful presence in Aiden's world. Her birthday would have been next month. It would be an ideal time. You had the idea yourself last week. Remember?"

Alice's mind searched her memory but came up blank.

"No one is asking you to be Lydia," Karen said smoothly. "But you are Mrs. Chandler now. Certain... expectations come with that role. Honouring Lydia would go a long way in showing everyone that you understand those expectations."

The air seemed to thicken around Alice, her pulse quickening. She wanted to argue, to push back, but Karen's gaze was unwavering, her tone firm. It wasn't a suggestion—it was a directive.

"I'll think about it," Alice said finally, her voice hollow knowing the decision had already been taken.

"Of course," Karen replied, her smile faint and inscrutable. "Take all the time you need."

But as Karen turned and walked away, Alice couldn't shake the feeling that she was being boxed in—and that Evermere, Karen, and even Aiden were all complicit in keeping her trapped.

By the time night fell, Alice was exhausted. The day had passed in a blur of anxiety and paranoia, and now she lay in bed, staring at the ceiling. Aiden still wasn't home. He had texted earlier to say he'd be working late, but his absence only made Evermere feel more menacing.

She rolled onto her side, pulling the blanket tightly around her, and tried to focus on the sound of the ocean outside. The steady rhythm had always been comforting, but tonight, it felt distant, as though nature itself were conspiring with the house to isolate her.

Just as she was beginning to drift off, a faint sound jolted her awake. It was coming from the bedroom mirror.

Alice sat up, her heart pounding as she stared at the glass. A faint glow emanated from the surface, and then Lydia's face appeared, her voice crackling through the speakers.

"Welcome to our home," Lydia said, her tone warm and inviting. "I hope you'll be as comfortable here as I am."

Alice screamed, scrambling out of bed and backing against the wall. "Turn off!" she shouted, her voice shaking. "Turn off!"

The mirror ignored her. Lydia's image continued to speak, her words growing distorted and echoing as if from a great distance.

"Evermere is a very special place," Lydia said, her smile widening. "Soon you'll see it for yourself."

"Stop it!" Alice yelled, tears streaming down her face.

The mirror went dark, plunging the room into silence. Alice stood there, trembling, her breath coming in ragged gasps. She felt like she was losing her mind. The house wasn't just malfunctioning. It was taunting her, tormenting her, driving her to the edge.

She grabbed her phone and dialled Aiden again, but it went straight to voicemail. Desperate, she left a message this time, her voice shaky and urgent.

"Aiden, something's wrong with the house. It's not just glitches. It's—it's Lydia. I don't know how, but it's her. Please call me back. I'm scared."

She hung up and sank onto the floor, wrapping her arms around her knees. Evermere loomed around her, vast, threatening and silent, its walls closing in. Alice felt like a stranger in her own life—a ghost haunting someone else's house.

And she couldn't shake the feeling that Evermere itself wanted her gone.

12

The chandelier above the ballroom glittered like a cascade of frozen stars, its light refracting off the polished glass and polished surfaces. Evermere had been transformed for the evening, every inch of it adorned with white roses and subtle, elegant touches that spoke of wealth and sophistication. The event to honour Lydia Chandler's legacy was in full swing, but Alice felt as though she was standing at the centre of a hurricane.

Guests milled about in dazzling designer gowns and sharp tuxedos, their laughter and murmured conversations blending into a low hum that filled the room. Alice stood near the edge of the crowd, gripping a crystal flute in one hand, her other resting stiffly at her side. The dress she wore—a sleek, floor-length gown in emerald silk was elegant, and striking, and seemed tailored perfectly to fit her frame. She had hoped it would make her feel confident, like she belonged. But it didn't.

As she moved through the room, she noticed the glances. Whispers rippled through the crowd, subtle but impossible to miss. Women leaned toward one another, their eyes darting toward Alice, while men raised their eyebrows and exchanged knowing looks. A few brave guests smiled at her, but even their smiles felt forced, tinged with pity or something worse.

Beth was one of the few familiar faces in the sea of strangers. She stood near the bar, her arms crossed, and her lips pressed into a thin line as she watched the proceedings with a look of open disdain. When Alice approached, Beth arched an eyebrow, her expression softening only slightly.

"Quite the spectacle," Beth said dryly, gesturing toward the room with her glass of wine. "I don't think I've seen this many diamonds in one place in my entire life."

"Beth, please," Alice murmured, glancing around nervously. "Not tonight."

Beth's gaze softened, but her tone remained pointed. "I'm just saying, Alice. This isn't you. This whole thing... just isn't you."

Alice didn't respond. She couldn't. She wanted to argue, to defend the choices she'd made, but the truth was, Beth was right. The event didn't feel like hers—not really. It felt like another chapter in the ongoing story of Lydia Chandler.

As if on cue, Ian Carlisle appeared, his painted smile as sharp as ever. He approached with a glass of whiskey in hand, his presence as unwelcome as it was inevitable. "Mrs. Chandler," he drawled, his voice dripping with mockery. "You look... radiant tonight."

Alice stiffened. "Thank you, Ian."

"But I must say," he continued, his eyes gleaming with mischief, "your choice of gown is... bold."

Alice frowned. "What do you mean?"

Ian's smile widened, and he leaned in slightly, his voice lowering to a conspiratorial whisper. "Surely you know... That dress—it's the same one Lydia wore to the Cannes gala five years ago. The photos were everywhere. It's iconic."

Alice's stomach dropped. She stared at him, her pulse

quickening as the weight of his words sank in. "I didn't know," she said quietly.

Ian tilted his head, feigning sympathy. "Ah, I see. An honest mistake, then. Still, I imagine the guests will find it... interesting."

Before Alice could respond, he disappeared into the crowd, his laughter trailing behind him like smoke. She stood frozen, her mind racing as she replayed his words. Her hands trembled, and she set her glass down, afraid she might drop it.

She scanned the room, her gaze darting from one group of guests to another. The whispers seemed louder now, the glances sharper. She caught snippets of conversation as she passed—a woman murmuring something about "poor taste," a man chuckling about "trying too hard," and another voice whispering "silly bitch".

The dress, the whispers, the way the women's eyes lingered on her—she couldn't escape it.

Her mind flashed back to the moment she'd walked into the room, Karen's brief but knowing glance. Someone must have known. Someone must have seen the connection. But no one told her. They let her walk into the lion's den dressed like that.

Her breath quickened, the silk of the dress suddenly feeling too tight, too suffocating against her skin. She wanted to rip it off, to run back upstairs and hide. But instead, she forced herself to keep moving, her legs unsteady.

And then she saw Aiden.

He stood near the center of the room, surrounded by a group of business associates. When their eyes met, his expression darkened, his mouth falling slightly open. He excused himself from the group and strode toward her, his movements swift and deliberate.

"Alice," he said sharply, his voice low but laced with anger. "Is this some kind of sick joke?"

"It's just a dress," she said, her voice trembling. "I didn't know—it was in the wardrobe..."

"You didn't know?" he interrupted, his tone incredulous.

Alice swallowed hard, a lump catching in her throat. "No one told me, Aiden. I—"

"You should have asked," he snapped, his words cutting. "Do you have any idea how this looks? The press will eat this up." He hissed.

"I didn't mean to—I didn't know..."

"Enough," he said, his tone final. "We'll talk about this later. Just... try not to draw any more attention to yourself. You're a fucking embarrassment."

With that, he turned and walked away, leaving Alice standing alone in the middle of the room. Her vision blurred, and the noise of the crowd seemed to swell around her, a cacophony of judgment and disdain. She felt small, exposed, and utterly humiliated.

She glanced down at the dress, the emerald silk glinting mockingly in the light. The knowledge that Lydia had once worn it made her feel sick. It felt as though the ground beneath her feet had crumbled away entirely.

She wanted to scream, to tear the dress from her body and run, but she couldn't move. She was rooted to the spot, her humiliation pinning her in place.

Beth appeared at her side, her expression a mix of anger and concern. "Come on," she said quietly, taking Alice's arm. "Let's get some air."

Alice let herself be led out onto the terrace, the cool night air a welcome relief from the stifling heat of the ballroom. She leaned against the railing, her hands gripping the cold metal to steady herself.

"I told you," Beth said, her voice soft but firm. "This isn't you, Alice."

Alice shook her head, her tears threatening to spill over. "No. This isn't me. This is Lydia." She looked down at the dress. "I don't know what to do," she whispered. "I thought I could handle it. I thought I could be what Aiden needed. But I can't... I can't live like this."

Beth placed a comforting hand on Alice's shoulder. "Then maybe it's time to stop trying to be what everyone else wants you to be and start being who you are."

Alice didn't respond. She stared out at the ocean, the waves crashing against the cliffs below, and she wished the world would swallow her whole.

13

The storm began in the late afternoon, rolling in from the ocean like a living thing. Heavy clouds gathered on the horizon; their grey edges tinged with an ominous green. By the time the first drops of rain began to lash against the glass walls of the estate, the wind had picked up, howling around the cliffs like a restless spirit.

Alice stood in the living room, staring out at the turbulent waves below, the image of herself wearing Lydia's dress tormenting her. The ocean had transformed from its usual placid beauty into a churning, violent expanse, the whitecaps frothing as they crashed against the jagged rocks.

Evermere felt darker than usual, its sleek, modern lines casting sharp, angular shadows in the dim light. The smart system had activated the interior lighting automatically, but the soft glow of the recessed fixtures did little to dispel the unease she felt. The glass walls, usually a source of awe and beauty, now felt like a vulnerability, leaving her exposed to the relentless storm outside.

As the rain intensified, drumming against the glass in a relentless rhythm, Alice's thoughts turned back to the notebook she had found in Lydia's closet. The scribbled notes, they painted a picture of a woman far removed from the glamorous, composed figure Lydia had presented to the world. And Aiden's journal had only deepened the mystery. His words, so controlled and measured, hinted at a marriage that was anything but perfect.

The words from his journal, that she'd snuck into his office and read, replayed in her mind, circling like a hurricane: *"She is always looking for something more—I don't know how to keep her here."*

What had he meant by *"Keep her here"*? Had Lydia been planning to leave him? Alice had spent weeks feeling like she was living in Lydia's shadow, but now it felt like that shadow was alive, strangling her.

A sharp crack of thunder split the air, and Alice flinched, the sound reverberating through Evermere. The lights flickered, dimming for a moment before stabilising, but the brief darkness left her pulse racing. She glanced around the room. The house, so pristine and controlled, now felt alive—its walls closing in, its corners darker than they should be. She could feel its presence, watching her, waiting.

She moved to the kitchen, hoping the familiarity of the space would steady her nerves. The rain streaked down the glass panes, distorting the view of the torrent outside.

A soft chime echoed through the house, startling her. The smart system had detected something. "Motion detected: rear terrace," the automated voice announced, calm and detached.

Alice froze, her breath catching in her throat. She turned slowly toward the rear terrace, her heart pounding. The curtains had been left open, and beyond the glass, the rain-slicked tiles of the terrace were empty, save for the relentless rain pounding against them. She stared for a long moment, her eyes scanning the space, but there was nothing there.

"It's just the rain," she whispered to herself, though her voice sounded unconvincing even to her own ears.

She reached for her phone, wanting to call Aiden, but she hesitated. He'd been distant lately, distracted by work, and she didn't want to give him another reason to brush her off. Instead, she checked the security system on her phone, watching the live feed from the cameras. The terrace was empty, just as she'd seen, but the motion alert still sat at the top of the screen, a reminder that something—or someone—had triggered it.

A loud bang echoed from upstairs, and Alice nearly dropped her phone. Her pulse skyrocketed as she turned toward the staircase, her body rigid with fear. The sound hadn't been thunder. It had come from inside the house.

The thought sent a shiver through her. She stood frozen, every muscle in her body tense, as she strained to hear any noise. Evermere was silent, save for the muffled roar of the wind and pelting rain outside. Slowly, she set her glass down on the counter and forced herself to move toward the stairs.

Her bare feet made no sound against the cool wood as she ascended, her hand gripping the railing tightly. The hallway at the top of the stairs was dimly lit, the recessed lights casting eerie shapes onto the walls. She paused, her eyes and ears straining for any sign of movement.

Alice moved toward the master bedroom, her heart pounding harder with each step. The door was slightly ajar, and she pushed it open cautiously, expecting to find something—or someone—waiting for her.

The room was empty. The bed was neatly made, the curtains drawn tight against the weather outside. Everything was as she had left it. She stepped further into the room, her gaze scanning every corner, every shadow. And then she saw it.

The mirror.

It was glowing faintly, its surface illuminated with soft,

shifting light. Her reflection stared back at her, but there was something off about it—something she couldn't quite put her finger on. She stepped closer, her breath catching as the glow intensified.

And then the image changed.

Lydia's appeared in the mirror, her expression serene but distant, as though she were looking past Alice rather than at her. She was wearing the emerald dress. The sight of her sent a jolt through Alice's body, and she stumbled back, her heart racing.

The words appeared next, etched across the glass in bold, glowing letters:

You don't belong here.

Alice gasped, her hands flying to her mouth. She blinked, hoping the words would disappear, but they remained, stark and unyielding. Her knees felt weak, and she sank onto the edge of the bed, her breath coming in shallow, panicked gasps.

"This isn't real," she whispered, shaking her head. "It's not real."

The mirror continued to mock her. The image so vivid, so real, that Alice could almost smell her perfume. Her heart pounded as she watched, unable to look away.

And then Lydia turned, her gaze locking onto Alice's. Her lips moved, forming words Alice couldn't hear.

Get out.

Alice scrambled to her feet, her breath hitching as she backed away from the mirror. She turned and fled the room, her footsteps echoing loudly in the empty hallway. She didn't stop until she was back in the living room, her chest heaving as she tried to catch her breath.

The house felt colder now. The storm outside raged on and Alice felt a deep certainty that she wasn't safe here. Not from the weather, not from Evermere, and certainly not from whatever—or whoever—was trying to drive her out.

She grabbed her phone and dialled Aiden's number, her hands trembling. The call went straight to voicemail.

"Aiden, something's wrong. The house—it's not just the wind and the rain. There's something here. I need you to come home. Please. Please call me back."

She hung up and sank onto the sofa, wrapping her arms around herself as she stared out at the downpour and somewhere in the depths of Evermere, a low, creaking sound echoed through the halls.

Alice closed her eyes, her mind racing. The journal, the notebook, the mirror—it was all too much. She felt like she was losing her mind, like the house was swallowing her whole. And for the first time, she wondered if Lydia was more than a shadow —if there was something far darker, something she couldn't escape.

She moved through the house, her bare feet silent against the floor, and found herself standing outside Aiden's office once again. The thunder raged beyond the glass, lightning illuminating the room in brief, blinding flashes.

The office felt different now, the dark wood and leather furnishings lending it an oppressive atmosphere. She crossed to the bookshelf, her fingers brushing the spines of the books as she searched for the leather-bound journal.

It was still there, tucked neatly among the others. She pulled it from the shelf and opened it, flipping through the pages with trembling hands. Aiden's words, his frustration and desperation leaping off the pages.

She's slipping. I don't know how to help her.

I don't know if I can do this anymore.

A loud crack of thunder shook Evermere, and Alice jumped, the journal slipping from her hands and landing on the floor with a dull thud. She crouched to pick it up, her heart pounding, when something caught her eye—a small slip of paper sticking out from the back cover. She pulled it free, her breath catching as she unfolded it.

It was a photograph. Lydia and Aiden, standing on the deck of a yacht, their arms around each other. Lydia was smiling, her golden hair swept back, but there was something in her eyes—something Alice couldn't quite place. It wasn't joy, or even contentment. It was something darker.

Alice stared at the photo, her mind racing. The yacht. Lydia's yacht. She traced the edge of the photo with her finger, hoping it might reveal something.

She turned the photo over, her heart skipping a beat when she saw the faint writing on the back. It was Lydia's handwriting, delicate and precise:

July 14th. Never again.

Another flash of lightning lit up the room, and Alice felt a chill race down her spine. What had happened on July 14th? What did Lydia mean by *"Never again"*?

The sound of footsteps in the hallway made her freeze. She clutched the photograph and the journal to her chest. The footsteps were slow, deliberate, and they stopped just outside the door.

"Mrs. Chandler?" Karen's voice cut through the heavy silence, cold and precise.

Alice quickly slid the photo back into the journal and placed it on the desk before turning to face Karen. The older woman stood in the doorway, her hands clasped neatly in front of her, her fixed expression unreadable.

"I didn't realise you were in here," Karen said, her tone carrying a hint of disapproval.

"I was just... looking for something," Alice said, her voice shaky.

Karen's eyes flicked to the desk, then back to Alice. "It's not like you to spend time in Mr. Chandler's office."

"I needed a quiet space to think," Alice replied, trying to steady herself.

Karen stepped into the room. "Storms can be unsettling," she said, her tone almost sympathetic. "But this house is secure. There's nothing to worry about."

Alice nodded, though her hands trembled at her sides. Karen's gaze lingered on her for a moment longer before she turned and headed toward the door.

With that she headed back to her cottage on the estate, leaving Alice alone. She let out a shaky breath, her heart still racing as she stared down at the journal on the desk. The photograph burned in her mind, its cryptic message eating away at her.

The wind howled louder, and the house groaned in response. Alice's eyes darted to the windows as rain lashed against the glass. She couldn't shake the feeling that she was being watched—not just by the house, but by something unseen, something waiting in the shadows.

As another crack of thunder shook the estate, Alice made a silent vow. She would find out what had happened to Lydia. She would uncover the truth, no matter what it took.

Because if she didn't, she feared she might completely lose herself.

14

The rain had passed by morning, leaving the air crisp and damp with the scent of rain. The sky was clear now, but Alice's anxiety remained. She couldn't let it go—the photograph, Lydia's haunting handwriting, and the secrets that seemed to seep from every corner of the house. The more she uncovered, the less she felt she truly knew about her husband, her new life, or the woman whose shadow still loomed over everything.

She needed answers.

The garden stretched out behind the house like an oasis. Rows of roses, hydrangeas, and perfectly trimmed hedges created a labyrinth of beauty, a stark contrast to the cold, modern lines of Evermere. Dew clung to every petal and leaf, sparkling in the early morning sunlight, and the air hummed faintly with the buzzing of bees darting from bloom to bloom. The scent of the flowers was heady and sweet, almost overwhelming, as if the garden was trying to lull her into a false sense of security.

Alice followed the stone pathway through the rows of greenery until she found David Steinberg near the far edge of the garden. He was crouched beside a sprawling rosebush, a pair of shears in his gloved hands as he carefully pruned the plant. Despite the stoop in his shoulders and the silver of his dark hair, there was a steadiness to his movements that spoke of years of experience. His presence was calming, like the earth itself—solid, dependable, and wise.

"David," Alice called softly, not wanting to startle him.

He straightened slowly, wiping his gloves on his pants before turning to face her. His expression was unreadable, his deep-set eyes studying her with a quiet intensity that made her feel both seen and scrutinised. There was a kindness in his gaze, but also something guarded, as if he were weighing something up.

"Mrs. Chandler," he said, his voice low and gravelly. "What can I do for you this morning?"

Alice hesitated, glancing around the garden. The roses swayed gently in the breeze, their vibrant colours a sharp contrast to the muted grey of the estate in the distance. The stone path beneath her feet was slick with rain, and she could hear the faint trickle of a fountain somewhere nearby. Despite the beauty of the setting, she couldn't shake the tension coiled in her chest.

"I wanted to ask you about Lydia," she said finally. "I know I've asked before, and I am sorry if it makes you uncomfortable..."

David's expression didn't change, but she noticed the subtle way his shoulders tensed, his grip tightening on the shears. "Lydia?"

"Yes." Alice stepped closer, lowering her voice as if the garden itself might overhear. "I've been... thinking about her. About her disappearance. And I feel like there are things I don't know—things I need to understand."

David sighed, slipping the shears into the pocket of his worn gardening apron. He looked away for a moment, his gaze sweeping over the roses as if searching for an escape. When he finally spoke, his voice was careful, measured. "What is it you're hoping to learn, Mrs. Chandler?"

"Anything, everything," Alice said, the desperation in her voice surprising even herself. "What was her relationship with Aiden like?"

David studied her for a long moment, his expression thoughtful. "Lydia was... complicated," he said at last. "She was brilliant, no doubt about that. Ambitious, driven. She had a way of lighting up a room, of making people feel like they were part of something special. But there was another side to her, too—a colder side."

"Cold?"

David nodded, his gaze drifting to the roses. "Lydia was good at getting what she wanted. She had a sharp mind, and she knew how to use it. But sometimes, that meant using people. She could be calculating, ruthless even, when it suited her."

Alice felt a chill creep up her spine, despite the warmth of the morning sun. "Did Aiden see that?"

David hesitated, his brow furrowing as if he were choosing his words carefully. "Aiden admired her," he said finally. "Respected her. But love is a complicated thing."

Alice's heart pounded, her mind racing with questions. "Do you think Aiden loved her?"

David's lips pressed into a thin line. "I think he wanted to. But Lydia had her own way of doing things, and Aiden... Aiden likes control. It created tension."

The words hung in the air between them, heavy with implication. Alice felt like she was standing on the edge of a precipice, peering into a void. "Tension," she repeated, her voice trembling. "What kind of tension?"

David's gaze sharpened, and for the first time, Alice saw a flicker of something in his expression—fear, perhaps. "They argued," he said simply. "More than most people knew. Lydia had her own ideas about how things should be, and Aiden... well, he didn't always agree."

Alice swallowed hard, her pulse quickening. "Do you think that's why she disappeared? Because of an argument?"

David's lips tightened, and he glanced around the garden as if ensuring they were alone. "Be careful, Mrs. Chandler," he said quietly. "You're asking questions that don't have easy answers."

Her breath caught, the weight of his words settling over her like a heavy cloak. "What do you mean?"

"I mean," David said, his voice low, "that Lydia's gone. And the truth about what happened to her... It might be best left alone."

Alice stared at him, her chest tightening. "Do you know something, David? Something you're not telling me?"

David shook his head. "I know enough to keep my distance and my mouth shut. But if you're determined to dig deeper, there's someone you could talk to."

"Who?" Alice asked, her voice full of urgency.

"Maria Valdez," David said. "She was a member of staff here for years. She worked under Karen. She knew Lydia better than anyone. If there's anyone who can tell you the truth, it's her."

Alice nodded, a flicker of determination sparking within her. "Where can I find her?"

"She lives in the city now," David said. "I can give you her address. But tread carefully, Mrs. Chandler. Not everyone's eager to talk about the past."

David's words lingered in Alice's mind as she watched him return to his work, his movements deliberate and unhurried. There was something about him—something she couldn't quite put her finger on. He was kind, yes, but there was an air of mystery about him. The way he spoke about Lydia, the way he hesitated before answering her questions—it all felt like pieces of a puzzle that didn't yet fit together.

The garden seemed smaller suddenly as she turned to leave, the scent of roses cloying in the air. She glanced back at David one last time, his figure half-hidden among the flowers, and Alice thought for a moment, how nice it would be to just disappear.

That evening, Alice sat in the library, the address David had written for her folded neatly in her lap. The room was dim, lit only by the soft, golden glow of a single lamp on the desk. The heavy linen curtains were drawn, shutting out the night and enclosing her in the brooding quiet of the house.

The paper felt heavier than it should in her hands, the words *Maria Valdez* and the neatly written address staring back at her. David's warning echoed in her mind: *Be careful, Mrs. Chandler. Not everyone's eager to talk about the past.* She turned the paper over in her fingers, hoping it might somehow erase the conflict inside her.

Alice leaned back in the leather chair, staring at the dark, glossy wood of the desk and let out a long sigh. The smart system hummed faintly, its sensors glowing like tiny, watchful eyes. A breeze rustled faintly through the vents, brushing against her skin like a whisper. Evermere seemed to breathe around her, an entity, alive with the memories.

Memories of Lydia. The thought struck Alice like a blow. Lydia had once sat in this very library. She had been the centre of this world, admired, feared, envied. And now she was gone, her absence leaving a vacuum that Alice had been sucked into.

And yet, it wasn't just Lydia's legacy that haunted Alice. It was Aiden. The man she had fallen for had become a stranger, his kindness increasingly tempered by control, overshadowed by cold pragmatism. She had tried to ignore it but the journal entries, the photographs, they whispered of tension between

Aiden and Lydia and painted a picture she could no longer ignore.

Her fingers tightened around the piece of paper as she fought against the rising doubt. Part of her wanted to throw the address away and pretend she had never asked David. She could be the wife Aiden wanted her to be—gracious, supportive, unburdened by curiosity. She could stop digging, stop questioning, and focus on building the life they said they wanted.

But another part of her—the part that refused to be silenced—knew that wasn't possible. She couldn't unsee the cracks in the facade. She couldn't ignore the feeling she had every time she looked at Aiden. The truth was a thorn lodged in her mind, and no matter how hard she tried, she couldn't stop it from festering.

Maybe Aiden's right, she thought, guilt flickering across her face. *Maybe I should let it go. Maybe this is what marriage is—choosing to trust, even when you don't have all the answers.*

But trust wasn't easy when the questions kept multiplying.

The clock struck midnight, the chime startling Alice from her thoughts. The sound seemed to reverberate through the room, each toll a reminder of the passing time, the choices she couldn't avoid. She glanced down at the paper in her lap.

She rubbed her temples and thought of Aiden, of the way he had held her hand on their wedding day. She thought of the way he had looked at her during the gala, his disappointment cutting deeper than any insult. She thought of his anger when she had mentioned the gallery, his insistence that her place was by his side.

And she thought of David's words, the quiet warning laced with concern. *The truth about what happened to her... It might not be what you want to hear.*

The truth. That was what it all came down to. Alice didn't know if she could handle it, if she could face whatever lay hidden in the past. But she knew she couldn't remain in Evermere without finding out.

Her hands shook as she reached for her phone. The address was still in her lap, the name *Maria Valdez* etched into her mind like a beacon. She stared at the screen for a long moment, her thumb hovering over the dial pad. The air around her seemed to grow heavier, the silence heavy like a weight around her neck.

Finally, she took a deep breath and dialled the number David had given her. The phone rang once, twice, three times. But then there was a click, and a woman's voice.

"Hello?"

Alice swallowed hard; her throat dry. "Is this Maria Valdez?"

There was a pause, and Alice could hear the faint sound of a television in the background. "Who's asking?"

"My name is Alice Chandler," she said, her voice trembling. "I'm—" She hesitated, unsure of how to explain. "I'm married to Aiden Chandler. I live in the house where you used to work."

Another pause, longer this time. When Maria spoke again, her tone was wary but laced with something else—curiosity, perhaps, or caution. "What do you want, Mrs. Chandler?"

Alice's grip on the phone tightened. "I want to know about Lydia," she said, her voice firm despite the fear curling in her stomach. "I want to know the truth." She realised how dramatic she sounded and instantly regretted it. She didn't want to scare Maria off.

The line went silent, and for a moment, Alice thought Maria had hung up. But then the woman sighed, the sound heavy with resignation.

"All right," Maria said. "I'll tell you what I know."

Alice's heart pounded as she nodded. "I'm ready," she said, though she wasn't sure if it was true.

Maria gave her an address and a time, then hung up without

another word. Alice sat in the silence; the phone still pressed to her ear. The reality of what she had just done settled over her, a mix of dread and determination.

As she set the phone down, she glanced at the clock. It was early evening, and the house was quiet, but she couldn't shake the feeling that it was listening, waiting. The secrets she had been chasing were closer now, but so was the danger. And as she sat alone in the library, she knew there was no turning back.

15

The coffee shop was a cozy nook tucked away from the busy city streets; its large bay windows fogged with condensation from the early morning air outside. Inside was warm and thick with the aroma of roasted coffee and baked pastries. The walls were lined with mismatched bookshelves, crammed with well-worn novels and forgotten memoirs. Small wooden tables were scattered across the room, some occupied by solo patrons with laptops, others by pairs chatting in low, conspiratorial tones. It was trendy. The kind of place Clara might hang out. The kind of place Alice felt she didn't belong.

Alice adjusted her pale pink scarf nervously as she walked in, her eyes scanning the room. She spotted a woman, sitting in a corner. Maria nodded for her to approach.

She had an air of quiet authority about her—her posture straight, her hands wrapped around a plain ceramic mug. She wore a faded blue cardigan over a crisp white blouse, her thick, dark hair pulled back into a practical bun that revealed the fine lines etched into her face. Her eyes, sharp and watchful, tracked Alice as she approached.

"Mrs. Chandler," Maria said, standing and offering her hand.

Her voice was low and steady, carrying the experience of someone who had seen and endured much. Her handshake was firm, her palm calloused.

"Please, call me Alice," she said with a faint smile, still not used to being so easily recognised by strangers, thanks to the press and the limelight she resented.

Maria studied her for a moment before nodding. "Alice, then."

Alice sat across from her, the chair scraping against the wooden floor. She was aware of the way the room seemed to quiet around them, the low hum of conversation fading into the background. She pulled the sunglasses down from her head over her eyes, covering half of her face. She wanted to be invisible.

The waitress approached, and Alice ordered a latte. Maria declined a refill as if accepting might somehow put her in harm's way.

"I wasn't sure you'd agree to meet me," Alice broke the silence.

Maria's eyes narrowed slightly. "I almost didn't."

"I just... I need to understand. Lydia, she's everywhere. I feel like I'm drowning, but no one will tell me the truth. And strange things keep happening in that house."

Maria leaned back in her chair, her gaze drifting to the window. The rain from the previous night had left streaks on the glass, blurring the view of the bustling street beyond. She sighed, a long, weary sound, before turning her attention back to Alice.

"Mrs Chandler was a force," Maria said, her voice tinged with both admiration and something darker. "The first Mrs Chandler, I mean," she apologised. "Ambitious. Brilliant. But her brilliance came at a price. She didn't just want to succeed—she wanted to dominate. She had a way of making people feel like they were the most important person in the room, but it was all a strategy. Everything she did, everything she said, was calculated."

Alice noticed suddenly the scent of stale cigarette smoke coming from Maria's breath. She frowned, leaning forward slightly. "Calculated how?"

Maria hesitated, her painted fingernails tapping lightly against the edge of her mug. "She knew how to get what she wanted, and she wasn't afraid to manipulate people. If you were useful to her, she would charm you, flatter you, make you feel indispensable. But the moment you crossed her—or outlived your usefulness—she'd cut you loose without a second thought." Her Mexican accent was thick and smooth.

Alice was curious. "Did Aiden see that side of her?"

Maria's lips pressed into a thin line. "He must have. They fought often enough. Mrs Chandler had high expectations, and Mr Chandler... well, he's not the kind of man who likes being controlled."

"Why did you leave Evermere?" Alice asked.

"Lydia fired me. She said I was taking things from the house. A pack of lies, of course." Maria blushed. "They were both good at putting on a show. To the world, they were perfect. Behind closed doors..." She trailed off, shaking her head.

"Behind closed doors, what?" Alice pressed feeling a lump growing in her throat.

Maria glanced around the room, as if checking for eavesdroppers, before leaning closer. Her voice dropped to a whisper. "It wasn't always love and light, if that's what you're hoping to hear. Mrs Chandler could be ruthless. And Mr Chandler... he has his own demons. Their fights were intense, and there were times I wondered if there were more than just words."

"Do you think it ever—" Her stomach churned, she

hesitated, lowering her voice further. "Do you think it ever got physical?"

Maria's expression hardened. "I don't know. And if I did, I wouldn't say." She glanced toward the door, her unease evident. "But I'll tell you this—Mrs Chandler wasn't always the victim. She was just as capable of hurting others, in her own way."

Alice nodded slowly, trying to piece together the conflicting images of Lydia she'd been given. The perfect wife, the ruthless manipulator, the woman who might have been caught in a volatile marriage. It didn't add up.

"There's something else," Maria said after a long pause, leaning closer and speaking in a hushed tone, "I think Mrs Chandler was having an affair." Maria sat back in her chair triumphantly and crossed her arms across her large heaving chest.

"With who?"

Maria shook her head. "I don't know. But there were signs—secret phone calls, unexplained absences, little things that didn't add up. I found a cufflink once, under the bed in their room. It wasn't Mr Chandler's."

The revelation was huge. She tried to picture Lydia, the woman who had seemed untouchable, sneaking around behind Aiden's back. It didn't fit the polished image Lydia had so carefully crafted. But then Alice was starting to realise that image wasn't everything.

"Why are you telling me this?" Alice asked, suddenly doubting Maria's true intensions.

Maria leaned closer, her sharp eyes locking onto Alice's. "Because you need to understand what you've got yourself into. I see the news. The papers. These animals, they pick at you like you are a carcass. A toy to be played with. It's not right." She puffed out her cheeks. "These people—the Chandlers, their circle—they're powerful. They'll do whatever it takes to protect their image, their wealth, their secrets. If you keep digging, you might find answers, but you'll also make enemies. Dangerous ones."

Alice swallowed hard, Maria's warning settling over her. "What would you do if you were me?"

"I'd stop," Maria said without hesitation. "Walk away. Leave the past in the past. Live your life. Forget about this. Move on."

Alice looked down at her latte, hoping to find answers in her reflection shimmering faintly on the surface. She knew Maria was right—knew she should let it go. But she couldn't

"I can't," Alice said finally, her voice quiet but firm. "I have to know."

Maria sighed, shaking her head. "Then be careful, Alice. This world eats people like us alive. Don't let yourself become the next victim."

The blast of air outside the coffee shop hit Alice like a slap, pulling her from the haze of her conversation with Maria. She couldn't shake the feeling that she was being watched. The bustling street felt too loud, too crowded, as if every passerby might be someone sent to follow her. She clutched her coat tightly around her and quickened her pace, Maria's warning echoing in her mind.

This world eats people like us alive.

The bustling city street, which had seemed almost charming when she'd arrived, now felt overwhelming—noisy, chaotic.

Her car was parked just a block away, tucked into a narrow side street. She quickened her pace, but she couldn't ignore the uneasy sensation. Maria's words echoed in her mind, a constant loop of warning and doubt. *Don't let yourself become the next victim.*

As she rounded the corner and approached her car, she

heard a burst of laughter from behind. She turned to see a group of teenage girls loitering outside a boutique, their arms filled with shopping bags.

One of them—a tall, willowy girl with sleek hair and a designer puffer jacket—was staring at Alice, her phone held up in front of her face.

"That's her," the girl whispered loudly to her friends. "That's Aiden Chandler's wife."

Alice's heart sank as the rest of the group turned to look at her, their eyes raking over her like she a curiosity in a circus. They huddled together, giggling and whispering, their phones pointed in her direction, tracking her every move. The unmistakable sound of a camera shutter made Alice feel sick.

"Wow, she really isn't like Lydia," one of them said, her voice carrying over the noise of the street.

"She's so... plain. Look at her clothes," another added, the sneer in her tone cutting through Alice like a sharpened knife.

Alice froze, her breath catching in her throat. She wanted to say something, to defend herself, but the words wouldn't come. She ached with humiliation as the girls continued to laugh, their voices dripping with cruelty.

"Look at her coat," one of them muttered, loud enough for Alice to hear. "Does she even know who she's married to? Tramp."

Alice turned sharply and unlocked her car, the sound of their laughter ringing in her ears as she climbed inside. Her hands trembled as she fumbled with the keys. The sting of their words would linger long after she drove away.

As she finally started the engine and pulled away from the curb, she glanced in the rearview mirror. The girls were still watching her, their phones raised, their laughter fading into the distance.

The city blurred passed her as she drove, the streets

unfamiliar and suffocating. She couldn't stop replaying the scene in her mind—the sneering looks, the harsh comments, the cruel comparison. She felt exposed, as if the world could see straight through her, stripping away every layer of protection she'd tried to build for herself.

And then there was Maria's voice, haunting her thoughts. *She wasn't the woman you think she was. She was manipulative. Cold. She had secrets, and those secrets didn't die with her.*

Alice tightened her grip on the wheel, her mind racing. What had she become? Her life was spent under the scrutiny of strangers. Even teenagers now got the better of her.

The road stretched ahead of her, the city giving way to quieter neighbourhoods. The sun was rising in the sky, casting a peach hue onto the pavement.

Alice felt vulnerable, exposed, and utterly alone.

By the time she pulled into the driveway of Evermere, the sky was a deep, bruised blue. The house loomed before her, its glass walls glowing softly in the light. It should have been comforting—a sanctuary from the outside world—but instead, it felt like a prison.

Alice sat in the car for a long moment, her hands still gripping the wheel while she tried to settle the hurricane gathering momentum inside.

Finally, she stepped out of the car and walked toward the house, her footsteps heavy against the gravel. She paused at the front door, glancing over her shoulder. The sensation of being watched continued to follow her.

Inside, the house was silent, its sleek interior bathed in the glow of automated lighting. The smart system chirped a greeting as she entered, but it only made her feel more alone. She dropped her bag on the console table and made her way to the living room, collapsing onto the sofa as the weight of the morning finally caught up with her.

Alice closed her eyes, Maria's warnings still echoing in her mind. *Be careful, Alice.*

She didn't know if she had the strength to keep digging, to uncover whatever it was everyone around her seemed so desperate to hide.

As Evermere settled around her, Alice stared at the glass wall that framed the deep ocean beyond. The very ocean that had swallowed Lydia and was threatening to take her down too.

16

Alice woke up with a throbbing headache. The humiliation from the previous day lingered like a bitter taste in her mouth, but it had done something unexpected—it had steeled her. The girls with their sneers—they had underestimated her. If the answers about Lydia weren't going to come to her, she would chase them.

She stepped into the small office adjoining the library, a room Aiden rarely used. The air inside was still and slightly stale, like a space forgotten by the house's careful curation. The mahogany desk sat at the room's centre, its surface polished but unused. The bookshelves, lined with hardbacks, loomed over her like silent judges.

As she settled at the desk, Alice couldn't shake the feeling that she didn't belong here. This was Aiden and Lydia's world—their house, their history, their secrets. And yet, as much as the house seemed to resist her presence, she couldn't leave. She needed to understand the truth, not only for herself but to reclaim a sense of control over a life that felt increasingly not her own.

Alice opened her laptop, her fingers trembling slightly as she navigated to the bookmarked articles she had saved. The first thread she pulled at was the lawsuit with Catherine Reese. She had heard Aiden mention the name once, in passing, but he had dismissed it as a minor dispute. Now, as Alice read through the sparse court records and articles, it was clear there had been nothing minor about it.

Catherine had accused Lydia not only of stealing her ideas but of actively sabotaging her career. The settlement had been kept out of the public eye, the details sealed, but the rumours surrounding it had persisted. A former employee quoted in one article had described Lydia as "relentless," a woman who "would destroy competition with a smile on her face."

The questions came faster now, tripping over each other.

Alice leaned back in the chair; her gaze fixed on the rows of books lining the shelves. Her head throbbed. Every new piece of information felt like another thread unravelling the already fragile tapestry of her marriage.

She rubbed her temples, her thoughts spinning in circles. Aiden rarely shared details, always quick to change the subject when Lydia's name came up. Was that because he was grieving —or because there were things he didn't want Alice to know?

Her mind wandered to Maria's warning: *Lydia wasn't always the victim. She was just as capable of hurting others.* And then there was the suggestion that Lydia might have been having an affair.

Her gaze drifted to the window, where the grey sky pressed heavily against the glass. The house felt eerily quiet, the silence broken only by the faint hum of the smart system. She couldn't shake the feeling that the house was watching her, its very walls alive with a secret history. This wasn't just a home—it was a stage. And Lydia had been the star.

But stars burn out, Alice thought grimly, her fingers tightening on the edges of her laptop. Lydia's perfect life had been a facade, one that had shattered long before her disappearance. The more Alice uncovered, the more she realised that Lydia's story wasn't just about ambition or success—it was about power. Power that she had wielded over others. Power that might have ultimately consumed her.

Alice turned back to her screen. She scrolled through interview transcripts and old blog posts, her eyes scanning for anything that might give her a clearer picture of Lydia's life. One post caught her attention: an interview Lydia had given shortly before her disappearance. In it, she had spoken about her marriage to Aiden, describing it as a "partnership built on mutual respect and shared goals." The words felt rehearsed and Alice couldn't help but wonder what had been left unsaid.

Was it mutual respect, or was it control? Alice thought. She thought of the journal entries she had found, Aiden's measured words hinting at frustration and strain.

Her breath quickened as the questions piled up, each one more unsettling than the last. She tried to push them aside, to focus on the facts, but her emotions were too raw, too tangled. She felt like she was standing on the edge of a precipice, peering into an abyss.

And yet, she couldn't stop. The answers were out there, buried beneath the layers of secrecy and lies. She had to keep digging, not just for Lydia's sake but for her own. She needed to understand the truth about the woman whose shadow loomed over her life—and about the man she had married.

Alice took a deep breath, her resolve hardening. She opened a new tab on her browser and began searching for any connections between Lydia and the people in her life. If Lydia had been unfaithful, there had to be a trail—texts, emails, something. And if Aiden had known... Alice didn't finish the thought.

As the hours passed, the sky outside darkened, the grey giving way to threatening indigo. The house grew colder, its silence deepening while Alice remained consumed by the search, as she pieced together fragments of a story that felt both distant and dangerously close.

She wasn't sure how long she had been working when the smart system chimed, its voice breaking the silence. "Good evening, Mrs. Chandler. Would you like me to adjust the lighting?"

Alice jumped, as she looked around the room. The voice was calm, neutral, but it felt intrusive, like the house itself was reminding her of its presence. She shook her head, trying to steady herself.

"No," she said aloud, her voice wavering. "I'm fine."

But she wasn't. The truth was dragging her deeper into a darkness she wasn't sure she could escape.

She leaned back in her chair, her gaze drifting back to her laptop screen. Lydia's secrets were out there, waiting to be uncovered.

The answer came to her almost by accident.

Continuing her quest, Alice was sorting through a box of old magazines she had found in one of the upstairs storage rooms. Most of them were lifestyle publications featuring Lydia smiling sickly on the cover. Alice flipped through them absently until a photo caught her attention.

It was a candid shot from a high-profile charity gala. In the photo, she was standing with Aiden on one side and Ian on the other. The caption read: *"Lydia Chandler with her husband, Aiden, and business partner, Ian Carlisle, at the inaugural gala for the Lydia Chandler Foundation."*

Alice stared at the photo, her eyes narrowing. Ian's body language was subtle but telling. He stood too close to Lydia, his hand resting lightly on the small of her back. The smile on his face wasn't one of a typical business partner—it was intimate. Lydia's expression, too, seemed different in this photo. There was a glint in her eye, a secretive smile.

A chill ran down Alice's spine.

She set the magazine aside and turned back to her laptop, her fingers flying across the keyboard as she searched for more photos, more evidence. The more she looked, the clearer the picture became. Ian was present at nearly every major event in Lydia's life. He wasn't just a business partner—he was always in the background, always lingering close enough to suggest something more.

Alice's heart raced as she stumbled upon an old blog post from a gossip site. The article was from years ago and speculated about Lydia's "close relationship" with Ian. It was vague, filled with conjecture and unverified claims, but it hinted at private meetings, late-night phone calls, and even a trip the two had taken to Europe under the guise of a business venture.

Her hands trembled as she read, her stomach churning. The pieces were falling into place, but the implications were staggering. If Lydia had been having an affair with Ian, what did that mean for her marriage to Aiden? And why had no one ever spoken about it?

That evening, Alice paced the library, her thoughts swirling. The house felt too quiet. She wanted to raise her suspicions with Aiden but thought better of it.

Instead, she called Maria.

"It's Alice," she said when Maria answered. "I need to ask you something."

There was a pause on the other end, and Alice could hear

the faint clinking of dishes in the background. "Go on," Maria said cautiously.

"Was it Ian?" Alice asked, her voice trembling. "Was he the man Lydia was having an affair with?"

Another pause, longer this time. When Maria finally spoke, her voice was low and measured. "Why do you think that?"

"I found some things," Alice said. "Photos, articles. They were... close."

Maria sighed; the sound heavy with resignation. "I suspected it for a long time," she admitted. "They were careful, but there were moments—little things you'd only notice if you were around them all the time. The way they looked at each other, the way Ian he was always there. And then there were the late-night meetings, the trips. It all added up."

Alice's throat tightened. "Did Aiden know?"

"I don't think so," Maria said. "Or if he did, he never let on."

Alice's mind reeled. The implications were staggering. It cast her marriage to Aiden in a new light. But more than that, it made Lydia's disappearance more suspicious.

"You need to be careful, Mrs Chandler," Maria said, her voice sharp. "Ian is a snake. I never liked him."

Alice swallowed hard. "I'll be careful."

As she hung up the phone. She knew she was getting closer to the truth. Lydia had played a dangerous game, and now Alice was caught in the same web.

17

The mornings had become a routine of awkward silences and polite distance. Alice sat at the sprawling marble breakfast bar; her hands wrapped around a steaming cup of coffee. Across from her, Aiden skimmed through his tablet, occasionally taking a sip of his protein shake.

The air between them was taut, each moment punctuated by the scrape of silverware against porcelain or the faint buzz of Aiden's phone as notifications rolled in.

"Busy day?" Alice asked, her voice light.

"Always," Aiden replied without looking up. He continued to scroll through his emails, his brow furrowed in concentration. "I've got back-to-back meetings this afternoon. Ian is flying in later for a strategy session."

Alice's stomach twisted at the mention of Ian. She forced a neutral expression, trying to sound casual. "You two seem close."

Aiden glanced up briefly, his expression unreadable. "He's worked with Lydia for years."

Alice nodded, taking a small sip of her coffee.

Karen entered briefly to refill Alice's mug of coffee, her presence a silent reminder of the meticulous order Aiden demanded in his life. He barely acknowledged her, his attention fixed on his tablet.

"Aiden," Alice said after a moment, her voice hesitant. "Do you ever think about Lydia?"

His hand paused mid-scroll, and he looked up at her, his expression hardening. "What kind of question is that?"

Alice felt a pang of regret. "I just mean... people still talk about her so much. It must be hard."

Aiden's set his tablet down with a soft thud. "Lydia is gone, Alice. What's hard is trying to move forward while everyone insists on dredging up the past."

His words stung, but his tone carried something more than frustration—something that sounded a lot like pain.

"If that's the case why are we surrounded by Lydia's things? Don't you think perhaps it's time to pack some of them away?"

Alice studied him for a moment, wondering if Aiden still carried the weight of Lydia's memory, just as she did. But before she could say anything else, his phone buzzed again.

"I'll be back late," he said abruptly, rising from his chair and grabbing his tablet. He leaned over to kiss her cheek, the gesture quick and perfunctory. "Don't wait up."

And just like that, he was gone, leaving Alice alone again. She stared down at her untouched breakfast, the knot in her stomach tightening. She'd lost her appetite.

Alice sat in the cavernous kitchen long after Aiden had left, the silence in the room bearing down on her. She stared at her untouched plate.

Karen re-entered briefly, moving silently as she tidied away the breakfast things. Alice watched her, wondering how much the staff knew—how much they had seen and overheard. She opened her mouth to say something, anything, to break the silence, but Karen moved away with a polite nod before Alice could say anything.

As the footsteps receded, Alice leaned back in her chair, staring out at the sky beyond. Rain streaked the glass in fine rivulets, mirroring the trail of her thoughts.

Her eyes drifted to the spot where Aiden's tablet had been, its absence leaving a strange emptiness. He had guarded it so closely, his fingers scrolling quickly through whatever had occupied his attention before her question interrupted him. It wasn't unusual—Aiden was always absorbed in his work or private matters—but today, there had been an urgency to it, something that felt different.

Alice rose from her seat and wandered to the window. Her reflection in the glass stared back at her, pale and uncertain.

The quiet whir of the smart system broke her reverie. "Good morning, Mrs. Chandler," it spoke softly, as though it sensed her turmoil.

"Stop," she murmured, more to herself than to the system. But the reminder of the house's omnipresence was enough to make her feel uncomfortable, even when she was alone.

Her eyes drifted toward Aiden's side of the house—the office, his private study, the places she rarely ventured. Curiosity began to take root, pulling her thoughts back to the tablet and the quick way he had shut her out. She knew Aiden valued his privacy, but the gnawing suspicion growing inside her was becoming unbearable.

She wandered toward his office. The door was closed, as it always was, and she hesitated in front of it. She could feel the house's stillness, as though it were holding its breath, waiting to see what she would do next.

She reached for the doorknob, turning it, half-expecting it to be locked. The door swung open, revealing the stark, minimal space within. Aiden's desk was as meticulously organized as the rest of Evermere, the surface almost unnaturally clean. A sleek monitor sat in the centre, its screen dark, and a series of files were stacked neatly to the side.

Alice stepped inside, her breath catching in her throat. She had been in his office before, but today, it felt different—charged, like the walls themselves were buzzing with something unsaid. She moved toward the desk. She wasn't sure what she was looking for, but the compulsion to search was irresistible.

Her gaze fell on a small drawer at the side of the desk. It was locked, the key nowhere in sight. She tried it again, her frustration mounting. The locked drawer only heightened her determination, her curiosity now a full-blown ache.

She knew she'd crossed a line as she closed the office door behind her, a cold sweat on the back of her neck. Evermere seemed darker now, silently condemning her. She hurried back to the kitchen, her mind a whirlwind of doubts and fears.

Aiden's words echoed in her mind: *"Lydia is gone. What's hard is trying to move forward while everyone insists on dredging up the past."* But it wasn't the past haunting him—it was something alive, pulsing beneath the surface of their lives like a wound that refused to heal. There was more to Lydia's story, more to Aiden's silence, and Alice was determined to uncover it.

The rest of the day passed in a haze. The house, with its gleaming surfaces and high-tech features, felt more unwelcoming than ever. Every time she walked past a screen, she half-expected it to flicker to life with another image or video of Lydia.

By late afternoon, Alice found herself back in the small office, where she had spent so many hours researching Lydia's life. She opened her laptop, her fingers hesitating over the keyboard before typing in the name of one of her favourite gossip websites. She told herself it was just a distraction, a way to escape the tension that pulsed through Evermere like a living thing.

But as the homepage loaded, her heart sank. There, on the front page, was a photo of her.

It was a candid shot, taken outside the coffee shop where she had met Maria. The caption read: *"Mrs. Aiden Chandler spotted downtown—trouble in paradise?"* The article speculated wildly.

The comments below were as cruel as they were predictable.

She looks so plain compared to Lydia. Aiden could do better.

Why does she always look so nervous? She's not cut out for this.

Bet she's already falling apart under the pressure.

She pushed the laptop away, the words blurring on the screen. It wasn't just the invasion of privacy that bothered her—it was the sense of exposure. Even her meeting with Maria, something she thought was private, had been twisted into tabloid fodder.

She stood and began pacing the room, her thoughts racing. If the paparazzi were following her, they might have seen Maria too. She needed to protect Maria, to make sure her name didn't get dragged into this mess. But more than that, she needed to figure out how much attention her digging might attract—and how to stay one step ahead.

That evening, dinner was as strained as ever. Karen had prepared a flawless meal, as she always did, and the dining room table was set with the kind of meticulous care that spoke more to presentation than comfort. Aiden was distracted, his phone buzzing intermittently with messages he couldn't seem to ignore.

Alice picked at her food; her appetite non-existent. She glanced up at Aiden, wondering if he had seen the article, but he gave no indication he had. His focus was elsewhere, as it always seemed to be these days.

"Did you know there's a photo of me online?" Alice asked.

Aiden glanced up, his brow furrowing slightly. "What kind of photo?"

"Paparazzi," she said, setting her fork down. "It was taken outside a coffee shop. They're already speculating about trouble in our marriage."

Aiden sighed, leaning back in his chair. "Ignore it. They're always looking for something to stir up."

"But it's not just gossip," Alice pressed. "They're following me, Aiden. They're watching everything I do."

"That's the price of being in this world," he said simply, as if that explained everything. "You'll get used to it."

Alice's didn't like his dismissiveness, but she forced herself to stay calm. "Do you think they'll stop at gossip? What if they dig into the past—into Lydia?"

Aiden's expression darkened. "Lydia's gone, Alice. Let it go."

His tone left no room for argument, but it only fuelled Alice's resolve. If Aiden wouldn't answer her questions, she would have to find the answers herself.

Later that night, Evermere was silent. Alice's footsteps echoed faintly as she made her way to the small office adjoining the library, a space she had claimed as her own.

She opened her laptop and settled into the plush leather chair, her fingers hovering over the keyboard. The gossip article she'd seen earlier still burned in her mind.

Alice searched for the article again, her heart sinking as the image loaded on the screen. The photo was sharp, the angle unflattering. She could see herself standing awkwardly outside the café, her expression tense. The caption was worse than she remembered: *Mrs. Aiden Chandler meeting a mystery woman.*

The comments below the article were a knife twisting in her gut.

She'll never be Lydia. Aiden deserves someone with charisma, not... this.

Why does she always look like she's on the verge of tears? Pathetic!

Can't handle the pressure?

Alice closed the laptop abruptly, unable to read another word. Her chest felt tight, her pulse pounding in her ears. She took a deep breath, wondering why she'd looked at it again. She glanced around the office, her gaze landing on a stack of magazines she had gathered earlier in the day.

She picked up one of them, flipping through the glossy pages until she found the photo she'd been searching for: Lydia, standing between Aiden and Ian at a charity gala. Her hair gleamed under the lights; her smile was radiant. But it wasn't Lydia who drew Alice's attention—it was Ian. His hand rested lightly on Lydia's shoulder; his posture angled toward her in a way that spoke of familiarity.

Alice stared at the photo.

She opened her laptop again, this time searching for Ian specifically. His name brought up hundreds of results: business articles, interviews, and photos from events. But the deeper she dug, the more patterns she noticed. Ian was always there—at Lydia's side during key moments in her career and at events where Aiden was conspicuously absent.

Her fingers battered the keyboard as she pieced together a timeline. There were rumours, subtle and buried in obscure blogs and forums. One article commented on a business trip that Ian and Lydia had taken to Paris, supposedly for a charity initiative.

The signs were all there, hiding in plain sight. Ian hadn't just been Lydia's business partner—he had been something much more.

Alice leaned back in her chair. If Ian had been having an affair with Lydia, what did that mean for her disappearance? Did Aiden know? And if he did, had he confronted Ian—or Lydia?

The room suddenly felt too small, too suffocating. She stood and moved to the window, staring out at the dark expanse of the ocean beyond the cliffs. The waves crashed against the rocks, their relentless rhythm a contrast to the chaos in her mind.

She reached for her phone, her fingers hovering over Maria's number. Maria had already warned her to be careful.

Alice's reflection stared back at her in the glass, pale and drawn. She couldn't stop now, not when she was so close to the truth. But for the first time, she felt the true weight of what she was uncovering—the danger, the secrets, the affair.

As the house settled into its nightly stillness, Alice turned back to her laptop, her determination hardening, even though she couldn't shake the feeling that someone out there was waiting for her to slip.

18

The wine bar was tucked away on a quiet side street in the city, its dim lighting and dark wood interior exuding an air of exclusivity. Alice arrived early, selecting a small, intimate booth near the back where she could observe the room while remaining mostly unseen. She had spent the entire day debating whether meeting Ian like this was a good idea. It wasn't, she knew that really, but her need had outweighed her caution.

The waiter approached, offering her the wine list. She ordered a glass of Malbec, something strong enough to steady her nerves, and waited. The minutes stretched and she began to wonder if Ian would even show. But then, just as her doubts began to take hold, he arrived.

Ian Carlisle entered the bar with his usual rehearsed confidence. His clothes marked him as a man who knew his power and wielded it with precision. He scanned the room before spotting Alice. His expression was neutral, but his eyes gleamed with curiosity—and something colder.

"Alice," he said smoothly as he slid into the booth across from her. "This is a nice surprise. To what do I owe this honour? I was intrigued when I got your message."

"Thank you for meeting me," Alice replied, keeping her voice steady. She offered a polite smile, though her hands gripped the stem of her glass tightly beneath the table.

Ian leaned back, studying her with an intensity that made her skin crawl.

"You said you wanted to discuss a business plan? Something I could help with?"

"Yes," Alice said, forcing herself to meet his gaze. "But first, I want to talk about Lydia."

Ian's expression didn't change, but his posture stiffened slightly. He reached for the menu, his movements slow and deliberate. "I'm not sure what you think I can offer."

"You knew her well," Alice pressed, her voice calm but insistent. "You were her business partner, but you were also... more than that, weren't you?"

Ian froze for a split second before placing the menu back on the table. He leaned forward, his eyes narrowing. "I don't know what you're implying, Alice, but I think you should choose your words very carefully. You're playing with the big boys now, or haven't you realised that yet?"

Alice swallowed hard, her pulse racing, but she didn't back down. "I've seen the photos. The articles. I know about the late-night meetings, the trips. You had an affair with her, didn't you?"

His temples throbbed, and for a moment, Alice thought he might deny it outright. But instead, he exhaled sharply, a bitter smile tugging at the corner of his mouth. "You're very bold, Mrs. Chandler. I didn't realise you had it in you."

"So, it's true," Alice said, her voice barely above a whisper. Ian's eyes darkened, and he leaned closer, his voice low and threatening.

"You don't know what you're talking about. And if you're smart, you'll stop right there."

Alice refused to look away. "Why? What are you afraid of?

That Aiden will find out? That someone might dig into what actually happened to Lydia?"

Ian's expression turned icy, the mask of civility slipping. "Listen to me carefully, Alice," he said, his voice dangerously quiet. "Lydia is gone. Whatever happened between us, it's in the past. Digging it up won't bring her back, and it won't do you any favours. If you value the life you have now, I suggest you stop playing detective."

Alice's hands shook beneath the table, but she kept her face as composed as she could. "You're not denying it," she said, her voice steadier than she felt.

Ian's lips curled into a cold smile. "I don't need to deny anything. Because whatever you think you know, you can't prove. And if you try to drag my name—or Lydia's—through the mud, I guarantee you won't like what happens next."

The wine bar's dim lighting cast Ian's sharp features in shadow, making him look more sinister as he leaned forward across the small table again. Alice's heart pounded in her chest, as her fingers clutched the stem of her wine glass. Ian's icy smile didn't waver, but his eyes burned with an intensity that made her feel off balance.

"You really don't know who you're messing with, do you?" he said, his voice low, almost a whisper. He leaned back in his seat, swirling his whiskey deliberately as though he enjoyed her discomfort.

"Then enlighten me," Alice replied, surprising herself with the firmness in her voice. "If Lydia wasn't the perfect wife everyone says she was, then what was she? And what were you to her?"

Ian's smile faded slightly, his gaze narrowing. "Lydia was ambitious. Ruthless. She didn't let anyone stand in her way—not me, not Aiden. If you think for one second that she was content being his little trophy wife, you're naiver than I thought."

Alice swallowed hard. "You're saying she wasn't happy?"

Ian's laugh was dry and humourless. "Happy? No, Lydia wasn't built for happiness. She was built for power. She had plans, Alice. Big plans. And trust me, Aiden wasn't part of them."

"What do you mean?"

Ian set his glass down with a soft clink, his expression hardening. "She was going to leave him. Take everything—his money, his reputation, the house, even the company if she could. She had it all worked out. She was meeting with lawyers, lining up allies, plotting behind his back."

Alice's blood ran cold. "Why would she do that?"

"Because that's who she was," Ian said simply. "She wanted control. She wanted to win. And Aiden, for all his charm and power, was just another obstacle in her way."

Alice's mind raced as she tried to process his words. It was a far cry from the idyllic picture the world had painted of Aiden and Lydia's marriage. If what Ian was saying was true, Lydia's disappearance wasn't just a tragedy—it was a powder keg.

"And you?" Alice asked, her voice barely above a whisper. "Were you part of her plan?"

Ian's lips curled into a smirk, but there was no warmth in it. "I was many things to Lydia. A confidant, a partner, someone who understood her. But even I knew better than to trust her completely."

The comment hung in the air like smoke, her mind unable to reconcile the image of Lydia as a cunning manipulator with the beautiful, enigmatic woman who still haunted ever corner of the Evermere estate.

"If she was planning to leave Aiden," Alice said cautiously, "why didn't she? What stopped her?"

Ian's expression darkened, his smile disappearing entirely. He leaned closer still, his voice dropping to a dangerous whisper. "That's the million-dollar question, isn't it? Maybe Aiden found out. Maybe he couldn't bear the thought of losing his perfect life, his perfect wife. Maybe he decided to take matters into his own hands."

"Are you saying... Aiden—?" Alice took a sip of her wine, trying to appear calm.

"I'm not saying anything," Ian interrupted, his tone sharp. "I don't have proof. But if I were you, I'd think long and hard about who you trust in that house. Lydia wasn't the only one who could be ruthless."

The words hit Alice like a punch to the gut. She stared at Ian, her mind racing with possibilities she didn't want to entertain. Could Aiden have been involved in Lydia's disappearance? Had he known about her affair with Ian? About her plans to leave him?

Ian stood abruptly, straightening his suit jacket with meticulous precision. "I've said enough," he said, his voice cold. "Take my advice, Alice. Stop digging. Walk away while you still can."

"Fuck you," she hissed as he placed a few bills on the table to cover his drink and turned to leave. Alice watched him go, her heart pounding so loudly she could barely hear the murmur of conversations around her.

Alice stared at her wine glass, the dark liquid swirling as she turned the stem absently in her hand. The bar's low hum of soft jazz music faded into the background, her thoughts consuming her. Ian's words repeated in her mind, their menace undeniable.

If you value the life you have now, I suggest you stop playing detective.

She took a sip of her wine, the sharp tang grounding her for a moment.

She knew keeping this to herself felt dangerous. Ian's threat wasn't empty—she could see it in his eyes. If she continued down this path, she would be putting herself in jeopardy.

Alice closed her eyes, letting out a shaky breath. The truth about Lydia was still just out of reach, tantalizing and elusive. But the more she uncovered, the more she realised that everyone around her had something to hide.

As the waiter approached to ask if she needed anything else, Alice shook her head and asked for the check. The wine sat heavy in her stomach as she gathered her things and left the bar, stepping out into the night air.

She slipped into her car and sat for a moment, gripping the steering wheel as she stared straight ahead. The night was still, but she couldn't shake the feeling that Ian—or someone else—might already be making moves to keep her quiet.

Her hands trembled as she started the car and pulled onto the street, her mind racing with questions.

As the city lights blurred past her, Alice knew one thing for certain: whatever she chose to do next, there would be no going back.

19

The house felt smaller than ever, its vast, echoing halls suddenly claustrophobic as Alice faced Aiden in his office. The air between them was charged, their gazes locked.

"You want the truth?" Aiden said, his voice cutting through the silence like a knife. "Fine. Lydia wasn't the woman the world thinks she was. She was..." He paused, his hands clenching into fists at his sides, as if he were physically grappling with the words. "She was the most dangerous person I've ever known."

"Dangerous? What do you mean?" Alice was taken back by his sudden honesty.

Aiden ran a hand through his hair, his movements agitated. "She wasn't just ruthless, Alice. She was calculated, manipulative, and she knew exactly how to hit someone where it hurt. She could smile to your face and destroy you behind your back—while making you believe it was your fault."

Alice swallowed hard, her voice barely above a whisper. "And what did she do to you?"

Aiden turned away, his hands bracing against the edge of his desk. The soft glow of the desk lamp cast illuminated lines on his face, making him look older, wearier. "She knew things about me," he said finally, his voice low and measured. "Things no one else knows. Mistakes I made when I was building the company—cut corners, deals I should never have agreed to. She found out, and she used it against me."

Alice's heart pounded. "She blackmailed you."

He nodded, swallowing hard, knowing he finally needed to admit the truth. "She didn't just want money, Alice. She wanted control. She threatened to go public with everything—leak documents, talk to reporters, ruin me. And it wouldn't have just destroyed the company. It would have destroyed me. My reputation, everything I'd worked for... She wanted it all."

Alice stared at him, the enormity of his words sinking in. "Why would she do that? She was your wife."

Aiden let out a bitter laugh, his eyes filled with something other than anger—hurt. "You think that meant anything to her? Lydia didn't love me. She loved power. She loved the idea of being married to someone like me, of being part of my world. But when she realised she could have all of it without me, she decided I was expendable."

Alice took a shaky step closer, her voice trembling. "You said she was planning to leave you."

"She wasn't just planning to leave," Aiden said, his voice sharp. "She was going to take everything. The house, the company, the foundation—everything. And she didn't even try to hide it. She wanted me to know."

"Why?" Alice asked, her throat tight. "Why would she do that?"

Aiden turned to her, his eyes burning with a mix of fury and pain. "Because she was cruel and she wanted to hurt me. She wanted to watch me squirm, to see me powerless. She even flaunted her affair with Ian, taunting me with it."

Alice's breath caught, the pieces of the story falling into place. "You knew about the affair."

"I suspected it for months. Question is, how do you know?" Aiden asked, his eyes narrowing, his voice laced with bitterness.

"I worked it out." She wasn't ready to admit how far she'd gone to get answer. "And when you found out?" Alice pressed.

Aiden's eyes darkened, and his voice dropped to a whisper. "She didn't even deny it. She wanted me to know. She wanted me to feel humiliated. She told me everything—how long it had been going on, how Ian was more of a man than I'd ever be. She even said..." He broke off, as he struggled to continue.

Alice stepped closer, her heart aching at the raw emotion in his voice. "What did she say?"

"She said I'd never touch her again," Aiden said finally, his voice trembling with suppressed anger. "That once she left, I'd be nothing. Just a man whose success was built on her brilliance."

The pain in his words cut through Alice like a blade. She had never seen Aiden like this—so exposed, so vulnerable. The man who had always seemed unshakable now stood before her like a shattered version of himself, the wounds his first wife had inflicted still fresh and bleeding.

Alice's voice softened. "Aiden... this doesn't make sense. I don't understand what you're telling me. I don't get it. Why?"

Aiden shrugged and slumped into his chair and for the first time in days she knew he was telling the truth. He didn't know.

"It's just what she did. Because she could." He sighed.

"What happened to her?" Alice asked cautiously.

Aiden's gaze hardened; his vulnerability replaced by a wall of steel. "She's gone, Alice. That's all that matters."

"That's not good enough. You must have—"

"Enough!" Aiden snapped, his voice echoing through the room. "You don't understand, Alice. You don't understand what it's like to have someone hold your entire life in their hands and threaten to destroy it. You don't understand the kind of person Lydia was—the kind of games she played."

Alice recoiled, her chest tightening at the force of his words. "I'm trying to understand, Aiden. But you're shutting me out."

Aiden exhaled sharply, running a hand over his face. "Because the truth won't help you, Alice. It won't change anything. Lydia's gone, and I'm finally free."

Before Alice could respond, the door creaked open, and Karen stepped inside. Her presence was like an arrow cutting through the tension in the room. She moved with her usual calm precision, her eyes flicking between Aiden and Alice with an almost imperceptible flicker of curiosity.

"Mr. Chandler," Karen said smoothly, her voice cutting through the silence. "I didn't mean to interrupt, but there's a call waiting for you. It's from the London office. They said it's urgent."

Aiden straightened, his expression hardening once more. "I'll take it in the study," he said curtly, brushing past Alice without another word.

Karen turned her attention to Alice, her face composed but her eyes sharp, as if she were calculating every detail of the scene she had walked in on. "Is everything all right, Mrs. Chandler?" she asked, her tone polite but probing.

Alice forced a nod, though her heart was pounding in her chest. "Yes. Everything's fine, Karen."

Karen's gaze lingered on her for a moment longer, her faint smile unreadable, before she turned and left, the soft click of the door bursting the atmosphere in the room. Alice stood there, her thoughts racing. She was sure Karen had been listening.

As the house settled into an uneasy quiet, Alice's mind spun with questions and doubts. Lydia had been far nastier than she had realised, but Aiden's pain, his anger—it didn't remove the possibility that he had been pushed too far. And now, with Ian's warnings still ringing in her ears, Alice felt more alone than ever.

The truth about Lydia was like quicksand, pulling her deeper with every step. And she wasn't sure if she'd ever be on solid ground again.

20

The morning light filtered through the glass walls of Evermere, but it did little to dispel the suffocating weight hanging over the house. Alice sat at the breakfast bar; her phone clutched in her hands. Her inbox was flooded with messages—links to an article, comments from strangers, and texts from people she barely knew, all asking the same question: *Did you see this?*

She had seen it. The article was everywhere, plastered across gossip sites and splashed all over social media. It painted her as a naive, incompetent trophy wife—out of her depth in a world of power players. Worse, it dredged up her lack of experience in running a gallery, suggesting that her "ambition" was nothing more than an attempt to capitalise on Aiden's success. How did they know she wanted to open a gallery?

But the most humiliating part was the photo. It was the same shot from outside the coffee shop where she'd met Maria, paired with a fabricated story about how she had been seen meeting "a questionable contact." The article implied she was hiding something, speculating wildly that she was either conspiring against Aiden or embarrassing him with some secret project.

Alice tossed her phone onto the counter. She couldn't prove

it, but she was certain Ian was behind it. The timing was too perfect, the angle too pointed. This was his retaliation for her confrontation at the wine bar, his way of reminding her just how powerful—and unpredictable—he could be.

She looked up as Aiden entered the kitchen, his usual calm veneer cracking at the edges. His tie hung loose around his neck, and the dark circles under his eyes hinted at a sleepless night. He glanced at her, then at her phone, his expression flat.

"I saw it," he said grimly, pouring himself a cup of coffee. "I've already had five calls from PR this morning."

Alice's voice was quiet but edged with frustration. "It's Ian, isn't it? He's sending a message."

Aiden hesitated, his hand gripping the coffee cup so tightly she thought it might shatter. "It wouldn't surprise me," he admitted. "Ian is... manipulative. Vindictive. He doesn't like being challenged, and he has a long memory."

"Then why do you keep him so close?" Alice asked, her voice rising. "Why do you let him have so much power over you?"

Aiden sighed, running a hand through his hair. "It's not that simple. Ian knows too much—about the company, about Lydia. Cutting him loose isn't an option."

"Why not?" Alice pressed, her frustration boiling over. "What does he know that's so dangerous?"

Aiden set his cup down and turned to face her, his expression strained. "He was there, Alice. He was part of Lydia's life in ways I didn't want to see. And now, he's part of mine in ways I can't undo."

Alice stared at him, her heart pounding. "Aiden, you're not making sense. What happened between them? What are you so afraid of?"

Aiden hesitated, his shoulders slumping. For a moment, he looked like a man on the verge of collapse. Then, as if something inside him finally broke, he spoke.

"She was pregnant," he said quietly, his voice hollow.

Alice froze, her breath catching in her throat. "What?"

"Lydia," Aiden continued, his eyes dark with pain. "She was pregnant when she disappeared."

Alice stared at him, her mind struggling to process what he was saying. "I don't understand. You never mentioned this before. Why didn't you tell me? What the fuck were you thinking keeping this a secret?"

"It wasn't that simple," Aiden pleaded, his voice trembling. "She told me about the pregnancy just a few days before she... before the yacht. But she wasn't sure who the father was."

Alice felt a chill run down her spine. "You mean it might have been Ian's?"

Aiden nodded. "That's what she said. She didn't know for sure, and she didn't care. She used it as another weapon—another way to hurt me."

"What happened? Tell me." Alice asked, her voice barely above a whisper.

Aiden turned away, pacing to the far side of the kitchen as if he couldn't bear to look at her. "We had an argument," he admitted. "The day she went sailing. It was... explosive. She threw it in my face, telling me the baby might not be mine, about how Ian was a great fuck."

Alice's chest tightened as she imagined the scene—Aiden and Lydia, locked in a bitter, devastating fight.

"I was fucking furious," Aiden continued, his voice cracking. "I said things I shouldn't have. She said things... vile things. And then she left. She walked out, went down to the yacht, and sailed off."

He turned back to Alice, his eyes filled with anguish. "She was an experienced sailor, Alice. She knew the waters better than anyone. But that thunderstorm... it came out of nowhere. By the time I realized she hadn't come back, it was too late."

Tears welled in Alice's eyes as she took a hesitant step toward him, feeling sickness settle in her stomach. "Aiden, why didn't you tell anyone?"

"Because I blamed myself," he said, his voice breaking. "I pushed her too far. I let the argument get out of control. And when they found nothing—no body, no yacht—it was easier to let people believe it was an accident. To let the world remember her as the version of herself she wanted people to see, not the woman she really was."

Alice reached for him, her hand resting on his arm. He flinched slightly at the contact but didn't pull away. "Aiden, you didn't make her go out there. You couldn't have known what would happen."

He shook his head, his eyes haunted. "But I let it happen. I let her win. She was ready to take everything from me, Alice. My dignity, my trust, and maybe even my child. And I'll never know if that baby was mine—my flesh and blood—or someone else's."

The raw pain in his voice broke something inside Alice. She had spent so long resenting Lydia, fearing her legacy, but now, she saw the truth: Lydia's awful shadow hung over Aiden just as much as it did over her.

Before Alice could say more, the sound of footsteps echoed in the hallway. Karen appeared in the doorway; her presence as calculated as always. She glanced between them, her expression blank, though her sharp eyes were taking in every detail.

"Mr. Chandler," she said smoothly, her tone calm but purposeful. "I didn't mean to interrupt, but the team from London is on the line. They're waiting for you."

Aiden stiffened, his walls coming back up. "I'll take it in the study," he said curtly, brushing past Karen without another word.

Karen lingered for a moment, her gaze settling on Alice. Her faint smile didn't reach her eyes. "Is everything all right, Mrs. Chandler?"

Karen had a way of always appearing at the worst moments.

Alice forced a nod, her throat tight. "Yes. Everything's fine," she snapped.

Karen's gaze lingered a moment longer before she disappeared down the hall. Alice stood frozen, her mind racing.

As Evermere settled back into uneasy quiet, Alice felt the weight of Aiden's confession. The truth about Lydia was darker than she had imagined, but it only left her with more questions.

The answers were out there, but Alice wasn't sure she was ready to face them.

21

Aiden's departure had left Evermere feeling even colder, more gloomy. Alice stood at the edge of the living room, staring out through the towering glass walls at the endless ocean. The waves crashed violently against the cliffs below, their relentless rhythm echoing her own turmoil. Evermere seemed to amplify her unease, its sleek design offering no comfort, only stark reminders of how out of place she was.

The fire alarm had gone off three times that morning for no apparent reason, its shrill beeping cutting through the silence like a scream. Each time, Karen had appeared with a calm efficiency, silencing the alarm and insisting it must be a glitch in the smart system.

"It's nothing to worry about, Mrs. Chandler," Karen had said with her usual faint, unreadable smile. "These things happen."

But Alice wasn't convinced. The alarms, the uneasy stillness of the house, the way Karen always seemed to be around every corner—it all felt deliberate.

Then there was the rat.

Alice had been walking past the infinity pool when she saw

it, floating lifelessly in the pristine, sparkling water. At first, she thought it was a leaf but as she got closer, she realized what it was. The bloated body of a rat, its tiny limbs splayed out, bobbed gently against the pool's edge.

She had called for Karen, her voice shaking, and watched as the housekeeper removed it with a practiced detachment. "It must have fallen in during the night," Karen had said, her tone infuriatingly calm. "I'll have the pool cleaned immediately."

But Alice couldn't shake the image of the rat, its lifeless eyes staring up at her. It felt like a message.

By midday, the tension had become unbearable. She needed answers, needed to feel like she had some semblance of control in a house that seemed intent on driving her mad. She called David and asked him to stop by, under the pretence of wanting to discuss the grounds.

When he arrived, his usual warm demeanour was a welcome contrast to the coldness that seemed to permeate every wall. He stood on the patio, wiping his hands on his work gloves, his expression cautious as Alice invited him inside.

"Tea?" she offered, already moving toward the kitchen.

David hesitated but nodded. "Sure, thank you."

They sat at the kitchen island, the steaming mugs between them. Alice stared at her cup, trying to build up the courage to speak. David sipped his tea, his weathered face calm but watchful.

"David," Alice began, her voice tentative, "can I ask you something?"

"Of course," he said, his tone suggesting he was bracing himself.

"I've been thinking a lot about... everything," she continued, choosing her words carefully. "I feel like I don't know the full story."

David set his mug down, his brow furrowing slightly. "What do you mean?"

Alice hesitated, then leaned in slightly, lowering her voice. "Ian. There is something about him I can't put my finger on." She stirred her tea. "I think he's untrustworthy. Aiden's hinted as much. But I don't understand why Aiden keeps him around. What do you know about him?"

David sighed, leaning back in his chair. "Ian Carlisle is a businessman, through and through. He's smart, cunning and he knows how to play the game. But trust? I don't think anyone really trusts Ian—especially not Aiden. Their relationship has always been complicated."

"Complicated how?" Alice pressed trying to sound relaxed.

David's gaze flicked toward the window, as if considering how much he should say. "Ian's been around for years. He was close to Lydia—too close, if you ask me. But it wasn't just personal. He and Aiden built a lot of their early success together. They made deals, took risks. Some of those risks paid off, others... not so much."

Alice's heart quickened. "What kind of risks?"

David hesitated, then shook his head. "I don't know the details, and I don't want to speculate. But there were whispers, back in the early days. Deals that skirted the edge of what's legal. Partnerships with people who... let's just say, weren't exactly above board."

Alice's mind raced, the pieces of the puzzle starting to shift again. She was so grateful to David for being so candid. "And Ian? Did he push Aiden into those deals?"

David shrugged. "Maybe. Maybe not. Ian's good at making people think his way is the only way. But Aiden's no fool. He wouldn't have gone along with anything he didn't think was necessary."

Alice bit her lip, her thoughts spinning. If they had been involved in shady business dealings, it could explain why Aiden felt so beholden to Ian. But it also raised more questions about Lydia. How much had she known? How deeply had she been involved?

"Do you think Ian had feelings for Lydia?"

David's expression darkened slightly. "I think Ian had feelings for what Lydia represented. She was beautiful, ambitious, and powerful. They were alike in a lot of ways—both willing to do whatever it took to get what they wanted."

"And Aiden?" Alice asked, her voice quieter now. "Did he know about their... connection?" She wasn't sure David would answer truthfully.

David hesitated, his gaze meeting hers. "I think Aiden knew everything. But Aiden's always been a man who values loyalty, even when it's misplaced."

Alice nodded slowly, the weight of David's words settling over her. She wanted to ask more, to dig deeper, but she held back. She couldn't let on about the pregnancy, not yet. Not until she knew more.

"Thank you, David," she said finally, her voice steady, realising she shouldn't push her luck. "I appreciate your honesty."

David nodded, though his expression remained cautious. "Be careful, Alice. This house, this life—it's not always what it seems. And the people in it... they're not always who they appear to be."

As he left, Alice stood in the doorway, watching him disappear down the path toward the gardens. The house loomed behind her gleaming in the afternoon light, but the shadows inside felt darker than ever.

The fire alarms, the cat, Karen's ever-present watchfulness—it all felt like pieces of a larger game. One she didn't fully understand.

She turned back toward the house, ready to face it. If no one was going to give her the answers she needed, she would find them herself.

22

The first letter had arrived two days after Aiden left for his latest business trip. Alice found it in the morning, slipped among the usual stack of mail that Karen had neatly stacked on the counter. The envelope was unmarked, the handwriting jagged and rushed. Inside was a single piece of paper, the message typed in bold, ominous letters:

You don't belong here. Leave.

At first, Alice thought it must be a joke—a cruel prank by someone who wanted to get under her skin. But when the second letter arrived the next day, her unease deepened. This one was more graphic, describing the "consequences" of staying, the words dripping with menace. By the third letter, there was no mistaking the threat. Someone wanted her gone, and they were willing to scare her into submission.

Aiden had been furious when she told him over the phone. "It's just some deranged fan," he had said, his voice tight. "Lydia had her share of obsessed admirers. They've probably fixated on you now because you're in her place."

"But why now?" Alice had asked, her voice trembling. "Why would they wait this long to target me?" She didn't appreciate

Aiden suggesting she'd taken Lydia's place. The press did enough of that already.

"Who knows." Aiden had replied, his tone dismissive and uninterested. "These people don't need a reason. They're irrational, unstable. Bored. Ignore them." He paused, "but promise me you won't go anywhere without telling me first. I need to know you're safe."

And then the calls began. Every few hours, Aiden would check in, his voice filled with concern. *"Where are you? What are you doing? Have you seen anything suspicious?"* At first, Alice found his protectiveness reassuring. But as the days wore on, his constant checking began to feel suffocating, as though the walls of Evermere weren't already closing in on her fast enough.

"You need to stay at home," he told her during one of their late-night calls. "It's not safe out there, Alice. The press is already circling like vultures. You're a target. You don't want to give them any more ammunition."

Alice had agreed, if only to end the conversation. But as she sat in the empty house, the silence broken only by the occasional noise of the smart system, she couldn't help but feel like a prisoner. The place seemed to pulse with Lydia's presence-reminders of her still lingering in the corners. And now, with the letters looming in the back of her mind, the house felt more like a trap than a sanctuary.

A few days later another letter arrived, this time slipped under the front door. Alice found it while pacing the foyer, her restlessness driving her mad. She hesitated before picking it up, the envelope heavier than the others. Her fingers trembled as she tore it open, revealing a single line scrawled in that same jagged handwriting:

"She's gone."

Alice's breath caught, her heart pounding in her chest. The message was so brief, so cryptic. Who was "she"? Lydia? Was this some cruel reference to her lingering presence in the house, or was it something more?

Her mind raced as she clutched the letter; her thoughts being pulled into the dark corners she'd been trying to avoid.

It seemed impossible—there had been no body, no trace of the yacht, nothing to suggest she had survived. But the more Alice thought about it, the more the question consumed at her.

Alice shivered, the air in the house suddenly feeling colder. She turned and paced to the kitchen, clutching the letter as though it might give her answers if she stared at it long enough. She had to tell Aiden, had to let him know what was going on in her head. But even as she reached for her phone, a part of her hesitated.

Aiden had been so certain, so adamant that Lydia was gone. And then there was the other possibility, the one she didn't want to entertain: What if Aiden knew more about Lydia's disappearance than he was saying? What if the letters weren't from a fan at all?

Her thoughts were interrupted by a quiet noise behind her —a creak of a door, barely audible but enough to make her stop and listen. She turned quickly but the kitchen was empty. Still, the feeling lingered. Evermere was too quiet, too watchful, as though its walls were listening.

And then there was Karen. Something about her made Alice feel uncomfortable. Like the housekeeper was the hostess and she was the guest. But lately, Alice had caught her watching from the corners of her vision, her gaze lingering just a moment too long. Karen's presence seemed amplified when Alice was alone, a presence that lingered even when she wasn't in the room.

Alice's phone buzzed, snapping her out of her thoughts. It

was Aiden. Of course it was. No one else ever messaged her these days.

"Hi," she said, her voice wavering slightly.

"Alice," he said, his tone brisk but concerned. "I just wanted to check in. How are you holding up?"

"I'm fine," she lied, glancing down at the letter in her hand. "Nothing new to report. How's Berlin."

"Good," he said, though his voice didn't sound convincing. "I don't want you leaving the house, okay? Not until we figure out who's behind this."

"I know," Alice said quietly. "I'm being careful." She rolled her eyes and tugged on the cuff of her jumper.

"Good," Aiden repeated. There was a pause, and then his tone softened. "I just want you to be safe, Alice. These threats—they're serious. And I don't want to lose you too."

The words caught her off guard, their sincerity cutting through her mounting paranoia. "I'll be fine," she said, though the tremor in her voice betrayed her as she wondered why he was finally taking it seriously.

After they hung up, Alice sat at the kitchen table, the letter now clutched in her hand again. She stared at it for a long time, the words burning into her mind. Whether it was the work of a crazed fan or someone closer to home, she was deeply troubled by the message. Inside, she wanted to scream.

As the night deepened, Evermere seemed to grow darker, its silence heavier. Alice felt like she was being watched—not by cameras or by Karen, but by something unseen, something lurking just beyond her reach.

The question that had given birth in her mind haunted her as she climbed the stairs to her room, the letter tucked under her arm like a talisman.

The house felt colder as the hours passed but it wasn't the physical temperature. It was the kind of cold that seeped into Alice's chest, chilling her from the inside out. The letter lay open on her dressing table in front of her, the words staring back like a taunt. She had reread it so many times the letters started to blur together.

Alice traced the edge of the paper with her finger, her thoughts spinning in endless circles. The possibility had always been there, tucked away in the back of her mind: Lydia might not be dead. It had felt absurd at first, a fleeting moment of paranoia, fuelled by whispers and the weight of the estate she now called home. But this letter, this ominous and simple declaration, was like a match struck in a dark room, illuminating corners of her mind she had tried to keep quiet.

She stood from the bed abruptly and began pacing, the windows framing the dark night outside. The sea beyond was black and turbulent, crashing against the rocks with ferocity. The vastness of the house, once a reminder of its grandeur, now felt haunted.

What if Lydia was alive?

The question wrapped itself around her mind like a vice, squeezing and refusing to let go. The whispers about Lydia seemed to follow Alice wherever she went. Was this all just a sick game?

Alice thought of the journals, the photos, the notes she'd uncovered—pieces of Lydia's life. The lies. The image. That perfect, fake image. And yet, if she had survived, what would drive her to remain hidden for so long?

Unless... she was planning something.

Alice's pulse quickened as her mind raced through the possibilities. What if the letters weren't just threats? What if they were a message—a warning or, worse. Lydia could be out there, pulling the strings, watching as Alice unravelled piece by piece. The thought made her feel sick.

She walked to the window, pressing her palms against the

cool glass as she stared out into the night. The darkness felt alive, as though something—or someone—was waiting just beyond the edge of the property. Watching. Waiting. The hairs on the back of her neck stood on end, and she felt certain she wasn't alone, even though she knew the house was empty, Karen long since retired to her quarters.

Lydia had been a master manipulator, as Maria and David had both suggested. She had controlled her image, her relationships, even her marriage. If Lydia was alive, then she was more than capable of orchestrating this—of turning Alice's life into a twisted maze of paranoia and fear.

Alice turned away from the window, her thoughts careening toward Aiden. She wished he was there with her. Even if she didn't really trust him. She felt safe with him most of the time. Most of the time.

Her chest tightened as doubt flooded her. Aiden had secrets; that much was clear. His guarded demeanour, his reluctance to talk about Lydia in anything more than vague terms—it all pointed to something buried, something he didn't want her to uncover. Perhaps this why he had been so insistent that she stay in the house, that she avoid drawing attention to herself. He was only trying to protect her. It wasn't about control. It was love she told herself forcing herself to remember the night they got engaged.

Alice's mind churned with questions she couldn't answer. She sank on to the bed, her legs feeling giddy beneath her. Why would Lydia fake her own death?

If Lydia was alive, then maybe she'd been watching Alice, waiting for the perfect moment to strike. And if Lydia was out there, then the child was alive. A child who might be Aiden's.

They had never discussed having children. The thought hit Alice like a physical blow.

She wasn't yet thirty, so there was plenty of time, but it occurred to her that it was odd they had never even discussed it.

The idea was absurd, but it made a sick kind of sense. Lydia had built this life, this legacy. There was no room for anyone else. There never would be. And Aiden showed no desire to welcome a child into the world either.

Twisting onto her side she cradled her face in her hands. She was just a placeholder, a pale imitation of the woman who had come before her.

Her phone buzzed on the table, startling her out of her destructive thoughts. She grabbed it quickly, her breath hitching as she saw Aiden's name on the screen again. For a moment, she considered ignoring the call, letting it go to voicemail. But the thought of his voice, his calm reassurance, was too tempting.

"Hello?" she said, her voice trembling.

"Alice," Aiden said, his tone brisk but warm. "Is everything all right?"

"I'm fine," she lied, her voice steadying. "Just tired." They'd only spoken less than an hour ago.

"Good," he said, his voice softening. "I know this has been hard on you. I'll be home soon, and we'll sort everything out. I promise."

As the call ended, Alice stared at her phone, blinking. Aiden might be willing to wait for answers, but she couldn't. The mystery was consuming her, and she couldn't rest until she knew the truth. Whether it was the ramblings of a deranged fan or the work of Lydia herself, Alice needed to face it.

Taking a deep breath, she folded the letter and tucked it into her pocket. She didn't know where this path would lead her, but she knew one thing for certain: she couldn't run from Lydia's shadow any longer. If Lydia was out there, pulling the strings in a sick game, then Alice was going to find her—and put an end to it.

23

The days at Evermere were beginning to bleed into one another, a haze of paranoia and fear that wound itself around Alice like a tightening noose. Every creak of each door, every distant noise made her jump. She tiptoed through the sprawling, sterile halls, afraid to disturb the silence, yet unable to escape the cloying weight of it. Lydia's presence was everywhere—suffocating, omnipresent. She wished she had the bravery to remove all traces, but she didn't. She was afraid of upsetting Aiden and terrified of angering whatever else was plotting against her.

Lydia's polished aura clung to every room like an unshakable ghost and Evermere itself seemed to conspire against her. The fire alarms continued to go off at random intervals, their shrill beeping jolting her from restless sleep or moments of pretend calm. Lights flickered unexpectedly, and the temperature controls would shift without warning, leaving rooms icy cold or unbearably warm. The smart home system felt more like a sentient force playing tricks on her.

Then there were the letters. Every day Alice found herself dreading the arrival of the mail, her heart pounding as she sifted through the envelopes, like a woman possessed. She hadn't told

Aiden about the latest one—another cryptic warning, this time implying that her time in the house was running out. The message was chilling:

Your days are numbered.

Alice stared at it for hours, unable to throw it away. She couldn't understand why she felt as though the sender was speaking directly to her—not just to Aiden's new wife, but *her*. Someone seemed to know how much Lydia's shadow haunted her. The letters felt personal, as though they were cutting directly into her deepest fears. The idea of Lydia still lingering, perhaps alive and angry, became harder to push aside.

She'd asked David to check the security camera's, hoping to find evidence of who was tormenting her, but her persecutor remained unknown. Even the private detective Aiden had hired at her request couldn't shed any light on their identity.

The breaking point came one evening when Alice finally worked up the nerve to confront Karen.

She found the housekeeper in the kitchen, calmly organizing the pantry as though the world wasn't crumbling around them. Karen glanced up as Alice entered, her expression as smooth and polished as always, her faint, almost mocking smile firmly in place.

"Mrs. Chandler," she said smoothly. "Is there something you need?"

Alice's hands trembled as she gripped the edge of the counter. "I need to talk to you about the CCTV," she said, her voice shaking slightly.

Karen raised an eyebrow, setting down the jar she was holding. "What about it?"

"Why wasn't it working the night the last letter was delivered?" Alice demanded. "I checked the footage, and there's nothing. Just a blank screen."

Karen shrugged, her tone calm. "It must have been a tech issue. These systems aren't infallible."

"A tech issue?" Alice repeated, her voice rising. "Do you realise how ridiculous that sounds? This house is state-of-the-art. How could the system just... fail?"

Karen gave her a placating smile, the kind that only fuelled Alice's anger. "Even the best technology can malfunction, Mrs. Chandler. I'm sure Mr. Chandler can have someone look into it when he returns."

Alice's fists clenched at her sides, her frustration boiling over. "You don't understand," she snapped. "Someone is out to get me. These letters, the alarms, the rat in the pool—this isn't random. Someone is trying to scare me, and now the CCTV just happens to stop working? It's not a coincidence!"

Karen's expression didn't change, but there was a flicker of something in her eyes—curiosity, perhaps, or a hint of disdain. "I'm sure you're under a lot of stress, Mrs. Chandler," she said carefully. "Maybe you're overthinking things. Evermere can be... overwhelming, especially when Mr. Chandler is away."

Alice felt like she'd been slapped. "I'm not imagining this," she said, her voice cracking as she waved the latest letter in Karen's face. "I know what's happening. Someone is watching me, Karen. Someone is *here*. Look at the evidence."

Karen didn't respond immediately. Instead, she picked up the jar she had set down earlier and returned it to the shelf with deliberate precision. "If you'd like, I can stay closer to the main house in case you need anything," she offered, her tone polite but patronising. "But perhaps you should focus on resting. Stress can do strange things to the mind."

Alice's vision blurred with tears, but she refused to let them fall. She spun on her heel and rushed out of the kitchen, her chest tight with rage and humiliation. Karen's calm, dismissive demeanour only made her feel more isolated, more trapped in a house that seemed determined to unnerve her.

By the time Aiden returned from his trip to Berlin a few days later, Alice was a wreck. She hadn't slept properly in days, her nerves frayed from the constant tension of living in a house that felt like an adversary.

Aiden entered the foyer, his suit wrinkled, his tie undone. Alice ran to meet him, her arms hugging herself as though she were trying to hold herself together.

"Alice," Aiden said, his brow furrowing as he took in her dishevelled appearance. "What's going on? You look—"

"Someone's after me," she interrupted, her voice quivering. "The letters, the alarms, the CCTV going out—it's all connected, Aiden. Someone is trying to scare me."

Aiden sighed, running a hand through his hair. "Alice, we've talked about this. It's probably just a crazed fan. A looney. They're trying to get a reaction out of you. Don't give it to them." He sighed, exhausted from jetlag.

"But why now?" Alice demanded. "Why would they wait until now? And how do you explain the CCTV? Or the rat in the pool?"

Aiden hesitated, his expression darkening. "I don't know," he admitted. "But I'll look into it. I promise. Just... stay calm. I'm here now. You're safe."

His words were meant to reassure her, but they felt hollow.

Later that evening, Alice overheard a quiet conversation between Aiden and Karen in the next room. She hadn't meant to eavesdrop, but their voices carried through the open doorway, their tones low and serious.

"She's not herself, Mr. Chandler," Karen was saying. "She's under a lot of stress, and it's starting to affect her. She was very upset about the CCTV issue, almost hysterical."

"I know," Aiden replied, his voice heavy with concern.

Karen hesitated, then said softly, "Perhaps it would be best for her to take a break. Maybe spend some time away, somewhere quieter. It might help her... clear her head."

Alice's blood ran cold. She clutched the armrest of a nearby chair, her nails digging into the fabric. Karen was painting her as unstable, fragile. And Aiden—his silence was worse than any words.

Alice walked away, not wanting to hear any more. She wouldn't let Karen push her out of Evermere and wouldn't let her turn Aiden against her. But as she made her way to her bedroom, the doubt began to creep in.

Alice closed the door behind her. Somewhere in the back of her mind, a single, haunting question whispered: *Perhaps Lydia's ghost is haunting you —or perhaps the threat is something far more real.*

24

The soft knock on the bedroom door barely registered through the pounding in Alice's skull. She lay curled up on the bed, the heavy blackout curtains drawn tight to block out the late morning sunlight. Her head throbbed relentlessly; a migraine so sharp it made it hard to breath.

"Mrs. Chandler?" Karen's voice drifted through the door, calm and measured as always. Alice groaned in response, unable to summon the energy for anything more.

The door opened silently, and Karen entered, carrying a silver tray laden with tea, toast, and a small vase holding a single white rose. The gesture, while considerate on the surface, felt oddly performative—like everything Karen did.

"I thought you might not feel up to coming down," Karen said, placing the tray on the bedside table. "You need to eat something. It'll help with the headache."

Alice turned her head slightly, her eyes barely cracking open. "Thank you," she murmured, her voice hoarse. She hated how vulnerable she felt.

Karen moved to the wardrobe, pulling open the doors and retrieving a stack of freshly laundered clothes. "I noticed the clean laundry piling up," she said lightly, as though trying to fill the silence. "I'll just put these away."

Alice didn't respond, watching Karen through half-closed eyes. The housekeeper moved with her usual precision, each gesture conscious and efficient.

"You're lucky," Karen said suddenly, breaking the silence. Her tone was conversational, but her words carried an edge that made Alice tense. "You have everything anyone could ever want. This house, Mr. Chandler, the kind of life most people can only dream of." There was something about her presence today that felt a bit different—less detached, more... human.

Alice blinked, unsure how to respond. "It doesn't always feel that way," she mumbled.

Karen turned, her lips curving into a controlled smile that didn't reach her eyes. "That's because you've always had it," she said. "You don't know what it's like to fight for respect, for security."

Alice frowned, the bitterness in Karen's tone surprising her. "You have?"

Karen sighed, smoothing the hem of a blouse before hanging it in the closet. "I wasn't born with a silver spoon in my mouth," she said. "I grew up in a house that was falling apart, with parents who could barely keep the lights on. My father drank. My mother... well, let's just say she wasn't much better."

Alice's headache seemed to dull slightly as curiosity took over. "That sounds awful," she said, her voice soft. "How did you get out of it?"

Karen gave a small, humourless laugh. "I didn't have a choice. I worked. Hard. I took every job I could find, no matter how demeaning, no matter how little it paid. I clawed my way out of that life because I refused to let it define me."

She paused, turning back to face Alice, her eyes sharp calculating. "That's why this job means everything to me," she continued. "This house, this family—it's not just a paycheck. It's my life. Aiden gave me purpose when I didn't have one. He trusted me when no one else would. I owe him everything."

Alice shifted slightly, her head pounding again. "You're very loyal to him," she said carefully.

Karen's smile returned, faint and enigmatic. "Loyalty is the one thing I have to offer. Some people deserve it. Some don't. Some are incapable," she paused, tilted her head and looked at Alice. "Aiden has been through more than you know. So has this house."

"And Lydia?" Alice ventured, the name tasting bitter on her tongue refusing to acknowledge the reference to the house. "You were loyal to her too?"

Karen's expression flickered, just for a moment, before she turned back to the closet. "Lydia was... someone I once loved," she said, her voice quieter now. "She was the kind of woman who commanded attention. She could walk into a room and make everyone feel like they didn't matter, unless she decided they did."

Alice's stomach twisted, the familiar knot of insecurity tightening. "You admired her."

"I did," Karen admitted. "But admiration doesn't equal perfection. Lydia had her flaws, like everyone else. She could be difficult, demanding. She pushed people away without realising it."

"Did she push you away?" Alice asked holding her breath.

Karen hesitated, her hands lingering on a hanger. "She trusted me," she said finally. "She relied on me. And I... I wanted to protect her."

The words hung in the air. Alice's chest tightened as she stared at Karen, trying to read the emotion behind her carefully guarded expression and trying to ignore her throbbing head.

"Protect her from what?" Alice pressed, the pulse of blood in her head threatening to explode.

Karen turned back to her, her faint smile returning like a mask slipping into place. "From the things that come with a life like this," she said simply. "The pressure, the scrutiny, the people who would do anything to tear you down."

There was something in her tone that made Alice shiver. It was the way Karen spoke of protection, of loyalty, as though they were absolutes—principles that justified any action, no matter how extreme.

Karen moved to the tray, adjusting the teacup and napkin. "You should rest, Mrs. Chandler," she said, her voice gentler now. "Stress won't help your headache. I'm here if you need anything. Just call."

Alice nodded weakly, watching as Karen left the room. The door closed with a quiet click, leaving Alice alone with her thoughts.

Karen's words lingered in her mind like shards of glass, sharp and unsettling. There was something Karen wasn't saying, something she was holding back.

As she lay there, her migraine throbbing dully.

The house seemed to exhale around her, its ghosts stretching as the day slipped toward evening. Karen's voice echoed in her mind; a quiet warning cloaked in polite conversation.

Loyalty is the one thing I have to offer.

Alice closed her eyes again. She didn't trust Karen, not fully. And she didn't trust Evermere.

Somewhere, deep in her gut, Alice knew she was missing something—something Karen wasn't saying, something no one would say, something that tied all the loose threads together. And until she found it, the house, Karen, and Lydia's memory would continue to haunt her, the threat growing more dangerous with each passing day.

25

The letter was waiting on the marble-topped console in the foyer. Alice stopped, her gaze falling on the plain, unmarked envelope resting on the silver tray where Karen always left the mail along with her breakfast.

She knew what it was before she even touched it. As she opened it the soft crinkle of the paper sounded impossibly loud in the cavernous space.

This time, the message was shorter, more direct, and far more chilling:

You'll never replace her. Stop trying.

The words punched through her chest like a physical blow. Alice's knees weakened, and she leaned against the console table for support. The scent of Lydia's lingering perfume seemed to rise out of nowhere, clinging to the air like a restless ghost. Outside, the thunder rumbling low and ominous, as if it, too, respected the weight of this moment.

Alice glanced at her reflection in the window. She barely recognised herself. Her hair, unwashed for days, hung limp around her face, the strands tangled from restless nights spent in bed tossing and turning. Her skin was pale and blotchy, her face bare of makeup, the dark circles under her eyes standing out like bruises. She tugged at the oversized cardigan she had thrown on, its shapeless form swallowing her frame. She looked tired, dishevelled, and completely unlike the polished woman who had once stood proudly at Aiden's side. Aiden who was now sleeping in one of the many guest bedrooms. Aiden who hadn't touched her for weeks.

She was still absorbed in her own reflection when he appeared in the kitchen, his sharp suit and immaculate appearance a stark contrast to her own. His eyes immediately went to the envelope in her hand, his expression hardening.

"What's that?" he asked, his voice low as his eyes landed on the envelope. "Another one?"

Alice nodded; her voice caught in her throat. She held out the letter, unable to speak. Aiden snatched it from her hand, his movements tense and abrupt. He scanned the note quickly, his face darkening as the vein in his temple pulsed.

"Damn it," he muttered, crumpling the paper in his fist. "This has to stop."

"It's getting worse, Aiden," Alice said, her voice trembling. "Whoever is doing this—they're escalating. I can't live like this. We need to go to the police."

Aiden shook his head sharply, turning away from her. The rain outside pounded harder against the glass. "No. That's not an option."

"Why not?" Alice demanded, her frustration boiling over. "This isn't just some prank, Aiden. This is serious. We need help —real help. My life is in danger."

Aiden tossed the crumpled letter onto the counter, his back to her as he ran a hand through his hair. "Don't be so melodramatic. For God's sake. Get a grip of yourself. Don't you understand?" he said, his voice tight and full of disgust. "If we involve the police, they'll start digging. They'll look into everything—into my business, into Lydia. And I can't risk that. For fuck sake," his chest rose as he let out a puff of hot air.

Alice froze, her chest tightening. "You're afraid of what they'll find. You're not worried about me."

Aiden turned to her, his eyes blazing. "I'm protecting us," he said firmly. "You don't know what it's like to have your every move scrutinised, every decision questioned. The police won't help us—they'll turn this into a circus. And then whoever is behind this will have won."

"Aiden, I'm scared," Alice said, her voice cracking. "Don't tell me I don't know how it feels. I am living in this nightmare now. I can't keep it up. I feel like I'm being watched all the time, like I'm not safe anywhere. What am I supposed to do?"

"I'll take care of it," Aiden said, his tone softening as he stepped closer to her. He reached out, his hands resting gently on her shoulders. "I'll hire private security. A team to monitor the estate around the clock. They'll make sure no one gets close to you."

Alice stared up at him, her eyes searching his face. He seemed sincere, his concern genuine, but a flicker of doubt lingered in the back of her mind. "Private security?" she repeated. "You think that's enough?" The most highly revered private investigator had found nothing.

"It'll be more than enough," Aiden assured her. "They'll install new cameras, patrol the grounds, and watch for anything suspicious. You'll be safe here, Alice. I promise."

For a moment, she allowed herself to believe it. Maybe private security was the answer. Maybe they could put an end to the letters and the threats without the risk of involving the police.

But as the day wore on, that flicker of doubt grew into something more. Aiden's insistence on keeping the police out of it bothered her. It wasn't just about protecting his reputation.

There was something else, something that he didn't want uncovered.

Then there was the security itself. At first, the idea had comforted her—the thought of professionals watching over Evermere, keeping her safe. But the more she thought about it, the more it began to feel like another layer of confinement. Cameras in every corner, guards patrolling the grounds—was it really about keeping dangers out? Or keeping *her* in?

That evening, Alice sat on the edge of the bed as she listened to the relentless drumming of the rain.

She still wasn't used to the speed that things could happen if you had wealth. That morning they'd discussed it. By that evening it was done.

The new security cameras dotted the corners of the estate, their little lights blinking rhythmically. They were meant to make her feel safe, Aiden had said. She caught herself glancing at them, wondering who was watching her, who might be reviewing the footage. She vowed not to get undressed in her bedroom as long as they remained in place.

She glanced at the envelope on the nightstand, the latest letter folded neatly inside. The words tattooed on her brain: *Get out while you can.* The cryptic message had twisted itself into her thoughts, making it impossible to think of anything else.

Alice stood abruptly, unable to bear the stillness any longer. She padded to the window, wrapping her arms tightly around herself as she looked out at the torrential downpour. Lightning forked across the sky, illuminating the grounds for a split second. It was beautiful and for a blissful moment she was distracted.

Then she thought she saw movement near the tree line—a

shadow, fleeting and insubstantial—but when the light faded, there was nothing but darkness.

Her breath hitched as she stepped back from the window. “It’s nothing,” she whispered to herself, her voice cracking, “Just the wind.”

The newly installed cameras only added to the paralysing atmosphere, their lenses fixed and unblinking.

Alice’s phone buzzed on the nightstand, making her jump. She reached for it, her hands trembling as she saw Aiden’s name flash across the screen.

“Hi,” she said, her voice shaking slightly.

“Alice,” Aiden said, his tone calm but laced with concern. “I just wanted to check in.” He was in a room on the other side of the house.

“I’m fine,” she lied, glancing at the letter again. “The cameras are all set up. The guards are outside. Everything’s fine.”

“Good,” he said. “I know this is hard for you, but I need you to trust me. This is for your safety.”

“I know,” Alice said quietly, though the words felt hollow. She hesitated, then added, “Thank you for doing this for me. I do appreciate it. I just need to be alone now. I need time to think. To work this all out.” She paused before putting her hand into the fire. “Aiden... do you think she could still be alive?”

The silence on the other end of the line was deafening. When Aiden finally spoke, his voice was distant. “Alice, we’ve talked about this. Lydia is gone. You need to let this go.”

“But the letters—”

“They’re from someone trying to scare you,” he interrupted, his tone firm. “That’s all. Don’t give them the satisfaction of believing their lies.”

Alice bit her lip, her chest tightening. “Lies? Do you even know what the truth looks like?”

Aiden exhaled; the sound heavy with frustration. “Alice,

you're letting your imagination run wild. Lydia isn't coming back. She can't."

The finality in his voice sent a chill through her. She wanted to believe him, wanted to trust that he was telling her the truth. But the doubts wouldn't be silenced.

"I could come back to our room," Aiden said, his tone softening slightly. "Be with you."

"Not tonight. Maybe tomorrow," Alice murmured, though she wasn't sure if she meant it.

After the call ended, Alice sat in silence, the weight of Aiden's words. The relentless assault on the house continued, the storm sending a warning while her husband slept in another room, down the long corridor. She turned her gaze back to the envelope, her fingers brushing over the paper yet again.

A sudden thud echoed from somewhere downstairs, the sound muffled but unmistakable. Alice froze, her pulse quickening. She strained to hear over the sound of the rain, her breath catching in her throat. The thud came again, louder this time, followed by the faint creak of a door.

Someone was in the house. And she knew it wasn't Aiden.

Her mind raced as she stood, her legs trembling beneath her. She reached for her phone, her fingers fumbling as she dialled Aiden's number. The call went straight to voicemail.

"Damn it," she whispered, her heart hammering in her chest.

The noise came again, closer this time. Alice stepped back toward the bed. She could feel her pulse in her ears, every instinct screaming at her to run, to hide, to do something.

And then, just as suddenly as it had started, the noise stopped. The house fell silent, the weather outside a faint backdrop to the stillness. Alice's breathing was shallow.

"Hello?" she called out, her voice barely above a whisper. "Is someone there?"

No response. Just the red lights from the cameras blinking in silent observation.

Alice sank to the floor, her back pressed against the bedframe. The letters, the cameras, the secrets. It was all too much.

And as the rain raged on, Alice couldn't shake the feeling that the puppet master behind it all was closer than she dared to imagine. Lydia's spirit wasn't just a memory—it was alive, lurking in the corners of the house, pulling her deeper into despair.

26

The house was deathly still when Alice woke, her breath catching in her throat as she blinked into the darkness. The rain had subsided, leaving an eerie silence that felt louder than the overnight storm. But something had stirred her—a sound, faint and persistent, like the tap-tap-tap of fingers against a chalkboard.

She sat up slowly, the sheets gathered around her waist as she strained to listen. There it was again, muffled but unmistakable. A rhythmic clicking that was coming from somewhere down the hall.

Her gaze darted to Aiden, who had joined her in bed when she was in a frenzy and unable to settle. He was sound asleep, his breathing slow and even, oblivious to the noise that had jolted her awake. For a moment, Alice considered shaking him, but something stopped her. She felt drawn to the sound, her curiosity outweighing her fear.

Sliding out of bed so as not to wake him, she padded barefoot across the room. The air was cool against her skin as she stepped into the hallway. She felt exposed, standing there in her silk nightdress. The noise grew louder as she approached

Aiden's office, a faint glow spilling out from beneath the closed door.

Alice's heart was thumping as she reached for the door handle, her fingers tentative. Slowly, she pushed the door open, the faint creak of the hinges breaking the silence.

Aiden's computer was on, its screen illuminating the dark room with an otherworldly glow. Words appeared on a blank document as if an invisible hand were typing them. The keys clicked softly, though the desk chair was empty and the room was devoid of life.

You don't belong here.

The words appeared one by one, slow and deliberate, the typing precise and steady.

You don't belong here.

You don't belong here.

You don't belong here.

Alice's breath hitched; her feet frozen to the floor. She wanted to turn and run, but she couldn't tear her eyes away from the screen.

You don't belong here. Leave now.

The cursor blinked for a moment before the next line appeared.

Or suffer the same fate as her.

Alice's blood turned to ice. She knew exactly who "her" was. Her hand flew to her mouth to stifle a scream, but the sound escaped anyway, a strangled cry that rippled through the house like an earthquake.

Then the screen flickered, and the words vanished as abruptly as they had appeared.

Without thinking, Alice turned and fled, her bare feet slapping against the cold floors as she raced back to the bedroom. Bursting through the door, she rushed to Aiden's side and shook him violently.

"Aiden!" she cried, her voice high and panicked, the tears choking her. "Aiden, wake up!"

He stirred groggily, his brow furrowing as he opened his eyes. "Alice?" he murmured, his voice thick with sleep. "What's wrong?"

"You have to come—now!" she said, tugging his arm. "It's your office. The computer—it's—someone's typing on it! It's a message."

Aiden sat up slowly, rubbing his face. "Alice, calm down. What are you talking about?"

"I'm not crazy," she insisted, sounding as unstable as she felt. "There were words on the screen, threatening words. They said I'd end up like Lydia." Her hair was wild, her eyes unable to meet his.

Aiden's expression shifted, as he swung his legs over the side of the bed. "Show me," he said, his tone firm.

Gripping his hand tightly, Alice led him back down the hallway to the office, her heart pounding so loudly she was sure he could hear it. The door was ajar, just as she had left it, the glow of the computer no longer visible.

When they stepped inside, the room was silent. The computer was off, its screen black, the desk chair pushed neatly under the desk. There was no sign of the document, no trace of the message.

"It was on," Alice said desperately, pointing at the monitor. "I saw it. The words—they were there."

Aiden sighed, running a hand through his tousled hair. "Alice," he said gently, "you've been under so much stress. Are you sure you didn't just dream it?"

"No!" she snapped, her voice rising. "It wasn't a dream. I was awake. I heard the typing—I saw the words!"

Aiden placed a hand on her shoulder, his touch meant to soothe but only fuelling her frustration. "Your mind is playing tricks on you," he said softly. "The letters, the house... it's bound to have an effect. You've hardly slept. It's no wonder you're seeing things."

Alice stared at him, her chest heaving with ragged breaths. She wanted him to be right, for his words to wash away the terror clawing at her. But the image of the screen—the threat was real.

"Aiden," she whispered, her voice breaking, "What if I'm not imagining it? What if someone is trying to scare me? To hurt me?"

"I won't let that happen," he said firmly, pulling her into his arms. "You're safe, Alice. No one can hurt you here."

He pushed a stand of hair off her face, wanting to see her better even if she preferred to remain hidden.

"No one can get past the security. There is no way this computer was hacked." He was trying to reassure her but she wasn't listening.

As he led her back to the bedroom, her mind continued to race with doubts.

She lay in bed next to him, her body stiff, her mind restless, Alice stared at the ceiling. Evermere was alive around her.

She closed her eyes, her heart pounding as she replayed the message on the screen again and again.

Suffer the same fate as her.

Next to her, Aiden's breathing deepened as he continued to sleep, leaving Alice feeling alone with her terror.

She didn't know what scared her more: the possibility that she was losing her mind, or the thought that Lydia's fate might be her own.

27

The house that had once seemed so impossibly vast, now felt like nothing more than a small cage. The walls pressed closer with each passing day, the darkness deepening and shifting, whispering secrets Alice wasn't allowed to hear.

She couldn't take it anymore.

Putting on a woman's coat she didn't recognise as her own, she stepped outside for the first time in days. The cold, bracing wind bit at her face as she walked across the manicured lawn and toward the cliffs. The clouds had cleared, but the sky was still heavy with angry purple clouds, a pale sun struggling to pierce through. The salty tang of the sea filled her lungs as she pulled the jacket tighter around her, her steps slow and deliberate.

Alice reached the edge of the cliffs, the waves calling her from the rocks below. She stopped, staring down into the rolling water, the foam churning like the mess in her mind. The idea crept in, soft at first, then louder, more insistent, until it was the only thought in her head.

Her breath caught as she took a small step closer to the edge, the whispering wind pushing against her like a taunting hand.

The rocks below were jagged and unforgiving, the waves surging, retreating, calling to her.

She teetered there, her heart pounding, the weight of relentless fear pulling her forward. She was not longer in control of herself.

"Mrs. Chandler!"

The voice cut through her thoughts. She turned to see David standing a few feet behind her, his expression alarmed but calm, his hand held out slightly as if approaching a frightened animal.

"What are you doing?" he asked gently, stepping closer. "You shouldn't be out here. It's dangerous this close to the cliffs."

Alice swallowed hard, her voice trembling. "I just needed air. I just... I needed to get out of the house."

David nodded, his posture careful, his concern evident. "I understand," he said softly. "But this isn't the place to clear your head. These cliffs are unpredictable. One strong gust, and..."

His words trailed off, but the unspoken warning clear. Alice looked back at the waves, hypnotised once more by their deadly pull. She felt them calling, but David's presence anchored her, his steady gaze drawing her back from the brink.

"Come on," he said, edging closer and still holding out a hand. "Let's get you back inside."

Alice hesitated, stepping away from the edge, but refusing to take his hand. She followed David back along the path, trembling with adrenaline as she hugged herself tightly.

The sharp buzz of a motor cut stopped Alice in her tracks. "What's that?" she asked, looking for a source of the sound.

David frowned, scanning the sky. "A drone," he said, his tone wary, his finger pointing at the sky.

The small device hovered over the cliffs, its blades slicing through the air with a high-pitched whine. It paused for a moment, its camera lens glinting as it focused in on Alice. Then it swooped down lower, with surprise speed, its movements deliberate and controlled.

Alice stumbled back, unsteady on her feet. "What's it doing? Why is it here?"

Before David could answer, the sound of footsteps thundered behind them. Aiden appeared, his expression hard and unyielding, a handgun clutched in his hand pointing directly at the foreign object.

"Get inside, Alice!" he barked, his voice unapologetic and commanding as security guards appeared in the distance, running towards them.

Alice froze, her eyes locked on the weapon. "Aiden, what are you—?"

"Inside. Now!" he reiterated.

Alice stepped backward, her gaze darting between Aiden and the drone as it buzzed lower, circling above her like a frantic bat. Aiden raised the gun with steady hands, his jaw clenched as he aimed.

"Aiden, no!" Alice cried, her voice breaking.

The shot rang out, deafening in the open air. The drone wobbled mid-flight, sparks flying as the bullet hit its mark. It spiralled downward, crashing into the rocks below with a metallic crunch.

Alice's hands flew to her mouth as she stared at Aiden, her breath coming in short gasps. "You have a gun?" she whispered, her voice loaded with shock.

Aiden turned to her. "It's a precaution," he said curtly, lowering the weapon. "We've had threats before."

"You never told me," Alice said, her whole body trembling. "You never said anything about having a gun."

Aiden stepped closer, his eyes narrowing slightly. "Because I didn't think it was necessary for you to know. I keep it locked away. I only brought it out because of this," he said, gesturing toward the cliffs where the drone had crashed.

David, who had stood silently during the exchange, cleared his throat. "I'll check the wreckage," he said, his tone calm but pointed. "See if we can figure out where it came from."

Aiden nodded, but his focus remained on Alice. "Are you alright?" he asked, his tone less harsh.

Alice nodded numbly; her mind was racing. The sight of the gun in Aiden's hand, the way he fired without hesitation—it unnerved her more than she cared to admit. She followed him back toward the house, her steps faltering as the questions in her mind grew louder.

As the house loomed closer, its exterior gleaming ominously in the fading light, Alice felt her unease deepen.

And as she crossed the threshold, the echoes of the gunshot still ringing in her ears, she wondered if the danger wasn't just outside the house.

28

The house, once a fortress, now felt more like a cage than ever. Alice sat at the kitchen table. Her tea untouched. Outside, the cliffs loomed, the ocean below a restless expanse of grey and white. Inside, the silence was thick, broken only by the noise from the refrigerator. She had barely slept the night before.

Karen's footsteps broke the quiet. The housekeeper appeared in her usual composed manner carrying a plate of biscuits, that she placed in front of her. There was a peculiar intensity behind her gaze.

"Mrs. Chandler," Karen began, her voice soft, "I've noticed you've been... struggling."

Alice stiffened, her fingers tightening around the mug. "I'm fine," she said quickly, though the tremor in her voice betrayed her. "It's just... everything. I have a lot on my mind."

Karen tilted her head slightly, her faint smile unwavering. "Of course, it's understandable. Anyone in your position would feel the same. This house has seen so much. It carries... memories."

"Memories?" Alice echoed.

Karen's smile remained in place. "Mrs. Chandler left her

mark here. Her presence lingers. For someone like you, stepping into her world... well, it's bound to feel overwhelming."

Alice hated hearing Lydia's name. "I don't feel overwhelmed," she lied. "I just—" She was unsure how to finish the sentence. "I'm adjusting."

Karen's expression changed, her voice a tone that was almost maternal. "Adjusting is difficult when you're not at your best. You've barely eaten, you're not sleeping... You have a lot to manage, Mrs. Chandler."

Alice stiffened, Karen's words striking a nerve. "I'm not losing my mind, if that's what you're suggesting."

"Of course not," Karen said smoothly, her tone soothing. "But even the strongest minds need rest, and clarity. Stress like this—it can cloud your judgement; make you see things that aren't there. Or miss things that are."

Alice looked up sharply, the weight of Karen's words settling uncomfortably in her chest. "What are you trying to say?"

Karen leaned slightly closer, her voice dropping to a conspiratorial whisper. "I'm saying you need help, Mrs. Chandler. Rest. Proper care. Dr. McAllister is very discreet, as I mentioned before. He can prescribe something to help you sleep, to ease your nerves. He's been a loyal associate of the family for some time."

Alice hesitated, her heart pounding in her chest. "I don't need a doctor. I just need... space. Time to figure this all out."

Karen's smile tightened, a flicker of frustration crossing her face. "Time won't fix this, Mrs. Chandler. You're exhausted, frayed. You're trying to carry a weight that no one person should bear. Let me help you. Let Dr. McAllister help you."

"I don't need medication," Alice said firmly, though her voice betrayed her. "I'm fine."

Karen's eyes narrowed slightly, the calm mask slipping for just a moment. "Forgive me for saying so, but you're not fine,

Mrs. Chandler. I've seen what happens to people who ignore the signs. Stress like this—I would hate to see you... suffer unnecessarily."

Karen's words made Alice's skin crawl. "What do you mean by that?"

Karen straightened, her composure snapping back into place. "I mean only that I've worked in this house for many years. I've seen what it can do to people. The isolation, the pressure... it can take a toll."

Alice swallowed hard, her gaze dropping to the mug in her hands. "I just need to focus," she said quietly. "I'll be fine."

Karen hesitated, then reached out to place a hand lightly on Alice's arm. The gesture was unexpected, almost too intimate, and Alice flinched at the contact.

"Please, Mrs. Chandler," Karen said softly, her tone almost pleading. "You don't have to do this alone. Let me call Dr. McAllister. Let me help you. One appointment, that's all I ask."

Alice pulled her arm back, her voice firmer now. "I said no, Karen. I appreciate your concern, but I don't need a doctor."

For a moment, Karen's expression was unreadable. Then she nodded, her fake smile returning. "Of course, Mrs. Chandler. I only want what's best for you."

Karen picked up the untouched plate of biscuits and left. As her footsteps faded down the hall, Alice let out a slow breath. The conversation had left her more unsettled. Karen's insistence, her veiled warnings—they felt less like concern and more like a warning.

Later that evening, as the sun dipped below the horizon and shadows stretched across the lawn, Alice paced the living room.

The sound of a voice outside caught her attention. She moved to the floor-to-ceiling windows and peered out. Aiden stood on the patio, his phone pressed to his ear, his posture rigid. She couldn't hear everything he was saying, but his tone was crisp, his words clipped and angry.

"...don't care what it takes," Aiden was saying, his voice carrying faintly through the glass. "This has gone on long enough."

Alice stopped breathing for a moment, her pulse quickening. She pressed closer to the glass, straining to hear.

"You think you're untouchable?" Aiden continued, his tone cold and threatening. "If you don't back off, you'll end up just like she did. At the bottom of the ocean. Do you understand me?"

Alice's heart stopped. Her hands trembled. Her mind raced. The words echoed in her head, so chilling they seemed to reverberate through her entire body.

Her stomach churned as a thousand possibilities flooded her mind and her knees wobbled as she stepped away from the window. She turned, her breath coming in short, shallow gasps. And that was when she saw her.

Karen stood in the doorway to the dining room, her arms folded neatly in front of her, her expression calm but watchful. She didn't say a word, but her gaze held Alice's with an intensity that made Alice's blood run cold.

For a moment, neither of them moved. The silence between them was oppressive, filled with tension. Then Karen inclined her head slightly, her faint smile returning, as if to say, *I see you.*

Alice's mouth opened, but no words came out. She took a step back, her mind screaming at her to do something. But Karen turned and walked away as if nothing had happened.

Alice stood frozen, her entire body trembling. She didn't know what she had just witnessed or what it meant.

Outside, the lawn stretched like a dark, yawning void under

the faint light of a crescent moon. Aiden's voice carried through the glass again, sharp and low, filled with anger.

"... I'll arrange it," he said, pacing along the patio, his phone pressed to his ear. The edge in his tone was unmistakable.

Alice leaned closer, her heart pounding. Her breath fogged the glass as she strained to hear, desperate to make sense of his words.

"You'll get what's coming to you," Aiden hissed, his body rigid with tension. "If you don't back off, you'll end up just like her. Do you understand me? *Just like Lydia.*"

The name struck Alice like a slap, her stomach twisting into knots. She gripped the curtain tighter, her nails digging into the fabric. *Just like Lydia.*

The air around pressed against her chest as she struggled to breathe. Aiden ended the call abruptly, shoving his phone into his pocket and glaring out at the dark horizon. His profile was etched in harsh lines, his expression unrecognisable.

Alice stumbled back from the window, her mind racing with questions she didn't dare voice. As she turned, her pulse still hammering in her ears, she found Karen was standing in the doorway again, her arms folded neatly in front of her. She tilted her head slightly, her face calm but her eyes cold. She appeared taller, more imposing somehow.

The silence enveloped them both like a straitjacket. Finally, Karen spoke, her voice smooth and measured, like a knife cutting through the fragile air.

"Is everything all right, Mrs. Chandler?" she asked, her tone carrying a faint, almost mocking edge.

Alice's throat was dry, her voice barely a whisper. "What... what are you doing here still?"

Karen's lips curved into a faint smile. "You seemed... upset."

"I—" Alice stammered, her mind struggling to form coherent thoughts. "I thought I heard something."

Karen's gaze flicked toward the window, then back to Alice. "I see. Was it Mr. Chandler? He often makes calls outside when he doesn't want to disturb you."

Alice didn't like Karen's knowing tone. "He... he was talking about Lydia," she said hesitantly, her words spilling out before she could stop them.

Karen's smile didn't falter, but there was something predatory in her expression now, a subtle shift that made Alice's skin crawl. "I'm sure Mr. Chandler would never say anything that wasn't entirely justified," she said smoothly. "He's always been protective of his family. And of you, Mrs. Chandler."

The way she emphasised the last word hit a nerve. "Protective?" she echoed, her voice shaking. "From what?"

Karen stepped closer. "From those who don't understand their place," she said softly. "Evermere has seen its share of threats, Mrs. Chandler. Mr. Chandler has always done what's necessary to ensure the safety of those he cares about."

Alice felt her legs go weak beneath her. "Are you saying... ?"

Karen cut her off, her smile sharpening. "I'm saying you're fortunate to have a husband who takes care of things, so you don't have to worry. Stress isn't good for you, Mrs. Chandler. Especially not in your current... state."

Alice's breath caught. "What state? What are you talking about?"

"You've been under a great deal of strain," she said. "The letters, the house, everything... it's no wonder you've been seeing and hearing things that aren't there. Perhaps it's time to speak with the doctor. I can arrange for him to visit tomorrow if you'd like."

"I'm not imagining this!" Alice snapped, her voice cracking. "I heard him, Karen. I heard what he said."

Karen's smile faded slightly, her gaze turning colder. "And what exactly do you think you heard, Mrs. Chandler?" she asked, her tone sharp but still polite. "That Mr. Chandler would harm someone? Or that he's doing what's necessary to keep you safe from the people who wish you harm?"

Alice's chest tightened. "I don't know," she admitted, her voice barely above a whisper. "I don't know what to think anymore."

Karen stepped even closer, her presence looming. "Then perhaps it's best not to think too much," she said quietly. "You have everything you need here. You're safe. You're cared for. Isn't that enough?"

Alice stared at her, the question settling over her like a shroud. There was no kindness in her tone, no genuine concern —only a cold, calculated warning.

Karen straightened, her painted smile returning. "I'll leave you to your thoughts, Mrs. Chandler," she said, her tone brisk once more. "If you change your mind about the doctor, just let me know."

Without waiting for a response, she turned and walked away.

She glanced back toward the window. Aiden was still outside, his silhouette barely visible in the inky dark

Alice sank into a nearby chair, her head in her hands. It was all too much. She didn't know who to trust anymore.

And as the night deepened around her, the house seemed to be closing in on her from all sides.

29

The announcement came at breakfast, over the clinking of silverware and the rustle of the morning newspaper. Alice sat at the far end of the dining table; her plate untouched as she pushed her food around with her fork. Aiden was his usual composed self, sipping his coffee and scrolling through his tablet, his expression giving away nothing.

Karen moved seamlessly between them, pouring coffee and setting down a fresh basket of pastries.

"Karen," Aiden said suddenly, his tone brisk but calm. "I've been thinking. You've been working so hard lately. I think it's time you took a break."

Karen froze, the coffee pot poised mid-pour. She turned to face him, her expression neutral but her eyes narrowing slightly. "A break, Mr. Chandler?"

"Yes," Aiden said, setting his tablet aside. "You've been running this house without pause for years. I can't remember the last time you had time off. You deserve it."

Karen's lips pressed into a thin line, her hands tightening slightly around the coffee pot. "I appreciate the sentiment, Mr.

Chandler, but I'm perfectly capable of managing my duties. The house—"

"The house will be fine," Aiden interrupted, his tone firm. "You've trained the staff well. But you all deserve time to yourselves. I insist."

Alice looked up from her plate, her brow furrowing as she glanced between them. Karen's expression had shifted subtly, her calm veneer cracking just enough to reveal resistance simmering beneath the surface.

"I'll arrange for someone to cover any critical tasks," Aiden continued, sensing Karen's hesitation. "Take a week, maybe two. It's not a request, Karen. It's a decision."

Karen's smile was faint, almost forced. "Of course, Mr. Chandler. If that's what you'd prefer."

"Good," Aiden said, returning to his coffee as though the matter were settled and as if the request wasn't highly unusual.

Alice could see the tension in Karen's stance, the way her hands tightened around the tray. "I'll start making arrangements," Karen said, her tone carefully controlled. "Though I should remind you, sir, that this is a particularly busy time, given the circumstances."

Aiden raised an eyebrow. "And yet, I'm confident everything will be handled. You've earned this, Karen."

"As you wish, Mr. Chandler."

"Good. You can take your leave tomorrow."

Aiden nodded, satisfied, and picked up his tablet again. Karen turned and left the room. Alice watched her go, a strange sense of dread settling over her.

Later that morning, Alice found Karen in the laundry room,

meticulously folding linens the way only she could. The normally unflappable housekeeper seemed unsettled.

"Karen," Alice said hesitantly, "Are you okay?"

Karen didn't look up, her hands smoothing the edges of a pillowcase. "I'm fine, Mrs. Chandler. Why wouldn't I be?"

"It's just..." Alice hesitated, searching for the right words. "You don't seem... thrilled about the time off."

Karen gave a soft, humourless laugh, finally looking up. "I suppose I'm not used to the idea," she admitted. "This house has been my life for so long. It feels strange to leave it, even for a little while."

Alice leaned against the doorframe, watching Karen closely. "How long have you work for Aiden?"

"Nearly fifteen years," Karen said, a distinct note of pride in her voice. "I've seen this house through every season, every challenge. It's more than just a job to me."

"And Lydia?" Alice ventured cautiously. "You were close to her too."

Karen's hands stilled for a moment, her gaze shifting. "Lydia was... unique," she said carefully.

Alice felt a pang of jealousy. "You must have a lot of memories of her."

Karen's eyes flicked to Alice, sharp and assessing. "I do," she said simply.

There was an edge to her words that made Alice's skin prickle. "You don't have to leave, you know," Alice said, her voice quieter now. "You could tell Aiden you're needed here."

Karen's lips curved into a faint smile, one that didn't reach her eyes. "It's not my place to question Mr. Chandler's decisions," she said. "But I'll admit, it feels... odd. Being asked to step away at a time like this." Karen's smile widened slightly, though her expression remained inscrutable. "Mr. Chandler always has his reasons," she said. "I've learned not to question them."

She turned back to the linens, her movements precise once more, as if the conversation had never taken place.

30

The house was quiet. The uniformed guards, their constant patrols, and the red blinking cameras had become an uneasy comfort to Alice over the past few weeks. Now, their absence felt like another layer of vulnerability. Aiden had assured her it was safe—that the letters had stopped and the drone incident was a one-off.

"Whoever it was," Aiden had said, "they've clearly lost interest."

But Alice wasn't so sure. As she moved through the house's vast, empty rooms, the sense of isolation chipped away at her. It felt strangely empty without any staff. Although Karen was the only member of the housekeeping team Alice or Aiden ever dealt with, she was aware a much larger machine was as work to keep the house spotless.

That morning, Alice sat in the living room, her laptop balanced on her knees. The ocean beyond the glass walls shimmered under a watery sun, the beauty of the view lost on her. Her attention was fixed on the screen, her fingers scrolling idly through news articles. She wasn't even sure what she was looking for—distraction, maybe, or some reassurance that the outside world wasn't as hostile as it felt.

Then she saw it.

The headline was bold, flashy, designed to grab attention:

Ian Carlisle's New Tech Venture: The Multi-Million Pound AI Startup That's Already Turning Heads.

Alice clicked the link, her curiosity piqued. The article detailed Ian's move into artificial intelligence, an ambitious platform aimed at revolutionising the way businesses operated. The piece was filled with glowing quotes from investors and industry experts, all predicting Ian's meteoric rise to even greater heights.

But what caught Alice's attention wasn't the product or the praise—it was the staggering amount of money Ian had secured in funding. The article mentioned private investors, but no names. Where had Ian managed to raise such an astronomical sum so quickly?

When Aiden entered the room, his phone in hand, Alice looked up. "Aiden, did you see this?" she asked, turning the screen toward him. "Ian's launching a new company."

Aiden glanced at the laptop briefly, his expression unreadable. "I'm aware," he said, his tone dismissive.

"It's impressive," A note of scepticism crept into her voice. "But where do you think he got the funding? I mean, that kind of money doesn't just appear overnight."

Aiden's shoulders stiffened. He slid his phone into his pocket and crossed the room to pour himself a glass of juice. "Ian has his ways," he said flatly, not looking at her.

Alice frowned, closing the laptop. "Don't you think it's strange? I mean, private investors? That's vague, isn't it? And after everything with Lydia, and the affair—"

Aiden slammed his glass onto the counter, the sound

reverberating through the room. "Enough!" he barked, his voice cutting through the air like a whip. "Know when to stop."

Alice flinched, her heart racing as she stared at him in shock. Aiden turned to face her, his expression dark and furious. His eyes blazing with a mixture of anger and something else.

"Why are you so obsessed with Ian?" he demanded, his voice rising. "Do you think I don't already know what kind of man he is? Do you think I don't see exactly what he's doing?"

"I just—" Alice stammered, her voice trembling. "I just think it's worth asking questions. After everything that's happened—"

"Stop," Aiden snapped, pointing a finger at her. "You don't know what you're talking about, Alice. Ian is not your concern."

"But what if—"

"Be quiet!" Aiden roared; his face contorted with rage. He took a step closer, and Alice shrank back into her seat. "I don't want to hear another word about him, do you understand? Not one more word."

The room fell into a tense silence, the only sound the faint clinking of ice in Aiden's untouched drink. Alice's chest rose and fell rapidly, her hands gripping the edge of the couch as she tried to steady herself. Aiden stood over her, his breathing heavy, his fists clenched at his sides.

Finally, he straightened, running a hand through his hair, an attempt to summon his normal cool. "I'm sorry," he muttered, his tone no less tense. "I didn't mean to yell. It's just... Ian isn't someone you need to worry about. Trust me."

Alice didn't feel reassured.

Aiden picked up his drink and downed it in one go, then left the room leaving Alice alone in the stifling silence.

The rest of the day dragged on, Alice carrying the memory of

Aiden's anger. After his outburst, he retreated to his office and locked the door, leaving her to stew in her thoughts.

Alice tried to distract herself, first by reading, then by attempting to sketch in the sunroom where she had once found solace. But her hand refused to cooperate. Her thoughts kept returning to Aiden's face, the flash of fury in his eyes when she'd mentioned the article.

She gave up on the sketch and wandered aimlessly through the house, looking for comfort but finding none.

By the evening, the atmosphere in the house had grown unbearable. Alice barely touched the dinner Karen had left in the fridge before departing, and Aiden didn't emerge from his office to join her.

She tried to call her sister, Beth, but the call went unanswered. The loneliness pressed down on her like a physical weight, and by the time she climbed into bed that night, she was too exhausted to do anything but close her eyes and hope for sleep.

But sleep didn't come.

That night, as she lay in bed staring at the familiar spot on the ceiling, the house felt more like a prison than ever.

She glanced at Aiden, who was already asleep beside her, having moved permanently back into their bedroom, his face relaxed and peaceful in a way that felt foreign after the rage she'd seen earlier. For the first time, she felt a sliver of fear—not of the house, or the letters, or the threats—but of the man lying next to her.

Alice tossed and turned, the blankets tangling around her

legs as her mind refused to quiet. Every time she closed her eyes, images flickered behind her lids—dark, murky, haunting.

She saw Lydia.

At first, the visions were vague, disjointed. A flash of Lydia's radiant smile, her golden hair gleaming under the sun, her carefree beauty. But the images twisted, growing more vivid and terrifying.

Alice imagined Lydia on her yacht. The waves lapped gently at the hull, the sound soothing and rhythmic. Lydia's silhouette stood at the edge. Her posture confident.

But then the water changed. The waves grew choppier, angrier. The sky darkened, clouds rolling in like an unstoppable tide. The wind picked up, tugging Lydia's hair and clothes, and her expression shifted—from calm to panic.

She saw Lydia struggling at the helm, her hands gripping the wheel. The yacht rocked violently, the once-pristine deck slick with rain and seawater. Lightning split the sky, illuminating Lydia's terrified face as she shouted into the void, her words lost to the roar of the storm.

The image shifted again. Water flooded the cabin, surging through the narrow corridors and sweeping away the physical evidence of Lydia's life. Alice saw Lydia scrambling, her movements frantic as the boat tilted dangerously to one side.

The yacht was nearly submerged, its once-proud bow sinking beneath the waves. Lydia clung to the edge, her face pale and streaked with tears, her mouth open in a silent scream. Then the water consumed her, dragging her under, the surface closing over her head.

Alice bolted upright in bed, her heart pounding, her skin clammy with sweat. The room was dark and still, the only sound her ragged breathing. She glanced at Aiden, sleeping peacefully, his face serene in the faint moonlight.

The images of Lydia sinking into the depths refused to fade, clinging to her mind like a waking nightmare.

Alice glanced toward the window, where the ocean stretched out beyond the cliffs, vast and endless. It was beautiful, but in the dark, it felt menacing, as though it, too, held secrets it refused to reveal.

As she sat there, staring into the void, the questions, the doubts, the fear—they were all building, crashing against her like the relentless waves that had swallowed Lydia, leaving behind no trace.

31

Alice woke to the pale, grey light of morning. Its weak glow doing little to chase away the darkness that lingered inside. Her chest felt heavy, her limbs weighed down by the remnants of her restless night. The nightmare clung to her, refusing to fade.

She sat up slowly, her hands gripping the edge of the bed as she tried to steady herself. Aiden's side of the bed was empty, the sheets neatly pulled back.

Boats didn't simply vanish without a trace. The thought refused to be silenced.

The dream felt like a memory that didn't belong to her.

She quickly found her robe and made her way downstairs, her feet dragging with exhaustion.

Aiden was at the kitchen island, his tablet propped up as he reviewed emails, a half-finished cup of coffee at his side. He looked up as Alice entered.

"Morning," he said, his tone neutral.

Alice didn't respond. She moved to the counter and poured herself a cup of tea. Aiden's gaze lingered on her.

"You didn't sleep well," he said, more of a statement than a question.

"No," Alice admitted, her voice flat. She took a seat at the island, her tea untouched as she stared into the steaming liquid. "I... I had a dream. About Lydia."

Aiden let out a pronounced sigh.

"It felt so real," Alice said, her voice trembling. "She was on her boat. I saw her struggling, trying to keep it afloat, and then... then she went under. The water just swallowed her up."

Aiden reached out, his hand covering hers. "Alice, it was just a dream."

"But why?" Alice asked, pulling her hand away. "Why am I dreaming about her like this? It's like she's trying to tell me something. Like she's... reaching out."

Aiden exhaled; his frustration barely masked. "You need to stop torturing yourself with this. Lydia is dead. You know that."

"Do I?" Alice said, her voice rising. "She disappeared, Aiden. There was no body, no wreckage. Just an assumption. What if—what if she's not?"

Aiden's expression darkened, his mouth pressing into a thin line. "Alice, listen to yourself. You're letting your imagination run wild. This is crazy."

Alice's chest tightened, her frustration boiling over. "I can't do this anymore, Aiden," she said, her voice breaking. "I can't live like this."

Aiden stood, his chair scraping against the floor as he moved to her side. He placed his hands on her shoulders, his grip firm but not unkind. "Alice, you need to stop," he said, his voice low but commanding. "You're losing it and I can't help you if you won't let go of this obsession."

Tears welled in Alice's eyes as she looked up at him, her desperation laid bare. "I'm not obsessed," she said, her voice trembling. "I'm trying to understand. I'm trying to make sense of all of this. But I feel like I'm drowning, Aiden."

Aiden's expression softened, and he pulled her into him.

"You're not drowning," he murmured. "I won't let that happen. You need to trust me, Alice."

As Aiden held her, whispering reassurances she couldn't bring herself to believe, Alice buried her face in his chest, her tears soaking into his shirt.

·

Alice pulled back from Aiden's embrace, her eyes red and brimming with desperation. "Aiden, please. I need to know the truth. What happened to Lydia?"

Aiden's clenched his teeth, his hands dropping to his sides as he stepped back. "Alice, we've been through this. She's gone. That's all there is to it. Please," he pleaded like a trapped animal.

"No," Alice said, her voice firmer now. "It's not all there is to it. I can feel it, Aiden. There's something you're not telling me. I'm surrounded by her memory, haunted by her absence. If you love me, if you care about me at all, you'll tell me the truth."

Aiden turned away, his back to her as he raked a hand through his hair. Alice's heart pounded as she watched him, the question hanging in the air like a thunder cloud about to break.

Finally, Aiden spoke, his voice low and rough. "You don't want to know the truth, Alice."

"Yes, I do," Alice said, stepping closer to him. "I need to know. Whatever it is, I can handle it."

Aiden laughed bitterly. He turned to face her, his eyes dark and tormented. "No, you can't," he said. "You think you want answers, but once you have them, you'll wish you never asked."

Alice stared at Aiden. His face was a canvas of emotions—anger, regret, fear—but beneath it all, she could see something else: guilt.

"Just tell me. This isn't going away. It's going to break us if you don't."

Aiden turned his back to her, his shoulders tightening as he braced himself, his knuckles white as he gripped the edge of the kitchen counter. “I argued with Lydia the day she disappeared,” he said, his voice low and hollow. “It was bad—worse than usual.”

Alice steadied herself. “What were you arguing about?”

Aiden shook his head, a resentful laugh escaping his lips. “Everything. Control. Her obsession with power. She’d threatened to leave before, but that day...” He paused, dragging a hand through his hair again, his eyes haunted. “That day, she wasn’t bluffing. She said she had everything ready—lawyers, evidence to ruin me. She said she was going to take the house, the company, everything.”

Alice’s chest tightened. “What happened, Aiden?”

He turned, meeting her gaze, his eyes hollow. “I snapped,” he admitted, his voice thick with emotion. “I told her I wouldn’t let her just walk away and leave me with nothing. We were shouting, yelling things we couldn’t take back, and then she pushed me. I pushed back.” He swallowed hard. “She fell. Hit her head on the edge of the coffee table.”

Alice’s blood ran cold. “What... what do you mean she hit her head? Was she—?”

“She wasn’t responsive,” Aiden said quickly, his voice cracking. “She was just lying there, motionless. There was blood on the floor around her head. I panicked. I didn’t know what to do. I rushed out to get bandages, to call for help. I swear, Alice, I was only gone for a minute.”

“And then?” Alice held her breath.

“When I came back, she wasn’t there.” His voice dropped to a whisper, filled with disbelief even after all this time. “The blood was still there, but Lydia wasn’t. I thought maybe she’d regained consciousness and gone to get help, but then... then I saw her boat.”

Alice’s breath hitched. “Her boat?”

Aiden nodded, his eyes distant, as if he were watching the

scene unfold all over again. "It was already out to sea by the time I reached the window. I called her phone, but there was no answer."

Alice felt like the ground was shifting beneath her. "You didn't try to stop her? Call the coast guard?"

"I didn't know what to do," Aiden said, his voice desperate. "I was in shock. One minute she was there, and the next... she was gone. I thought maybe she'd gone out on the boat to get away from me, to clear her head. But when the storm came, and they couldn't find her..." He trailed off, his eyes darkened by years of torment. "It was an accident. She'd gone out too far, underestimated the waves."

Alice stared at him, her mind racing.

"What if they find her body?" Aiden couldn't stop now, words pouring out of him, his voice sharp but edged with fear. "What if they find the wreck and think I killed her?" He dragged a hand over his face, his frustration boiling over. "That's what I've been terrified of. Since the moment I saw that boat disappearing into the horizon, I've carried this with me—the fear that they'll find her and think I did it."

Alice took a shaky step back, her mind spinning. "You never told anyone?"

"What was I supposed to say?" Aiden shot back, his voice cracking. "That we fought, that she fell, that I left the room, and she disappeared? Do you have any idea how that sounds? No one would have believed me. They would've said I staged it, that I wanted her gone." He clenched his fists, his entire body rigid with tension. "The media would have crucified me. The authorities would have torn my life apart. I couldn't take that chance, Alice."

Alice shook her head, tears welling in her eyes.

Aiden closed his eyes, and for the first time, Alice saw his composure crack. "Every single day," he said, his voice raw. "I see her face every time I close my eyes. I hear her voice, her threats. I wake up in the middle of the night, expecting to see her standing over me, accusing me. And every time a letter arrives, every time someone dredges up her name, it feels like the walls are closing in."

Alice felt her heart break at the vulnerability in his voice. She had never seen Aiden like this—so exposed, so weighed down by his own torment. "Why didn't you tell me?" she asked. "Why didn't you trust me with this?"

Aiden let out a bitter laugh. "Because I didn't want you to look at me like you are now. Like I'm a monster. Like I killed her."

"I don't think you killed her," Alice said quickly, her voice shaky. "But, Aiden, you didn't try to stop her."

"I was scared," Aiden admitted, his voice barely above a whisper. "Terrified. I couldn't take that risk, Alice. I've spent every day since trying to move on, trying to bury it. But it doesn't go away."

Alice could see the truth in his eyes, the guilt he had been carrying for so long. But she couldn't shake the image of Lydia's boat disappearing out to sea, of the blood on the floor, of the haunting possibility that Lydia wasn't truly gone or, worse still, that Aiden was hiding something even darker.

32

Alice sat up slowly, her mind sluggish from another night of restless sleep, her body aching from the tension of the previous night.

"Aiden?" she called, her voice hoarse and uncertain.

No response.

The quiet swamped her like a heavy blanket. Evermere was empty. She could feel it.

She wandered through the corridors, her steps tentative and slow, her eyes darting to every corner as if expecting someone—or something—to appear. But there was nothing. No sound of Aiden's voice, no distant hum of the coffee machine in the kitchen, no Karen gliding through the halls with her usual efficiency. The house, usually bustling with its quiet rhythms, was still.

Alice's thoughts whirled as she moved through the house, her steps taking her to the kitchen, the dining room, the sunroom where she rested her gaze on the cliffs beyond the glass. The ocean was calm today. It looked peaceful, but Alice knew better. Beneath that placid surface lay currents that could drag a body out to sea.

She pressed her hand against the glass, her breath fogging the pane as her thoughts turned to the yacht.

Alice's hand lingered on the cold glass, her reflection a faint blur overlaying the ocean. The memory of Aiden's confession replayed in her mind like a broken record: the argument, Lydia's fall, the blood, the boat.

The yacht had become an obsession for Alice in recent weeks. It wasn't the boat itself but what it symbolised: Lydia's final act. But the more Alice thought about it, the less sense it made. If she was injured, bleeding, why would she sail into a storm?

She wanted to believe Aiden—that he'd run to get help, that his fear had paralysed him, that Lydia's disappearance was a tragic accident. But her mind wouldn't stop conjuring other possibilities.

The sound of footsteps behind her made her jump. She turned quickly to see Aiden standing in the doorway.

"Couldn't sleep either?"

Alice shook her head, her hand dropping from the glass. "No. The house feels... different today."

Aiden stepped into the room, his eyes flicking briefly to the cliffs beyond the glass. "It's the quiet. I know I dismissed the staff but I didn't realise how strange it would feel."

Alice studied him, searching for cracks in his calm exterior. His confession had been so raw, so vulnerable, but now he seemed composed again, his walls firmly back up.

"Aiden," she began, her voice hesitant, "have you ever thought about... searching for the yacht?"

He stiffened, his gaze remained fixed on the horizon. "There's nothing to search for," he said finally, his tone clipped. "The coast guard looked. Private investigators looked."

"But what if they missed something?" Alice pressed. "What if—"

"What if what?" Aiden snapped, turning to face her. His eyes were hard, his stare challenging. "What do you think you'll find, Alice? The wreck? Her body? Do you think that's going to change anything?"

"I don't know," Alice admitted. "But I can't stop thinking about it. About her. About what happened that night."

Aiden exhaled, running a hand over his face. "I told you everything, Alice. I've carried this guilt—wondering if I could have done something, if I could have stopped her. But I can't change what happened. And neither can you."

Alice took a step closer, her voice soft but insistent. "Don't you think she deserves to be laid to rest?"

Aiden's eyes darkened, his expression closing off. "You're letting your imagination get the better of you," he said coldly. "Lydia is gone. That's the truth, whether you want to accept it or not."

Alice recoiled, hurt by his tone but unwilling to back down. "Don't you want to know, Aiden? Don't you want to be sure?"

"I am sure," he said firmly, his voice brooking no argument. "And you need to stop this. It's not healthy, Alice. It's not helping either of us."

Alice's throat tightened, tears prickling at the corners of her eyes.

Aiden stepped forward, his hands gripping her shoulders. "This is not your fight," he said, his voice softening slightly. "You need to let this go, Alice. For your sake. For mine."

Alice nodded reluctantly, rooted to the spot as Aiden left the room, his footsteps echoing faintly down the hallway. The sound faded into silence, leaving her alone once again. She turned back to the window, her hands pressing against the cool glass.

Aiden's account of that night replayed in her mind and something still didn't fit. The questions refused to leave her, at the edge of her thoughts like a persistent splinter.

A head injury, blood pooling on the floor. Aiden running to find bandages. And then, Lydia gone—her yacht slicing through choppy waters toward certain doom. It made no sense.

Alice tried to picture it: Lydia, disoriented and in pain, making the decision to stumble out of the house, climb aboard her boat, and cast off into the churning sea. She shook her head, trying to dispel the image forming in her mind, but it clung to her like a leech as a creeping sense of dread began to take hold. She didn't want to believe that Aiden was capable of such a thing, but the details of his story didn't add up.

And then there was the timing. Aiden had said he went to get help, to grab bandages and call for assistance. But how long could that have taken? A minute? Two? Would Lydia have had enough time to disappear without a trace?

Alice's breath hitched as another possibility crept into her mind, unbidden and unwelcome.

Her hands trembled as she stepped away from the glass, the room suddenly feeling colder, darker. The air thick with an almost suffocating weight. Alice tried to push the thought away, but the creeping fear was relentless. She thought of Aiden's demeanour that morning—calm on the surface, but with tension simmering underneath. He had seemed so certain, so adamant that she let this go.

Alice's gaze drifted back to the cliffs beyond the window, the memory of the stormy sea vivid in her mind. She could almost see it now—the waves crashing against the rocks, the yacht disappearing into the horizon.

The thought sent a fresh wave of dread washing over Alice who wrapped her arms around herself, trying to quell the shivers that wracked her body. She felt like she was standing on the edge of a precipice, the truth dangling just out of reach. If she leaned too far, she would fall—into what, she didn't know.

But the alternative was worse: to turn back, to pretend she hadn't seen the cracks in Aiden's story.

Alice turned away from the view, her footsteps hesitant as she moved toward the door. As she stepped into the hallway, she quickened her pace, her heartbeat thundering in her chest as she made her way to the library.

The room felt no safer, but at least it was familiar. She sank into one of the armchairs, her hands gripping the armrests as she tried to steady her breathing. She thought of Aiden, of his haunted expression as he recounted that night. The weight of the truth—or whatever twisted version of it lay hidden—felt dangerous now.

Alice didn't want to believe it, didn't want to think that the man she had married could be capable of murder. But the seeds of doubt had been planted, and they were growing fast, their roots twisting and tangling around her heart.

Alice realised she had a choice to make. She could confront Aiden again, demand answers and risk everything. Or she could bury her doubts, pretend she hadn't noticed the inconsistencies in his story, and try to move on.

But as she sat there, she knew deep down that she couldn't let this go. She also felt the creeping sense that she was no longer just searching for answers. She was fighting for her own survival.

She got up from the chair and caught sight of her reflection in the glass. She looked pale, hollow, a shadow of herself. Moving to the kitchen, she poured herself a glass of water. The clink of the glass against the counter echoed loudly in the empty room. She stared at the water, her reflection rippling on its surface, and felt a wave of nausea wash over her.

"What am I doing here?" she whispered to herself.

Her phone in her hand, Evermere loomed around her, its emptiness amplifying her thoughts. She stared at the screen for what felt like an eternity before summoning the courage to dial.

It rang twice before Beth's voice came through, warm and familiar. "Alice? Hey, it's so good to hear from you! How are you?"

The simple question made Alice's throat tighten. She swallowed hard. "I'm... I'm okay," she said, though the words felt hollow. "I just needed to hear your voice."

"Alice, what's wrong?" Beth asked, her tone immediately shifting. "You don't sound like yourself."

Alice hesitated, gripping the edge of the counter for support. "I don't know, Beth," she admitted finally. "I just... I feel like I'm unravelling. Like I'm trapped. This house, Aiden, everything..."

Beth's voice softened. "Oh, Alice. I knew something was wrong. You've sounded off the last few times we talked. Tell me what's going on."

"I can't..." Alice faltered, her words catching in her throat. She couldn't bring herself to tell her big sister the potential magnitude of her discovery. "It's hard to explain. I just feel like I don't belong here, like I'm drowning in a life that doesn't belong to me."

There was a pause on the other end of the line before Beth spoke again, her voice resolute. "Then come here. Come and stay with us for a while."

Alice blinked, caught off guard. "Beth, I don't know—"

"No arguments," Beth said firmly. "You need a break, Alice. Get out of that house, away from Aiden, and come spend some time with your family. The kids would love to see you. It'll do you good."

"I don't want to impose," Alice murmured, "You have so much on your plate already—"

"Don't be ridiculous," Beth interrupted. "You're my sister.

You could never impose. Besides, we miss you. It's been ages since you've spent time with the kids. They've been asking about you, especially since they see your face in the papers."

Alice closed her eyes, a wave of emotion washing over her. The idea of escaping, even for a little while, was like a lifeline. "Okay," she said finally, "I'll come."

"Good," Beth said, relief evident in her tone. "When?"

"I'll figure it out," Alice said. "I'll let you know as soon as I can."

"Perfect," Beth said. "And Alice? You're doing the right thing. Sometimes it's good to just step away and clear your head."

Alice nodded, even though Beth couldn't see her. "Thank you," she said softly. "I really needed to hear that."

They talked for a few more minutes, Beth's cheerful updates about her kids and day-to-day life providing a welcome distraction.

She didn't know how she would explain it to Aiden, but she didn't care. She needed to leave, to escape the grip of the house and the past. For the first time in weeks, she felt a flicker of hope.

33

Alice stood by the wardrobe, methodically folding clothes and placing them into the open suitcase on the bed. The soft sound of fabric rustling was the only noise in the room, but even that seemed unnaturally loud in the silence of the house. The tension that had dogged her for weeks felt different today—sharper, more urgent.

She paused, a sweater in her hands, and glanced at the door. The unease she couldn't shake had followed her all morning.

The faintest sound made her freeze. Her breath caught in her throat, her hands tightening around the sweater as she turned slowly.

"Hello, Alice."

Ian stood in the middle of her bedroom, his posture relaxed, his hands casually in his pockets. The sight of him there—so unexpected, so wrong—sent a jolt of fear through her chest. She stumbled back a step, her heart pounding.

"What—what are you doing here?" she stammered, her voice trembling. "How did you get in?"

Ian smiled, a slow, calculated expression that didn't reach his eyes. "Let's just say I have my ways."

"That's not an answer," Alice said, her voice firmer now, though her hands shook. "The alarm—how did you get past the alarm?"

He shrugged, stepping closer. "You'd be surprised how easy it is to bypass even the most sophisticated security systems when you know how."

Alice's throat tightened as her mind raced. The alarm had been silent all morning. She felt exposed, vulnerable in a way that made her skin crawl.

"You need to leave," she said, her voice rising as she tried to muster authority. "Right now. Aiden will—"

"Aiden," Ian interrupted, his tone turning cold, "is exactly why I'm here."

Alice's breath hitched. "What do you want?"

Ian took another step closer, his smile fading. "Your husband and I had a little chat recently. He's been making some very unwise threats."

Alice frowned, confusion and fear swirling in her chest. "What are you talking about?"

"Aiden and I have an arrangement," Ian said smoothly, his eyes narrowing. "Or rather, we did. He was supposed to back my new venture—a mutually beneficial partnership. But then he decided to get... difficult. Threatened to pull out, to cut me off entirely."

Alice's stomach churned. She thought of the article she'd read about Ian's new company, the staggering amount of funding it required, and Aiden's irritation when she'd mentioned it. "Why would he do that?" she asked cautiously.

"Because your husband has a habit of overplaying his hand," Ian said, his voice laced with contempt. "He thinks he can control everything, everyone. But I'm not so easily intimidated."

Alice's legs felt weak as she leaned back against the dresser for support. "What do you want from me?"

Ian's expression softened slightly, but there was no kindness in it. Only calculation. "You're in a unique position, Alice," he said, his tone almost conversational. "You can talk to him, reason with him. Convince him to honour his commitments."

Alice shook her head, her voice trembling. "I can't. You don't understand—"

"Oh, I understand perfectly," Ian said, cutting her off. "You see, I know things about Aiden. Things he wouldn't want the world to discover. But I'm not unreasonable. If he plays ball, we can both walk away from this with our reputations intact. If not..."

"I can't make Aiden do anything," Alice said, her voice cracking. "You're asking the wrong person."

Ian chuckled, a low, humourless sound. "Oh, I think I'm asking exactly the right person. You're his wife, Alice. Someone he wants to protect."

"Protect?" Alice spat, her fear giving way to anger. "You think he's protecting me? He's the reason—" She stopped herself, clamping her mouth shut before she said too much.

Ian's eyes gleamed with interest, his smile returning. "Now, that's interesting," he said. "What exactly were you about to say?"

"Nothing," Alice said quickly, her voice shaking. "You need to leave."

Ian studied her for a long moment, his gaze unnerving. Then he stepped back, his hands still in his pockets. "Think about what I said, Alice," he said casually. "You wouldn't want Aiden's... indiscretions to become public knowledge. That wouldn't be good for either of you."

He turned and strolled toward the door, pausing in the frame to glance back at her. "And by the way, you might want to get that alarm checked. Seems like a pretty big security flaw."

Alice sat frozen on the edge of the bed, her thoughts racing.

She stared at the door where Ian had just stood, her mind refusing to process the audacity of his intrusion. But then his voice echoed again, cutting through the fog of her thoughts as he reappeared in the doorway.

"One last thing, Alice," he said, leaning casually against the frame, his tone sharp with purpose. "You might as well know why your husband's so desperate to keep me quiet."

Alice's breath caught, her pulse quickening. "What are you talking about?"

Ian stepped back into the room, his presence overwhelming, his smug confidence twisting her stomach. "Aiden's not just a tech genius or a charming entrepreneur, as I'm sure you've noticed by now. He's also a man who likes to play dangerously when it suits him."

Alice narrowed her eyes, the fear in her chest mingling with anger. "If you're trying to scare me, it's not going to work. Just say whatever you came to say and leave."

"Oh, this isn't about scaring you," Ian said, his smirk deepening. "It's about making sure you understand what's at stake—for both of you."

He took a step closer, his hands still in his pockets, his voice dropping to a conspiratorial tone. "Lydia knew," he said, his eyes gleaming. "She found out about one of Aiden's less... savoury business deals. A partnership that shouldn't have happened. Something about bypassing regulations, bribing a few key players to keep things quiet, all to launch one of his big projects."

Alice felt the blood drain from her face. "Why are you telling me this?"

"Your husband isn't the squeaky-clean innovator he pretends to be," Ian said. "Lydia stumbled onto some proof—emails, financial records, the works. She used it to her advantage, of course. Blackmailing Aiden."

Alice's head swam as his words sank in. "You knew about this? You knew Lydia was blackmailing him?"

"Oh, I didn't just know," Ian said, his smile turning wolfish. "I made sure to get my hands on the same proof Lydia had. It's amazing what a little digging can uncover, especially when someone's suddenly no longer around to guard their secrets."

Alice's stomach churned, her thoughts tumbling over one another. "So that's why you're threatening him now," she said, her voice trembling. "You're using the same leverage she had."

"Exactly," Ian said, spreading his arms as if presenting himself as the ultimate opportunist. "Aiden's always been so concerned with maintaining his pristine image, with keeping the Chandler name untouchable. But I have no problem dragging it through the mud if he doesn't keep his end of the deal."

"You're disgusting," Alice spat, her voice shaking with anger. "You're just as bad as her—worse."

Ian chuckled, clearly unfazed by her outburst. "Call it what you want. I call it survival. Aiden's not the only one who knows how to protect himself."

"Is that why she's dead?" Alice asked, her voice trembling. "Because of this deal?"

Ian raised an eyebrow, his expression unreadable. "That's a question for Aiden, isn't it?"

The weight of his words hung between them. The implication clear. Lydia had been a liability, just as Ian was now threatening to become. And Aiden... Aiden had already proven what he was capable of when someone got in his way.

Alice stared at Ian, her chest heaving as she tried to process the enormity of what he had revealed. "What do you want from me?" she asked again, her voice barely above a whisper.

"I want you to remind Aiden of the consequences," Ian said, his tone casual, as though he were discussing a business arrangement instead of a threat. "Tell him to honour his commitments. To keep the investment he promised. Otherwise..."

"Otherwise what?" Alice demanded, her voice rising.

"Otherwise, the world learns what kind of man Aiden Chandler really is," Ian said smoothly. "And trust me, Alice, it won't just be his reputation that's ruined. The fallout will destroy you too."

Alice felt the walls of the room close in around her, her breath coming in short, shallow gasps. She wanted to scream, to throw him out, to make him disappear. But she was frozen, paralysed by his words and the horrifying truth they carried.

Ian stepped back toward the door, his smirk returning. "Think it over," he said, his tone almost cheerful. "I'm sure you'll make the right choice."

And then he was gone.

Alice collapsed onto the bed, her hands trembling as she pressed them to her face. The room spun around her, her thoughts a whirlwind of fear, anger, and betrayal.

Aiden had killed Lydia to protect himself. And now, the same secret that had destroyed his last wife was threatening to consume Alice too.

34

The sound of the front door closing startled Alice as she stuffed another sweater into her suitcase. Her mind was a haze of fear and indecision. She hadn't even heard Karen's car pull up. For a moment, she froze, listening as footsteps echoed through the hallway. When Karen's familiar figure appeared in the doorway, her calm presence was both a relief and an unwelcome reminder of the house she was so desperate to escape.

Karen's sharp eyes took in the scene at once: the half-packed suitcase, the dishevelled state of the room, and Alice's pale, tear-streaked face. Her expression remained unreadable as she stepped into the room and closed the door softly behind her.

"Going somewhere, Mrs. Chandler?" Karen asked, her voice steady.

Alice sank onto the bed, her composure cracking under Karen's watchful gaze. "I... I can't stay here anymore," she said, her voice trembling. "I'm going to my sister's. I need to get out of this house, away from all of this."

Karen tilted her head slightly, her gaze softening as she stepped closer. "What's happened?" she asked gently. "Why are you so upset?"

Alice shook her head, her hands clutching the edge of the bed. "I don't even know where to start," she whispered. "Everything's falling apart. Aiden, the house, me... everything."

Karen sat down in the chair across from her, folding her hands neatly in her lap. "Start wherever you need to, Mrs. Chandler," she said. "Sometimes it helps just to talk things through."

Alice hesitated, her thoughts swirling. She couldn't tell Karen everything—not about Lydia's pregnancy, not about Aiden's confession.

"Aiden's being blackmailed," she admitted finally, her voice breaking. "By Ian. He—he knows something, something damaging about Aiden's business. And he's using it against him."

Karen's expression didn't change. "I see," she said simply. "And does Mr. Chandler have reason to worry? Is this... information credible?"

Alice nodded. "It is. I don't know all the details, but it's bad, Karen. Really bad."

Karen leaned forward slightly, her tone calm but probing. "And what about you, Mrs. Chandler? What's making you want to leave?"

Alice hesitated, her hands twisting in her lap. "It's not just the blackmail," she admitted. "It's Lydia. I've learned things about her—about her relationship with Aiden, and with Ian."

Karen's gaze sharpened, though her expression remained composed. "What things?"

Alice bit her lip, the words tumbling out before she could stop them. "She was having an affair with Ian. It changes everything, Karen." Tears welled in her eyes. "And now Ian's using whatever he can to control Aiden. It's like I'm trapped in this nightmare. I can't take it anymore."

Karen sat back, her hands resting lightly on the arms of the chair. "I see," she said, her voice measured. "It's no wonder you're feeling overwhelmed, Mrs. Chandler. But running away won't solve anything."

Alice's head snapped up, her eyes widening. "What are you talking about? I'm not running away—I'm protecting myself. I need space, Karen. I need to think."

Karen's lips curved into a faint smile, though her eyes remained serious. "And what will happen while you're gone?" she asked. "Do you think Mr. Carlisle will simply stop? Do you think the memories of this house and its history won't follow you wherever you go?"

"I don't care," Alice said. "I just need to get out of here. I can't breathe in this house anymore. Everywhere I turn, there's another reminder. The past won't leave me alone."

Karen's smile faded, and she leaned forward, her gaze piercing. "Mrs. Chandler, I've seen many women try to run from their problems, and it never ends well. The truth has a way of catching up with you, no matter where you go. The question is, are you strong enough to face it?"

Alice's chest tightened, her tears spilling over. "I don't know," she whispered. "I don't know if I can."

Karen stood, smoothing the front of her skirt as she looked down at Alice. "You're stronger than you think," she said. "But you'll never find out if you keep running. This house, this life—it's yours now, Mrs. Chandler. You have to decide whether to fight for it or let it slip away."

Alice stared at her, her mind racing. Karen's words felt like a challenge, a subtle but undeniable push to confront the chaos surrounding her.

Karen moved to the door, pausing with her hand on the frame. "Think carefully about what you want, Mrs. Chandler," she said.

Alice sat motionless, Karen's words echoing in her mind.

The weight of the decision felt like it might break her as she stared at the open suitcase. Now, she wasn't sure whether leaving was the right choice.

Karen lingered for a moment; her gaze more piercing than before. "You know," she began, her tone casual but laced with something sharper, "I never liked Ian Carlisle."

Alice blinked, the unexpected statement snapping her from her thoughts. "What?"

Karen stepped into the room, folding her arms. "I never trusted him," she continued. "Even when Lydia was alive, he had... too much influence over her. Too much control."

Alice frowned. "In what way?"

Karen hesitated, her lips pressing into a thin line. "Lydia was a brilliant woman," she said finally. "Driven, ambitious, always thinking ten steps ahead. But when Ian was around, she changed. She became secretive, cautious, almost... deferential. It was unlike her."

Alice's pulse quickened. "Are you saying she was afraid of him?"

Karen tilted her head, considering the question. "I don't know if it was fear," she said slowly. "But there was something about him—something that made her second-guess herself. He has a way of making people feel powerless while acting as though he's doing them a favour. I saw it with Lydia more than once."

Alice felt the pieces of the puzzle shifting uncomfortably in her mind. "Was Aiden aware of this?" she asked.

Karen hesitated again, then nodded. "He must have been. Mr Chandler isn't the type to miss things like that, not when it comes to Lydia. But whether he acknowledged it or not, I couldn't say."

Alice's chest tightened. "Do you think Lydia loved him?" she asked quietly, the words almost catching in her throat. "Ian, I mean."

Karen's face hardened, her voice turning colder. "I think Lydia was a woman who liked to win. With Ian, it wasn't about love—it was about leverage. She was too smart to mix the two."

The room fell into a heavy silence as Alice processed Karen's words. The idea of Lydia being manipulated—or worse, controlled—by Ian only deepened the sense of unease. She opened her mouth to ask another question, but before she could speak, the room was filled with a sudden burst of sound.

A voice, warm and polished, floated through the air, startling both women.

"...and I have to say, I'm the luckiest woman in the world. Aiden and I have the kind of marriage most people only dream of. We're partners in every sense of the word."

Alice's blood ran cold as she recognised the voice. "Lydia," she whispered, her eyes darting around the room.

Karen stiffened, her head snapping toward the ceiling as the voice continued.

"...he's my rock, my greatest supporter, and my best friend. I can't imagine my life without him. We're building something beautiful together, something that will last forever."

The words echoed through the room, clear and unwavering, as though Lydia herself were standing there, delivering them in person. Alice's chest tightened, her breath coming in short, shallow gasps.

"Turn it off!" Alice screamed, her voice cracking. She stumbled back against the bed, her hands flying to her ears as if to block out the sound. "Karen, find it and turn it off!"

Karen, usually so composed, looked unsettled for the first time. She spun on her heel, scanning the room with sharp eyes. "It's coming through the speakers," she said, her voice tight. "It must be connected to the house's sound system."

"Then stop it!" Alice cried; her voice raw with panic. "I can't —I can't listen to this!"

Karen moved quickly, her footsteps echoing as she left the room in search of the system controls. But the voice continued, relentless and haunting.

"...and when I look at Aiden, I see everything I've ever wanted. Everything I could ever need. He's my forever."

Alice clutched her chest, tears streaming down her face as the words cut through her like a knife. The image of Lydia smiling, speaking those words to the world, juxtaposed with the knowledge of what had really happened to her, made Alice feel like she was drowning in a sea of lies.

Karen returned moments later; her expression grim. "The system's locked," she said tightly. "I'm trying to override it, but it'll take a minute."

"Why is this happening?" Alice whispered, her voice trembling. "Why?"

Karen didn't answer, her focus on the tablet in her hands as she worked to stop the recording. But the voice persisted, relentless.

"...I believe in love, in trust, and in building a life together that's worth remembering."

Finally, the voice cut off, leaving a heavy silence in its wake. Karen exhaled sharply, setting the tablet down on the dresser.

"It's off," she said, her tone clipped. "I don't know how it started, but it won't happen again."

Alice collapsed onto the bed, her hands shaking as she wiped at her tear-streaked face. "It's like she's everywhere," she whispered, her voice trembling. "Even now, she's still here. I can't escape her."

Karen stood over her, her expression unreadable. "Mrs. Chandler," she said slowly, her voice steady but laced with warning. "Evermere holds many memories, and not all of them are kind. But letting them consume you won't help."

Alice stared up at her, her heart pounding. "What am I supposed to do?" she whispered. "How do I live with this?"

Karen's gaze didn't waver. "You face it," she said firmly. "You face it head-on. Running won't make it disappear."

But as Karen turned and left the room, her words lingering in the air, Alice couldn't shake the feeling that Lydia's voice had been more than a cruel coincidence. It had been a warning—a reminder that the truth, no matter how deeply buried, would always find its way to the surface.

35

Alice sat on the edge of her bed. Her suitcase open but untouched. The clothes she had hastily packed earlier now seemed out of place, a half-formed plan she no longer intended to follow. She stared at her phone, Beth's last message glowing on the screen:

We'll be ready whenever you are. Just come, Alice. You need this.

She had meant to leave, to escape the house and all its secrets. But running away wouldn't solve anything. Lydia's shadow wouldn't disappear. The truth would remain, lurking in the corners of her mind, until she faced it head-on.

I'm not coming, she finally typed, the words feeling both heavy and liberating. *I need to stay and figure this out. I'll call soon. Love you.*

She hit send, then tossed the phone onto the bed. Her gaze drifted to the window, where the cliffs and the ocean beyond loomed dark and ominous. The house still felt heavy with Lydia's presence, but Alice's fear had shifted. It wasn't just about survival anymore. It was about more than that.

The boat. The body. The truth.

The thought settled over Alice like a cold, unshakable

certainty. Lydia's death had been buried in lies, her disappearance a mystery that remained unanswered. If Alice wanted peace—if she wanted to move forward—she had to find Lydia's boat. She had to find her body. Only then could Lydia truly be free, and only then could Alice escape her ghost.

Her hands shook slightly as she dialled David's number. He answered on the second ring, his voice calm and familiar.

"Mrs. Chandler," he said. "Everything all right?"

"I need your help, David," Alice said, skipping any pleasantries. Her voice was steady, though her heart raced. "Can you come to the house? I need to talk to you in person."

David hesitated, and she could almost hear his mind working on the other end of the line. "Of course," he said after a moment. "I'll be there shortly."

"Thank you," Alice said quietly before hanging up.

She stood and moved to the window, consumed by the same restless energy she had felt the night before, as if the ocean itself was calling to her, urging her to continue.

David arrived just over an hour later. His pickup truck crunched over the gravel driveway, the sound carrying through the stillness of the house. Alice watched from the window as he climbed out, his rugged frame moving with the quiet confidence she had always found reassuring. He carried himself like a man who had seen much and kept it all to himself—a quality she was counting on now.

When she opened the door, David's sharp eyes immediately scanned her face. "You look like you've been through hell," he said bluntly.

As David stood there, his presence steady and firm, something about him still made her uneasy.

"David," she said, her voice trembling slightly as she

gestured toward the sitting room. "Can we sit? I need to... I need to talk this through."

He nodded, following her into the room where she sank into the corner of the sofa. David stood for a moment, watching her, before taking a seat in the armchair across from her.

"I feel like I'm losing my mind," Alice admitted, her voice barely above a whisper. Her hands twisted together in her lap. Her knuckles white. "Every day, it gets worse. The letters, the way the house feels—it's like I'm being watched constantly. And Aiden—" She broke off, her voice catching.

David leaned forward, resting his elbows on his knees. "Aiden what?" he prompted gently, his voice calm but laced with concern.

Alice hesitated; the words heavy on her tongue. "I don't know if I can trust him. He's hiding things from me, David. I don't think he's telling me everything. I don't know what to believe anymore. And there's Ian," she bit her lip, "I don't know who I can trust."

David frowned, his expression tightening. "Ian's a snake," he said, his voice low. "I never liked the way he operated. Always circling people, looking for leverage. If he's got something on Aiden, if he's the problem..." He shook his head, his lips pressed into a thin line. "You're right to be wary of him."

Alice nodded, but her heart was pounding. "It's not just him, though. It's this whole place. Everything about it feels... wrong. I'm scared, David. Scared of what I'll find if I keep digging, but even more scared of what'll happen if I don't. I think my life is in danger. And my sanity—" She broke off, her voice cracking. "I'm hanging by a thread."

David's gaze softened, and he leaned back slightly in his chair. "You're not crazy, Alice," he said firmly. "I've seen what this place can do to people. Lydia... she had a way of twisting things, of making people doubt themselves. She was good at it, too good. And the people who surrounded her—people like Ian—they thrived on that chaos. Maybe it's not just the house, Alice. Maybe it's the people who built their lives here."

Alice swallowed hard, her eyes welling with tears. "But Lydia's gone. She's dead—or at least she's supposed to be. How is she still controlling everything? How is she still controlling me?"

David's face darkened, a flicker of something unreadable passing over his expression. "Because she was never really gone," he said quietly. "Not in the way you think."

"What do you mean?" Alice asked, her voice trembling.

David exhaled sharply, his gaze dropping to the floor. "Lydia had a way of leaving pieces of herself behind. Not just in this house, but in the people she touched. The things she did to Aiden, to Ian, even to me… she didn't just disappear. She made sure of that."

The room seemed to close in around Alice. "What did she do to you?" she asked, her voice barely above a whisper.

David hesitated, his hands tightening into fists before he relaxed them again. "She made me question myself," he said finally. "Made me wonder if I was part of her games, if I was just another pawn to her. I saw things, Alice. Things that didn't add up, things I wasn't supposed to notice. And when I did, she made sure I kept quiet."

Alice's heart pounded. "What things, David? What did you see?"

David looked up at her, his gaze sharp and piercing. "Things that would ruin people, if they ever came out. Lydia was smart—she didn't just hold secrets. She wove them into her life, into her relationships."

Alice stared at him, the weight of his words settling over her like a lead blanket. "Are you saying she was blackmailing you?"

David didn't answer immediately, his silence speaking volumes. "Let's just say Lydia knew how to keep people in line," he said finally. "And if she wanted something, she got it. No matter the cost."

Alice shivered, wrapping her arms around herself. "It feels like she's still here. Like she's still pulling the strings."

David leaned forward again, his voice low and urgent. "Then you need to decide, Alice. Are you going to take control of this?"

Alice blinked, her breath hitching as she searched his face. There was something in his eyes—something that made her hesitate. For a moment, she wondered if he was truly trying to help her, or if he was part of the web Lydia had left behind.

"I don't know who to trust," she admitted, her voice breaking. "Not Aiden, not Ian, not this house. And I want to trust you, David, but I don't know if I can."

David's expression didn't change, but his eyes softened slightly. "I don't blame you for that," he said quietly. "I'd feel the same in your position. But if you want my advice, Alice... trust yourself. Trust your instincts. They'll guide you better than anyone else can."

Alice nodded slowly, though her unease remained as she said, "in that case I have an idea but I am going to need your help."

David listened patiently as she explained and afterwards, he stood, his movements deliberate and calm and offered her his hand.

"You can do this," he said. "If there's anything out there, we'll find it. Together."

Alice hesitated. Something about him unsettled her, but she couldn't do this alone. Not anymore.

Alice couldn't shake the feeling that she was walking into a trap. Whether it was one Lydia had set or one that David was leading her into, she didn't know. But one thing was certain: the truth was waiting for her, and it wasn't going to let her go without a fight.

36

Alice sat at the desk in Aiden's office, the glow from the computer screen illuminating her determined expression. Her hands hovered over the keyboard, steady now where once they had trembled. Evermere was silent save for the faint hum of the heating system, but Alice felt anything but alone. For the first time in weeks, she felt in control, her purpose clear.

In the days since her conversation with David, she had spent hours poring over the threads of information she had quietly gathered. Aiden's shady deal, Ian's manipulations, and the breadcrumbs Lydia had left behind in her carefully constructed life—all of it led to one undeniable truth: Ian Carlisle had secrets of his own, and it was time for them to see the light.

Her plan had taken shape late one night, fuelled by equal parts fear and resolve. Ian had underestimated her, assuming she was Aiden's ornamental wife, too fragile and naïve to pose a threat. He didn't know that Alice had been watching, listening, and learning. And he certainly didn't know that she had no intention of playing by his rules.

Alice had combed through everything she could find on Ian: public records, financial statements, even whispers on obscure forums that hinted at his less-than-legal dealings. But it wasn't until she stumbled upon an encrypted file buried in Aiden's archives—a remnant of Lydia's digital trail—that she found her smoking gun.

The file contained a series of emails between Ian and several offshore accounts, detailing money laundering schemes, under-the-table deals, and bribes that would make even the most seasoned criminal blush. Alice didn't know how Lydia had gotten her hands on it, but she was grateful she had. It was enough to take Ian down without implicating Aiden—if she played her cards right.

Now, as she typed out the final details of her anonymous tip to the press contact she'd found online, Alice felt a surge of adrenaline. She was careful to redact any mention of Aiden or his company, ensuring that the focus remained squarely on Ian. The tip was precise, detailed, and damning enough to spark a full-scale investigation. But she didn't stop there.

Alice included carefully selected hints about Ian's pattern of manipulation—how he used fear and leverage to control those around him. She painted a picture of a man who had clawed his way to the top by stepping on the backs of others, and she made sure the story had teeth.

When she was satisfied, Alice leaned back in the chair, staring at the screen for a moment. Her finger hovered over the send button, a sliver of doubt creeping in. But then she thought of Lydia, of the lies and manipulation that had surrounded her life and death. She thought of Ian's smug smile, his veiled threats, and the way he had tried to turn her into another pawn in his game.

With a deep breath, Alice pressed send.

She leaned back in the chair, her pulse racing as the screen confirmed the message had been sent. The room around her felt strangely still, as though the house itself was holding its breath.

She exhaled slowly, trying to steady the adrenaline coursing through her veins. The glow of the monitor dimmed slightly, and for a moment, she let herself imagine what it might feel like to be free of Ian's shadow.

The fallout was swift.

The first article appeared within 24 hours, its headline bold and damning:

"Ian Carlisle Under Fire: Allegations of Corruption and Fraud Surface."

Within hours, the story spread like wildfire. News outlets picked up the narrative, each one digging deeper into the web deceit that Ian had spun. Former associates came forward with their own stories, emboldened by the sudden scrutiny. Even those who had once been loyal to him began to distance themselves, sensing the tide turning.

Alice watched it all unfold from the comfort of the estate, her laptop open as she sipped her tea. For the first time in weeks, she felt a sense of calm. Ian's empire was crumbling, his reputation in tatters, and his threats neutralised.

Aiden, who had been out of town on business, called her in a panic when the news broke. "Did you see this?" he asked, his voice strained. "Ian's finished. This could destroy everything."

"It won't," Alice said calmly. "The story doesn't touch you or the company. Ian made his bed—now he has to lie in it."

Aiden hesitated. His silence heavy with unspoken questions. "How do you know?" he asked finally.

Alice smiled. Her tone steady but firm. "Because I made sure of it."

. . .

That evening, Alice sat in the sunroom, staring out at the cliffs as the last rays of sunlight dipped below the horizon. The ocean was calm and for the first time in weeks the house felt still—not heavy or suffocating, but peaceful.

She knew this wasn't the end. There were still questions. But for now, she had won. She had outmanoeuvred Ian, protected Aiden's reputation, and taken back some of the power that had been stolen from her.

As the first stars began to prick through the velvety night sky, Alice rested back in her chair. She could feel a shift within herself—a quiet resolve settling over her, solid and unshakable.

For the first time in weeks, Alice felt like she had a sense of direction, a purpose. Ian's empire was unravelling, and she had played a part in it. The thought gave her strength, a reminder that she wasn't powerless. Not anymore.

Her phone buzzed on the table beside her, breaking the silence. She picked it up and saw David's name flashing on the screen. Taking a steadying breath, she answered.

"David?" she said, her voice calm but tinged with anticipation.

"I've got everything we need," David said, his tone confident but tinged with the seriousness of the task ahead. "Coordinates, tides, last-known sightings—everything. It's all pointing to a specific area about thirty miles offshore. That's where Lydia's boat likely ended up."

Alice's heart skipped a beat. "How did you find it?" she asked, gripping the phone tightly. "I thought the authorities searched everywhere and came up empty."

David chuckled softly, a sound that carried a hint of pride. "They searched, but they didn't have the resources you've got, Mrs. Chandler. With enough money and the right connections."

Alice swallowed hard, the enormity of what they were about

to do sinking in. "And you're sure? This isn't just another dead end?"

"As sure as I can be," David replied. "The currents in that area are tricky, and the conditions that night would have carried the boat further than the cops estimated. If the wreck is there, it won't be easy to find."

Alice glanced out at the ocean. "What's the plan?" Her voice was quiet but resolute.

"Meet me at the harbour tomorrow morning," David said. "I've chartered a boat and prepped the equipment we'll need. If the yacht's down there, we'll find it."

Alice exhaled, her grip on the phone tightening. "Thank you, David. For everything."

David's voice softened. "You don't need to thank me, Mrs. Chandler. Just be ready. It's going to be a long day."

Alice ended the call, set the phone down then sat in the quiet stillness until the faintest sound caught her attention. So slight she almost dismissed it. She turned her head, her eyes scanning the dimly lit room, but saw nothing out of place.

Alice couldn't shake the unnerving feeling that something or someone was always watching.

A muffled noise echoed from somewhere down the hall. Alice stiffened, her senses sharpening instantly. She turned her head toward the sound, her breath catching in her throat. The house, which had felt so silent and empty just moments before, now seemed alive with unseen movement.

She pushed the chair back slowly, the wheels gliding over the rug. Rising to her feet, Alice moved to the door of Aiden's office, her bare feet silent against the hardwood floor. She peered out into the dimly lit hallway, her pulse pounding in her ears.

"Aiden?" she called softly, her voice barely above a whisper.

No response.

Alice's grip on the doorframe tightened. It wasn't like Aiden to wander the house at this hour, and Karen was out. The thought of Ian creeping into the house again, his smug face twisted into something darker, sent a shiver down her spine.

Steeling herself, Alice stepped out into the hallway. The faint glow of the office cast her shadow long against the walls, and she found herself glancing over her shoulder every few steps. Evermere hummed with a low, almost tangible energy.

She reached the staircase and paused, listening. The sound came again—a faint, rhythmic movement like footsteps above, on the second floor. It was too deliberate to be the house settling. Someone was there.

Alice's heart raced as she descended the stairs; each step deliberate and careful. She turned toward the sitting room, where the flicker of the fireplace cast dancing images onto the walls. Her eyes darted around the space, searching for any sign of movement, but the room was empty.

She moved toward the back door, her hand brushing against the lock. It was secure, as were the windows she checked one by one. Still, the sense of being watched prickled at the back of her neck.

A sudden noise behind her—a sharp knock—made her jump. Alice spun around, her breath hitching. The sound had come from the front door. For a moment, she froze, her body refusing to move. Then, with trembling hands, she approached the door, peering through the peephole.

No one was there.

Her hand hesitated on the doorknob, her instincts screaming at her to lock herself in the bedroom and wait until morning. But the pull of curiosity—or recklessness—was stronger. Slowly, she turned the lock and opened the door a crack, the cold night air brushing against her face.

The porch was empty.

Alice stepped outside, the chill biting at her skin. She scanned the driveway and the edges of the estate, the faint glow of the garden lights barely illuminating the dense shadows. The wind howled, rustling the trees at the edge of the property, but there was no sign of anyone.

As she turned back toward the door, something caught her eye—a small, folded piece of paper wedged under the mat. She crouched down, her hands trembling as she picked it up. The paper felt damp and cold in her fingers, the ink smudged but legible.

Did you really think it would be this easy?

Alice's breath caught, her heart hammering in her chest. She stared at the note, her mind racing. The threat was clear, and it was aimed directly at her. Whoever had left this knew exactly what she had planned—and they were watching.

She stumbled back into the house, slamming the door shut and locking it. Her hands were shaking so violently she could barely turn the deadbolt. She needed help, but who could she trust? David—despite his reassurances—was an enigma she couldn't fully decipher.

Alice's eyes darted toward the staircase, her instincts screaming at her to retreat to the relative safety of her room. But something stopped her—a flicker of movement outside the window. She turned quickly, her breath catching in her throat.

For a split second, she thought she saw a figure standing at the edge of the garden, just beyond the glow of the lights. But when she blinked, it was gone.

The room seemed to tilt around her, her vision swimming. The fear was overwhelming, but beneath it was something else —a spark of defiance. She had come too far to back down now. Whoever was watching her, whoever thought they could scare her, didn't realise she wasn't the same woman she had been weeks ago.

Clutching the note tightly, Alice took a deep breath and made her way back to Aiden's office. She sat down at the desk, her hands still trembling but her resolve hardening. She opened her laptop, the glow of the screen lighting up her determined face.

If whoever this was wanted a fight, they would get one.

37

Aiden pushed open the front door. The house felt colder than usual, its silence unnerving. Normally, someone would have appeared by now, but the foyer remained empty, and no sound came from the rest of the house.

"Alice?" he called out, his voice bouncing off the high ceilings. Only silence greeted him.

He frowned, setting his briefcase down and loosening his tie. The journey home had been long, and all he wanted was a stiff drink and a moment to collect himself. But the emptiness of the house was filling him with a sense that something wasn't right.

Aiden checked the kitchen, the living room, the sunroom. Each one was immaculate, undisturbed, as if they had been frozen in time. The only sign of life was a faint trace of Alice's perfume lingering in the air.

He pulled out his phone and dialled Karen's number, but it went straight to voicemail. His attempt to call Alice yielded the same result. Frustration bubbled beneath his calm exterior, mingling with a growing sense of dread.

"Where the hell are they?" he muttered to himself.

Returning to the living room, Aiden poured himself a

whiskey and sank into one of the leather armchairs. He stared into the amber liquid, his mind racing with possibilities. Alice had been distant the last time they spoke, but she hadn't mentioned going anywhere.

His thoughts were interrupted by the faint sound of the television, which had been left on mute. The screen displayed a breaking news segment, the bold headline catching his attention: *"IAN CARLISLE UNDER FIRE: NEW SCANDALS EMERGE."*

Aiden grabbed the remote and unmuted the television. The reporter's voice filled the room, calm but carrying the weight of a significant revelation.

"...allegations of widespread corruption, including money laundering and offshore dealings, have surfaced against tech mogul Ian Carlisle. Sources indicate that the evidence is substantial, and legal experts predict this could mark the end of Carlisle's career..."

Aiden leaned forward; his drink forgotten on the side table. His stomach twisted as the broadcast continued, detailing Ian's fall from grace. The allegations were damning, every word slicing through the veneer of Carlisle's carefully constructed image. Aiden's hands gripped the armrests of the chair as the full scope of the scandal unfolded before him.

"...anonymous sources provided detailed documentation of Carlisle's involvement in several illegal activities, including bribery and tax evasion. While the identity of the whistleblower remains unknown, insiders suggest that the evidence was meticulously compiled and difficult to refute..."

As he stood in the empty house, Aiden couldn't shake the sensation that he was losing control. And for the first time in years, he wasn't sure how to get it back.

Aiden set the glass of whiskey back down, his throat dry despite the drink. The silence of the house bore down on him.

The faint echo of his own footsteps as he moved toward the main hallway only heightened his unease. Something was wrong, deeply wrong, and he couldn't shake the prickling sensation at the back of his neck.

As he walked further into the house, he froze. A single photo of Lydia, the one that always sat on the console table by the staircase, one of the few last remaining imagines of her in the house, was turned face down. His brow furrowed as he approached it, his hand hovering over the frame. He picked it up, staring at Lydia's familiar smile—bright, poised, and untouchable.

He placed the photo back in its original position and continued toward the kitchen, but as he passed the dining room, his steps faltered. Another photo of Lydia, this one on the mantel above the fireplace, was also face down. His stomach churned. It wasn't just one photo—every remaining picture of her in house, all deliberately flipped.

"Karen?" he called again, his voice louder now, his tone betraying the unease creeping up his spine.

He'd instructed her to return, so where was she?

Still, there was no answer. He moved further into the dining room, his eyes scanning the room with growing suspicion. The polished surface of the long dining table gleamed under the dim light, but it was what sat at the centre that made his breath hitch: Lydia's old photo album, the leather-bound one she had cherished, sat open, its pages exposed as if someone had been rifling through it.

Aiden approached cautiously, his hands trembling slightly as he closed the album. He didn't need to open it to know what it contained—pictures of their early years together, Lydia's carefully curated life captured in glossy snapshots. The thought of Alice or Karen poring over it in his absence made his chest tighten.

The sound of movement upstairs made him whip around, his eyes narrowing as he stared at the ceiling. He moved toward the staircase with purposeful steps, his heart hammering against his ribs.

As he ascended, each footstep on the stairs felt magnified. He reached the landing and turned toward the master bedroom, his hand brushing the wall as he steadied himself.

The hallway was dark, save for the faint glow of light spilling out from under the door to the guest room. He frowned. That room was rarely used, and Alice hadn't mentioned anything. Slowly, he approached the door, his pulse quickening.

He pushed it open, and the sight that greeted him made his blood run cold. Karen stood in the middle of the room, her back to him. In her hands was another photo of Lydia, its frame glinting in the dim light. She stared at it for a moment before deliberately placing it face down on the vanity. The room was unnaturally still, the air heavy with something Aiden couldn't name.

"Karen," he said, his voice sharp and cutting through the silence like a blade.

She turned slowly, her expression calm but her eyes unreadable. "Mr. Chandler," she said, inclining her head slightly as if his presence was expected. "I didn't hear you come in."

"What are you doing?" Aiden demanded, stepping into the room, his eyes darting between her and the turned photo. "What's going on? With the photos."

Karen's hands clasped in front of her, her posture serene despite the accusation in his tone. "The house feels... restless," she said carefully. "I thought it might help to—shift the energy."

Aiden's jaw tightened. "Shift the energy?"

Karen's gaze didn't waver. "It's not about erasure. It's about balance. The memories of Mrs. Lydia linger here, Mr. Chandler, and they're heavy. I know you feel it too. Mrs Chandler certainly does."

"I don't have time for this nonsense," Aiden snapped. "Where's Alice? And why haven't you been answering your phone?"

Karen hesitated for a fraction of a second, the kind of pause that spoke volumes. "Alice needed some space," she said finally, her voice even. "She's been... overwhelmed."

Aiden's eyes narrowed. "Where is she, Karen?"

"I don't know," Karen admitted, her hands still clasped. "But she asked not to be disturbed. She's trying to make sense of everything."

Aiden stepped closer, his frustration boiling over. "What exactly does that mean? What have you been telling her while I've been gone?"

Karen's expression didn't change, but her voice lowered, her tone almost soothing. "Alice is grappling with a great deal, Mr. Chandler. She's trying to find her footing in a house that doesn't quite belong to her yet. It's natural for her to feel lost."

Aiden clenched his fists, the tension in his body almost unbearable. "You're overstepping, Karen. I don't pay you to meddle in our lives."

Karen inclined her head again, but there was something defiant in her gaze. "I only want what's best for this household, Mr. Chandler. For you and for Alice."

Aiden stared at her for a long moment, his chest rising and falling with the effort to keep his temper in check. But as he was about to walk away, Karen's calm expression shifted, her gaze darkening as she picked up the photo once more, her fingers brushing over Lydia's face before setting it back down, face down, with deliberate precision.

Aiden stepped back, his eyes flicking once more to the photo on the vanity. Without a word, he turned and left the room, his footsteps heavy as he descended the stairs.

38

Alice pulled her scarf tighter against the bite of the morning chill. The harbour stretched before her, quiet save for the occasional cry of gulls and the lapping of water against the moored boats. It wasn't the idyllic scene she had pictured—grey clouds hovered low, promising rain, and the dampness in the air seemed to seep into her bones.

Her gaze locked on David, who stood by the gangway of a weathered navy-blue vessel. He leaned casually against the railing, his face set in a neutral expression, but the tension in his posture betrayed him. Alice hesitated at the edge of the dock, the water beneath her dark and shifting. This wasn't just another step in her search for answers—it felt like crossing a threshold she couldn't return from.

"Alice," David called, motioning her forward. His voice, steady as always, was a small comfort in the vast unease swirling around her. "Come on, let me help you aboard."

She forced a faint smile, taking his outstretched hand as she stepped onto the gangway. The boat swayed under her and she gripped David's arm tighter than she intended. Beneath her, the water churned in murky ripples, its depth unknowable, its secrets untouchable.

"Thanks," she murmured, glancing nervously at the waves before steadying herself. She adjusted her scarf, the breeze tugging at it as if trying to pull her back.

"Not a problem," David said, his tone light. But as she glanced up at him, she caught the flicker of apprehension in his eyes. Neither of them said it, but they both knew this mission wasn't just about finding Lydia's yacht.

The vessel itself wasn't what Alice had expected. Where Lydia's yacht, *The Governess*, had been all sleek luxury and shimmering opulence, this boat was utilitarian, built for endurance rather than beauty. The navy paint was chipped in places, and the deck bore the scars of countless missions. It wasn't comforting, but it exuded purpose. This was a boat that got things done.

David introduced her to the crew as they made their way to the cabin. Captain Miles, a compact man with weathered skin, gave her a firm handshake and a measured look. His piercing blue eyes seemed to size her up in an instant, and Alice felt gratitude that someone so competent was at the helm.

"Captain Miles," he said gruffly introducing himself, his voice carrying the weight of authority. "Welcome aboard. We'll be heading out shortly. Weather might give us some trouble, but we've handled worse."

"Thank you," Alice said, trying to match his steadiness.

"And this," David continued, gesturing toward a woman seated in front of a bank of monitors, "is Doctor Eloise Carter."

Eloise turned; her sharp features softened by a quick smile. Her hair was tied back in a practical ponytail, and her glasses perched on her nose. She looked like someone who thrived on precision, someone who found comfort in the clean logic of data.

"Alice, is it?" Eloise said, standing to shake her hand. Her grip was firm, her gaze direct. "David's told me you'll be observing. Don't worry—we'll keep you in the loop. I'll be running the sonar and the ROV. It's a lot of tech, but once you see how it works, it will all start to make sense."

Alice glanced at the array of monitors. Numbers scrolled across one screen, while another displayed sonar imaging—dark shapes outlined against a lighter background, the ocean floor rendered in ghostly relief.

Eloise followed her gaze. "This is where we'll get our first look. Sonar's great for mapping large areas, but the ROV—that's where we'll find the details. Wreckage, debris... anything that doesn't belong."

Alice nodded, her throat tightening. Somewhere out there, the boat that had carried Lydia to her end waited beneath the waves, its story unfinished.

Captain Miles appeared in the doorway, his boots thudding against the deck as he approached. "We'll be moving out in a few minutes," he announced. "Storm's brewing further out. We'll skirt its edge, but it's going to get rough."

David tensed beside her. "Is it safe?" he asked, his voice low.

Miles gave him a long, measured look. "Safe enough, if you trust the boat and me. But the sea doesn't take kindly to hesitation. If you're in, you're in."

Alice stepped forward; her determination unshaken. "We're in," she said firmly, her voice cutting through the tension. "We've come this far. We're not turning back now."

David hesitated, glancing between Alice and the captain. "I still think we should call Aiden. He should know—"

"No," Alice interrupted, her tone sharp. She turned to face him, her eyes blazing with conviction. "Aiden doesn't need to know. Not yet."

David sighed, running a hand over his face. "Fine. But if things go south—"

"They won't," Alice said, cutting him off.

Miles nodded approvingly. "Good. Then let's get to it."

The boat rumbled to life beneath them, the engine's growl vibrating through the deck. As they left the harbour behind, the waves grew choppier, the dark clouds on the horizon creeping closer. Alice stood at the railing, the cold spray of seawater stinging her cheeks.

Eloise's voice crackled through the cabin's intercom. "First scan will start in about thirty minutes. We'll begin with sonar, then deploy the ROV. It's going to be a long day, folks, so buckle in."

Alice gripped the railing tighter, her resolve hardening. The clouds loomed ahead, and the sea seemed to whisper its secrets just beyond her reach. She knew the risks, but she couldn't stop now. Somewhere beneath the waves lay the truth, waiting for her to uncover it.

David stepped up beside her, his expression tense. "You really think we're going to find something?" he asked, his voice low.

Alice didn't look at him. Her eyes were fixed on the horizon, where the clouds met the water in a dark, unbroken line. "We have to," she said quietly.

39

Aiden's breath came in ragged, uneven bursts as he stumbled along the narrow, overgrown path toward the cliffs. The wind screamed through the gnarled trees lining the way, tugging at his coat and tangling his hair, its icy fingers clawing at his exposed skin. His shoes skidded on the loose gravel, the earth beneath him uneven and treacherous, but he didn't slow. He couldn't.

Evermere, with its carefully cultivated grounds and pristine facade, seemed a world away now—a hollow shell of stability compared to the chaos he felt inside. Here, the land was wild, untamed, and dangerous. Each step felt heavier than the last, a weight pressing down on him with every thought of Alice. Her voice, her presence, her silences—they echoed in his memory, tormenting him.

Finally, he reached the edge, and the sight stole the breath from his lungs. The cliffs dropped away sharply, their jagged edges plunging into the violent sea below. The waves were monstrous, crashing against the rocks with a force that sent plumes of white foam spiralling upward. The scent of salt and brine filled his nostrils.

He took a tentative step closer, his shoes grinding against the gravel. The sheer drop made his stomach churn, and he instinctively leaned back, his body screaming at him to move away. But his eyes were fixed on the scene below. The rocks jutted out like jagged teeth, sharp and unforgiving, the waves surging and breaking over them in relentless fury.

"Alice!" he shouted, his voice raw and desperate. He cupped his hands around his mouth and shouted again, louder this time, the name echoing faintly before being swallowed by the endless roar of the sea.

Panic gripped him, tightening around his chest like a vice. His mind raced with possibilities, each one worse than the last. He scanned the shoreline below, his eyes darting over every shadow and crevice, searching for any sign of her. A flash of white among the rocks made his breath catch, his heart leaping into his throat. For a horrifying moment, he imagined seeing her broken body sprawled there, limbs twisted at unnatural angles, her hair plastered to her pale, lifeless face.

"No," he muttered, shaking his head violently as if to banish the image. His hands clenched into fists at his sides, his nails biting into his palms. "No, she wouldn't... she wouldn't do that." But the thought refused to leave him, coiling like a serpent in his mind, its venomous whispers growing louder.

He stepped closer to the edge, his legs trembling as he peered down again. The drop was dizzying, the churning water below a relentless reminder of how easily life could be claimed by the sea. His pulse thundered in his ears. Each beat a cruel metronome ticking away the seconds she might be lost.

"Alice!" he called again, his voice cracking. His breath hitched as he fumbled for his phone, his fingers clumsy with cold and panic. He dialled her number, pressing the phone to his ear as it rang. And rang. And rang.

"Pick up," he whispered, his voice trembling. "Please, Alice, just pick up."

But the call went to voicemail, and her calm, recorded greeting was like a dagger to his chest. He ended the call and immediately dialled again, his movements frantic. The same result. He swore under his breath, his frustration mounting.

The storm picked up with an almost sentient fury, as if the world itself were mocking his helplessness. He looked out over the sea, the horizon dark with churning clouds, and felt the weight of his own inadequacy weighing him down. Alice had been slipping away from him for weeks. He had tried to reach her, but it hadn't been enough. He hadn't been enough.

His hands trembled as he ran them through his hair, gripping handfuls in frustration.

He stared down at the rocks again, his vision blurring as tears stung his eyes. The thought of losing her, truly losing her, was unbearable. It was a grief that threatened to swallow him whole, a black hole of guilt and regret that he couldn't escape. He closed his eyes, his shoulders heaving as he struggled to steady himself.

"Alice," he whispered, the name a prayer, a plea. "Come back to me. Please."

As Aiden made his way back towards the house his phone vibrated an alert, telling him the intercom at the estate gates was being buzzed, the noise sharp and sudden. Aiden froze. He glanced back toward the cliffs, a knot twisting in his stomach. The intercom buzzed again, louder this time, insistent.

Relief flickered, quickly overtaken by dread. He jogged back toward the house, his unease sharpening into something darker.

By the time he reached the intercom controls inside the house, his hands were shaking. Pressing the button, he leaned close to the speaker. "Who is it?" His voice was taut, straining to sound calm.

"It's Ian," came the reply, sharp and cutting. "Open the gates, Aiden."

Aiden hesitated, his hand hovering over the control. His mind churned as he replayed the events of the last week—the leaked documents, the damning headlines. Aiden had known this moment was inevitable.

"What do you want, Ian?" he asked, trying to buy time.

"What do I want?" Ian's laugh crackled through the intercom, low and dangerous. "I want to talk. To you. Now."

"I'm not sure this is the right—"

"Cut the crap, Aiden," Ian snapped, his voice rising with barely contained fury. "I'm not here to exchange pleasantries. Open the damn gates, or I'll tear them down."

Aiden pressed the button reluctantly, releasing the lock. Through the window, he saw the sleek silver car glide up the drive, its tinted windows gleaming ominously under the brooding sky. He could feel the tension tightening around him like a noose.

The car stopped abruptly, and the door swung open. Ian stepped out, his tailored coat billowing in the wind. He looked every inch the man used to being in control, but his expression was thunderous, his jaw set like granite.

Aiden swallowed hard as Ian strode toward him, his polished shoes crunching on the gravel.

"You've got nerve," Ian said, his voice low and venomous as he stopped inches from Aiden. "Leaking those documents? Feeding the press? Did you think I wouldn't figure it out?"

Aiden raised his hands defensively. "I didn't—"

"Don't lie to me!" Ian's voice cracked like a whip, tight with raw anger. "Do you have any idea what you've done? How many years of work, of trust, you've destroyed? You've left me to bleed out in the public eye!"

Aiden took a step back, his mind scrambling for a response. "I didn't leak anything, Ian."

Ian's eyes narrowed, cold and calculating. "I've had every corner of my life gutted this week. My accounts frozen. Investors pulling out. And now, you're standing here denying your part in this?" He took a step closer, lowering his voice to a hiss. "If I find out you're lying, Aiden, I won't just destroy your life. I'll bury you."

The threat hung in the air, heavy and unrelenting. Aiden clenched his fists, trying to summon the courage to hold his ground. "It wasn't me. You're blaming the wrong person."

Ian's lips curled into a humourless smile. "Then you'd better hope you're right. Because if I find out otherwise..." He let the words trail off, his meaning unmistakable.

"You wouldn't want to lose another wife, would you Aiden. That would just be careless."

40

The boat slanted violently as another wave slammed against its hull, sending a spray of saltwater crashing onto the deck. The grey sky had darkened to a bruised black while every breath Alice took felt heavy, laden with salt and desperation, her stomach roiling as much from her anxiety as the rocking sea.

Inside the cabin, Eloise sat rigidly at her station, her fingers hovering over the keyboard as she glanced nervously at the growing torrent outside. The screens in front of her displayed rolling lines of sonar data and shifting maps of the ocean floor, but they had found nothing. No sign of *The Governess*. No sign of Lydia.

Alice stepped inside the cabin, her soaked hair clinging to her face, and clutched the doorway for balance. Her fingers were stiff with cold, her body taut as a bowstring, but her determination burned fiercely inside her.

"This is getting reckless," Eloise muttered, glancing over her shoulder at Captain Miles. "We need to turn back. The storm's intensifying, and if we lose control—"

"We're not turning back," Alice cut in sharply, her voice laced with a desperation that made Eloise flinch. Her eyes were wide, feverish, as though sheer willpower alone could force the ocean to surrender its secrets.

"Alice, listen to me," Eloise said, keeping her voice calm but firm. "We've covered the area twice already. There's no trace of the yacht, and this storm—"

"I don't care about that!" Alice snapped, slamming her hand down on the edge of the console. The vibration rattled through the cabin, silencing everyone. "We're close. I can feel it. We're not leaving until we find something."

Her voice cracked on the last word, and a tremor passed through her. She turned to the screen, her throat tight, her heart hammering in her chest. She needed to find the boat. She needed to know what had happened to Lydia—not just for the dead woman, but for herself. Because without answers, the doubt would consume her.

David shifted uncomfortably by the door; his broad shoulders hunched against the rising tension. Rain dripped from his jacket onto the cabin floor as he glanced between Alice and Eloise. He wiped his face with a shaking hand, his discomfort clear.

"Alice, maybe Eloise is right," he said carefully. "We're not going to be able to do much if this hits us full force. We can come back once it's passed."

"Come back?" Alice turned on him, her expression incredulous. "And what if the churn buries whatever's left of *The Governess* even deeper? What if we miss our chance?"

The words hitched in her throat. She clung to the edge of the console, her knuckles white, willing herself to stay strong.

Her mind raced as she stared at the screens, her breath shallow. If they found the yacht, it could finally confirm Aiden's innocence. It could prove, once and for all, that Lydia's death had been an accident, that the man she loved wasn't capable of the things her darkest thoughts whispered to her.

But another possibility loomed, just as vivid, just as unbearable. What if the wreck told a different story?

The thought chilled her to the bone. She could see Aiden's face now, the way he looked at her with those intense, unreadable eyes. She'd trusted him. She'd loved him.

"I can't stop now," she muttered under her breath, the words barely audible over the hum of the equipment and the howl of the wind. Her nails bit into her palms as she clenched her fists. "I have to see this through."

"Alice," Eloise's voice broke through her thoughts, softer now. "I understand how important this is to you but pushing further into this weather... it's dangerous. For all of us."

Alice's gaze darted back to the monitors, where the data continued to scroll uselessly. The patterns were meaningless, just a labyrinth of data and static that offered no answers.

"Then we keep looking," she said through gritted teeth. "Expand the search area. Double the scans. I don't care what it takes—just find it."

Eloise exchanged a glance with Captain Miles, who tightened his grip on the wheel. The boat pitched violently as another wave struck, and the captain cursed under his breath.

"You've got fifteen minutes," he growled, his voice taut with frustration. "After that, we're heading back, whether you like it or not."

Alice opened her mouth to argue, but before she could speak, Eloise stiffened in her chair.

"Wait," Eloise said, her eyes narrowing at the monitor. Her fingers flew over the keyboard, adjusting the feed. "I think I've got something."

Eloise's fingers darted across the keyboard, her eyes narrowing at the faint shadow on the screen. She leaned closer, her brow furrowing in concentration. The soft beeping of the sonar filled the cabin, a rhythmic pulse that seemed to echo Alice's racing heart.

"What is it?" Alice asked, as she leaned over Eloise's shoulder, her gaze fixed on the murky outline on the screen.

Eloise exhaled sharply, her lips pressing into a thin line. "It's hard to say. It could be a geological feature—a cluster of rocks or a ridge on the seafloor. But the shape..." She trailed off, adjusting the display to zoom in further. "The edges are too clean, too structured. It doesn't look natural."

Alice felt a surge of adrenaline. "So, it could be the yacht?"

Eloise hesitated, her fingers hovering over the controls. "It's possible. But I can't confirm that yet. We need more data—sonar isn't perfect. Sometimes shadows can play tricks on the imaging. It could just as easily be debris from another shipwreck, or even equipment left behind by fishing vessels."

"But it's close to the search area," Alice pressed, her voice rising. "That can't be a coincidence."

Eloise turned to face her; her expression measured but tinged with sympathy. "And that's why we're taking it seriously. But, Alice, I need you to understand something. Even if this is the yacht, we don't know what condition it's in. It could be buried under sediment, damaged beyond recognition. And if we do find it... it might not give you the answers you're hoping for."

Alice's chest tightened, her breath hitching. "I don't care what condition it's in. I just need to know. I need to see it for myself."

Eloise studied her for a moment, her sharp eyes softening. "I get it," she said quietly. "I really do. But I've been on dives like this before, and I've seen how hard it can be—how much it takes out of people. Sometimes finding the wreck doesn't bring closure. Sometimes it just raises more questions."

Alice's hands clenched into fists at her sides. "I'd rather have more questions than live with the ones I have now. I can't—" Her voice cracked, and she turned away, staring out the cabin window at the sea.

Eloise's gaze softened further. "I understand. And we'll do everything we can to get answers. But you need to prepare yourself. Even if we find the yacht, even if we find something conclusive..."

Alice turned back to her, her eyes blazing. "I'm not looking for comfort, Eloise. I'm looking for the truth."

Eloise nodded slowly; her expression unreadable. "All right," she said, turning back to the monitors. "Let's see what we're dealing with."

She adjusted the sonar imaging again, filtering out some of the background noise to bring the shadow into sharper focus. The shape became clearer—a long, narrow structure with what looked like broken edges on one side. Eloise's shoulders tensed as she analysed the image.

"It's long enough to be a yacht," she murmured, almost to herself. "And that break in the hull..."

Alice's breath caught in her throat. "You think it's *The Governess*?"

"I think it's a possibility," Eloise said cautiously. "But we won't know for sure until we send the ROV down to get a visual."

Alice nodded; her expression set with determination. "Do it." But as she stared at the dark shape on the screen, her resolve wavered. Was she really ready for what lay ahead?

41

The air inside Evermere was thick with tension. Aiden stood in the grand entryway, his fists clenched at his sides as Ian paced in front of him, his polished shoes echoing ominously against the marble floor. The sound grated on Aiden's nerves, each step stoking the fire of his already simmering anger.

"Cutting it a bit close, aren't we?" Ian drawled, his tone dripping with mockery. "I'd have thought you'd be on the defensive by now, scrambling to keep *your* precious empire from collapsing."

Aiden glared at him; his fists tight. "You seem awfully confident for a man whose name is plastered all over the news in connection with offshore accounts and bribery scandals. Shouldn't you be busy talking to your lawyers?"

Ian laughed, the sound low and infuriatingly amused. "Oh, I've got my lawyers working around the clock, don't you worry about that. But you and I both know I'll land on my feet. I always do. That's the difference between us, Aiden. I play to win."

Aiden leaned forward, his hands gripping the edge of the desk. "You're here for a reason, so why don't you stop wasting my time and get to the point?"

Ian's grin widened, his eyes glinting with malice. "The point is, I know you're behind this little crusade against me. All those files, the damning evidence conveniently leaked to the press—it has your fingerprints all over it."

"You overestimate my interest in your downfall," Aiden said coldly, though his pulse quickened. "I've got better things to do than dig through your dirty laundry."

"Do you?" Ian's voice took on a mocking edge. "Because I seem to remember a time when you and I weren't so different. Back when you were cutting corners, making deals under the table, bending the rules to get ahead. You think you've cleaned up your act, but I know better. You're still that same man, Aiden. You just hide it better now."

Aiden's lips pressed into a thin line. "I'm not the one under investigation."

"Not yet," Ian shot back. "But you and I both know there are plenty of skeletons in your closet. It'd only take one whistleblower, one disgruntled employee, to shine a light on all those carefully hidden secrets. And trust me, the world would love to watch the great Aiden Chandler fall."

Aiden forced himself to stay calm, though his hands itched to throw Ian out of his house. "What do you want, Ian? A confession? An apology? You're not getting either."

Ian tilted his head, his expression smug. "Oh, I'm not here for an apology. I'm here to remind you that I don't go down without a fight. And if I burn, I'll make sure you burn with me."

Aiden's patience snapped. "You think you can intimidate me? I've dealt with worse than you, Ian. You're just a relic—a parasite clinging to power you don't deserve."

"Careful, Aiden," Ian warned, his smirk fading. "You might want to watch your mouth. After all, you've got just as much to lose as I do. Maybe even more. I mean, what would your darling wife think if she knew just how deep your hands were in the muck?"

Aiden froze, his stomach twisting. "Leave Alice out of this."

"Why? Are you worried she'll start asking questions? Worried she'll look at you the way Lydia did, once she figured it out?"

Aiden's fists clenched, but Ian wasn't finished. He leaned forward, his voice dropping to a low, venomous tone. "Oh, don't look so surprised. Lydia and I talked about you all the time. She loved to complain about her 'brilliant, ambitious husband' who thought he could outsmart her. But you know what the best part was? When she'd crawl back to me, whispering all your dirty little secrets. That woman was a force of nature, Aiden, and she knew how to play you like a fiddle."

Aiden's vision blurred with rage. "Shut your mouth."

Ian's grin returned, taunting and cruel. "What's the matter? Can't handle the truth? Or is it the fact that Lydia and I didn't just talk? Because, trust me, she was just as good at certain other things as she was at manipulation."

Aiden shot to his feet, his fists slamming onto the desk. "I said, shut your mouth!"

Ian didn't flinch, his smugness only deepening. "Touched a nerve, have I? Relax, Aiden. Lydia was never yours to begin with. She was playing you from day one, and you were too blind to see it."

"You don't know anything about my marriage," Aiden hissed, his voice low and dangerous. "And if you ever so much as mention Alice's name again, I'll make sure you regret it."

Ian stood, smoothing his jacket with exaggerated calm. "Temper, temper. You should save that energy for when the wolves come knocking at your door. Because they will, Aiden. And when they do, I'll be there to enjoy the show. Lydia always said you were a brilliant liar. Let's see how long you can keep it up."

Aiden didn't move. His chest heaved as he fought to calm himself, but Ian's words lingered, digging into his mind like thorns. The mention of Lydia, of Alice—it was all too much.

"Do you know what your little leak has cost me?" Ian snarled, turning on Aiden with a ferocity that made him flinch despite himself. "Everything I've built, every ounce of credibility I've fought for—it's gone. And for what? A petty grudge? Some misguided sense of justice? All because I fucked your wife."

Aiden shot back, his voice trembling with equal parts fear and fury. "You'll regret saying that, Ian. Watch what comes out of your mouth."

Ian's face darkened, a vein in his temple pulsing visibly. He stepped closer, towering over Aiden. "You have no idea who you're playing with."

"I'm not playing!" Aiden snapped, the words spilling out before he could stop them. "You're the one who's been screwing everyone over for years, and now it's finally catching up with you. Don't blame me because you can't keep your own house in order."

The slap of Ian's palm against the nearest table was deafening. Papers and a crystal glass toppled to the floor, but neither man acknowledged them. Ian leaned in, his voice dropping to a dangerous whisper.

"If you think this is about me," he said, his eyes gleaming with malice, "then you're a bigger fool than I thought. This is about you. About Alice. And if you think for one second that I won't do whatever it takes to protect what's mine, you're sorely mistaken."

Aiden stiffened, his blood running cold. "What do you mean, 'whatever it takes'?"

Ian's lips curled into a cruel smile. "I mean I've tolerated her meddling long enough. She's a liability—one I won't hesitate to remove if she keeps sticking her nose where it doesn't belong."

Aiden's vision went red. The words hit him like a physical blow, and before he realised what he was doing, he was lunging at Ian. "You bastard!"

The impact of his shoulder sent Ian stumbling backward, but he quickly regained his footing, shoving Aiden off with surprising strength. "You think you can take me?" Ian sneered, his voice dripping with disdain. "You're even more pathetic than I thought."

Aiden didn't respond. Rage had overtaken him. He swung a wild punch, which Ian narrowly dodged, countering with a blow to Aiden's ribs that sent him staggering. The pain was sharp, but it only fuelled Aiden's fury.

The two men grappled, crashing into a side table that splintered under their weight. Ian had the advantage of size and experience, but Aiden's raw anger gave him an edge, his punches landing with a force that seemed to surprise even him.

"Stay away!" Aiden shouted; his voice hoarse as he pinned Ian against the wall. "If you so much as touch her—"

Ian twisted free, slamming Aiden against the wall in return. "Or what? You'll ruin me even more? You've already taken everything from me. Maybe it's time I returned the favour."

Both men were breathing heavily now, their faces flushed and their clothes dishevelled. Ian sneered, wiping a trickle of blood from the corner of his mouth. "You think you're protecting her, but all you're doing is making her a target. If you want to keep her safe, maybe you should stop acting like a hero and start thinking about the consequences of your actions."

Aiden's chest heaved, his hands trembling at his sides. "If you so much as look at her the wrong way, I'll kill you."

Ian laughed, a low, chilling sound. "You don't have it in you."

They stood there, glaring at each other, the weight of

unspoken threats filling the room. Finally, Ian straightened his coat, his movements deliberate and controlled.

"You're lucky I don't finish this now," he said, his tone icy. "But this isn't over, Aiden. Not by a long shot."

Aiden's hands were still trembling, his chest tight with lingering fury. He looked around at the shattered table, the fallen glass, the papers scattered like debris, and the suffocating silence of the house.

This isn't over.

Aiden exhaled shakily, leaning against the wall for support. Somewhere out there, Alice was fighting her own battle. And now, more than ever, he knew he had to find her—before Ian did.

With one final lunge, Aiden catapulted himself forward and flung open a draw. Spinning round to face Ian, he held the gun up and fired one deafening shot.

42

The boat groaned and shuddered, the storm screaming like a banshee through the rigging. Waves rose like walls of black water, crashing against the sides with a force that threatened to tear the vessel apart. Inside the cabin, Eloise sat hunched over her station, her face illuminated by the pale glow of the monitors. Her fingers flew across the keyboard, her focus unwavering despite the chaos outside.

Her words barely carried over the relentless drumming of rain on the metal hull. "It's big. The way the sonar's bouncing... it's fibreglass. Definitely not natural."

"Is it the yacht?" Alice demanded, gripping the edge of the console for balance as the boat pitched violently beneath her.

"It's the right size," Eloise replied, her tone cautious. "But I can't confirm until I get a visual."

"Then get the camera down there faster," Alice urged, her voice trembling. "Now."

Eloise hesitated, her gaze flickering to the window in earnest. The boat rocked again, nearly throwing her out of her chair. Captain Miles shouted from the wheel; his voice barely audible over the din.

"We're running out of time!" he bellowed. "If we don't turn back soon, we're not making it out of this alive!"

"Not yet!" Alice yelled back, her voice raw and desperate. "We're so close!"

She could see the captain's glare through the cabin door, his hands clenched around the wheel, his knuckles white. But she didn't care. Turning back now wasn't an option.

Eloise exhaled sharply, her fingers tightening on the controls. "Fine," she muttered. She reached for the joystick that controlled the ROV—a remotely operated underwater vehicle equipped with a camera. The small robotic unit hung off the back of the boat, tethered by a thick cable. Eloise pressed a series of buttons, releasing the ROV into the dark abyss below.

The screen lit up with the camera feed, a grainy view of murky water and particles floating in the current. The weather made the descent rough, the tether jerking as the boat swayed above. Eloise adjusted the controls with practiced precision, guiding the robot deeper.

"Come on," she whispered, her eyes glued to the screen.

Alice's own gaze was locked on the flickering monitor, her heart hammering against her ribs. Her breath came in shallow gasps, the air thick and suffocating in the cramped cabin. Her mind raced, a torrent of fear and obsession that refused to be silenced.

She couldn't bear the idea of leaving here empty-handed. Not after coming this far. Not after risking so much. The thought sent a wave of panic through her, and she clenched her fists, her nails digging into her palms.

But then, a darker thought slithered into her mind, coiling around her like a serpent.

Alice closed her eyes for a moment. She had told herself this was about finding closure. But deep down, she knew it was more than that. This search wasn't just about Lydia—it was about

Alice's own sanity, her need to unravel the twisted threads of her life before they strangled her completely.

The screen flickered, drawing her attention back. The ROV's camera was descending steadily, the beam of its light cutting through the inky darkness. Shapes began to emerge in the murk—rocks, seaweed, the occasional flicker of movement as a fish darted past. But nothing definitive. Nothing that looked like a yacht.

Eloise's fingers moved over the controls; her brow furrowed in concentration. Captain Miles shouted something from the wheelhouse—another warning—but his words barely registered.

Alice leaned closer to the screen, her eyes narrowing as she searched for anything. The camera's light swept over the ocean floor, revealing jagged ridges and depressions that seemed to stretch endlessly into the void.

And then, there it was.

A shadow. Faint at first, barely distinguishable from the surrounding darkness. But as the ROV moved closer, the shape began to take form—a long, slender hull partially buried in the silt. The beam of the camera caught the glint of metal, the curve of a railing twisted and bent by time and pressure.

Alice's breath hitched, her chest tightening as she gripped the edge of the console. "Is that—?"

Eloise didn't answer immediately. She adjusted the camera angle, bringing the shadowy figure into sharper focus. The screen flickered again, and then the image was clear: the remains of a yacht, its once-sleek design now battered and broken, the name barely visible on the side.

"The Governess," Eloise said, her voice barely audible over the crash of the waves.

Alice felt her knees buckle, and she sank into the nearest chair, her hands trembling. She stared at the screen, her mind a whirlwind of emotions—relief, fear, disbelief. They had found it. After all this time, they had found it.

But as the camera continued its slow exploration of the wreckage, another thought crept into Alice's mind, chilling her to the bone, while another wave struck the boat, slamming against the hull with a deafening crash. The force tilted the vessel dangerously to one side, sending a torrent of seawater rushing across the deck. David, gripping a railing near the cabin, nearly lost his footing as the cold water surged around his ankles. His breath came in short, panicked gasps, the relentless assault making it nearly impossible to think clearly.

"This is insane!" David shouted, his voice cracking with fear. "We're not going to make it back if this keeps up!"

His hands fumbled for his phone, slick with water as he tried to compose a message.

Aiden, we're in trouble. Out on a boat with Alice. Weather's worse than we thought. Might not make it to shore.

His hands trembled as he hit send, watching the spinning circle of a weak signal struggle to deliver the message. He didn't know if it had gone through and didn't have time to check. Another wave, higher and angrier than the last, loomed in the distance.

The lightning lit it up like a spectral wall of black water, its crest curling with malicious intent. David's stomach dropped. The wave was too big; it could swallow them whole. His grip on the railing tightened until his knuckles turned white. "We need to pull back!" he shouted, his words lost in the cacophony. "Alice, Eloise—whatever you're doing, stop now!"

"Not yet!" Alice's voice rose above the chaos, sharp and defiant. She stood in the cabin, her hair plastered to her face, her eyes blazing with something almost unhinged. Her hands were on the back of Eloise's chair, clutching it as if the connection to the controls could somehow anchor her in the madness of it all.

David could see the desperation etched into every line of her face. Her pale skin glistened with rain, her lips pressed into a thin, determined line. She wasn't afraid—not of the waves, not even of death. It chilled him to the bone.

"Alice!" David yelled again, his voice cracking. "You're going to get us killed!"

She turned to him briefly, her eyes fierce and resolute. "If we don't do this, we'll never know! We'll never know the truth!" Her voice broke slightly, but the conviction in it was unshakable.

David wanted to scream at her, shake her, make her see sense. But he knew it wouldn't matter. Alice was far beyond reason now. Her obsession had taken hold, driving her to the edge. She would rather die out here, than live with the questions that haunted her.

Inside the cabin, Eloise was hunched over her station, her face gaunt but focused. The monitors flickered and shook with the motion of the boat, the ROV feed distorted by the turbulence. Still, she worked with practiced precision, her hands flying over the controls as the camera moved closer to the shadowy mass below.

"There!" Eloise's voice broke through.

Alice's breath hitched; her eyes fixed on the screen. The fibreglass hull was barely visible, shrouded in sediment and marine growth, but it was there. A mass of man-made structure buried in the silt, tantalizingly close.

"Get closer," Alice commanded, her voice shaking with urgency. "We need to see it clearly."

"I'm trying!" Eloise shot back, her hands trembling as she adjusted the controls. The current was making the ROV's movements erratic, the tether jerking with every wave that rocked the boat. "It's partially buried..."

David stumbled into the cabin, drenched and wide-eyed. "We're going to capsize!" he shouted, his voice high with panic. "Captain Miles is signalling mayday! We need to turn back before it's too late!"

"Not yet!" Alice's voice was a raw scream, filled with a mix of desperation and fury. She turned on David, her eyes blazing. "We're so close! We can't turn back now!"

David was shaking, his hands flailing as he tried to reason with her. "Alice, listen to yourself!"

Her expression faltered for a moment, her lips parting as if to respond. But then she looked back at the screen, where the outline of the wreck was becoming clearer with every second. Her face hardened again. "If you don't want to be here, David, then go below deck and wait it out. But I'm not stopping."

David stared at her, his chest heaving with panic and frustration. He turned to Eloise, who was biting her lip, her fingers hesitating over the controls. "Eloise, please," he begged. "Tell her this is insane!"

Eloise glanced at Alice, then back at David, her face torn with indecision. "We're pushing it," she said, her voice strained. "If these waves gets any bigger, we won't be able to recover the ROV, let alone make it back to shore."

"I don't care!" Alice shouted, slamming her hands on the console. "We're not leaving until we have proof. I need to know. Don't you get it? I need to know what happened to her. I need to know the truth about Aiden!"

The cabin fell silent except for the beep of the sonar. David stared at Alice, his face pale with shock. He had known she was desperate, but he hadn't realised how deeply this obsession had consumed her.

"Alice..." he began, his voice barely audible.

But before he could say more, another wave struck the boat, larger than the last. The cabin lurched violently, throwing Eloise out of her chair and sending equipment crashing to the floor. The monitor flickered, the image of the wreck fading into static.

Captain Miles's voice bellowed from the wheelhouse. "We're out of time! I'm turning this ship around, and if you don't like it, you can jump overboard!"

Alice's eyes darted back to the monitor, her breath coming in ragged gasps. The camera feed sputtered back to life, showing the wreck for a brief moment before cutting out again. And then they saw it. The skeleton, at the bottom of the ocean, trapped within the ribs of the body of the boat wreck.

David reached out, his voice shaking. "Alice, please. We have to go."

For a moment, she didn't move, her eyes fixed on the static-filled screen. Then, slowly, she turned to face him. Her face was pale, her eyes red-rimmed, but the fire in them hadn't dimmed.

"She's really gone," she said quietly, her voice cold and unyielding. "I faced it. And now, she's really gone."

David nodded, swallowing hard, relieved it was finally over. Alice could stop now. She'd found what she was looking for, even if it might kill them all.

43

The rain lashed against the windshield, the relentless drumming drowning out the hum of the radio and the occasional chime of his phone's unanswered calls. Aiden gripped the steering wheel of his Lamborghini, his knuckles bone-white against the sleek leather. The wipers screeched across the glass, barely keeping pace with the torrent that blurred his view of the winding road.

Every twist and turn felt sharper, every puddle a potential hazard threatening to spin the car out of control. He tightened his grip, his teeth clenched as his mind raced with possibilities—each more terrifying than the last. His breath came short and ragged, matching the rhythm of his hammering pulse.

Lightning cracked across the sky, illuminating the rain-slicked road for a brief, searing moment. In the after flash, he saw her face—not Alice's, but Lydia's. Pale, frozen, her eyes wide with shock and betrayal. The memory hit him like a punch to the gut, making him recoil. His chest tightened, panic threatening to overwhelm him. He forced himself to focus on the road, pushing the car harder, faster, the engine growling like a caged animal.

"Alice, pick up," he growled, stabbing at his phone's screen with one hand while the other fought to keep the car steady. Her voicemail greeted him again, the sound cutting through his panic like a cruel taunt. He tossed the phone onto the passenger seat, cursing under his breath.

The harbour was still miles away, yet the distance felt insurmountable. He couldn't shake the image of Alice out there on the raging sea, the ocean dragging her down into its depths. The thought of her meeting Lydia's fate was unbearable. His hands trembled as he pushed the car even faster, the tires skidding dangerously on the waterlogged road.

Another flash of lightning illuminated the sky, and for a brief, haunting second, he imagined her. Alice, soaked to the bone, clinging desperately to the deck of a boat that was being tossed like a toy in the waves. Her hair plastered to her face; her eyes wild with fear. Or worse, her body submerged beneath the churning water, the darkness swallowing her whole.

"No," he muttered, shaking his head violently as if to dislodge the thought. "No, no, no." His voice rose with each repetition, the desperation in it raw and unguarded. He slammed his fist against the wheel.

The harbour lights appeared on the horizon, blurred and flickering through the rain. Relief surged through him, but it was fleeting, drowned out by the chaos that awaited him. He skidded into the parking lot, the car fishtailing before screeching to a halt. He barely waited for the engine to shut off before flinging the door open and stepping into the downpour.

The rain hit him like ice, soaking through his clothes in seconds, but he barely felt it. His breath came in sharp gasps as his eyes scanned the scene. The dock was a frenzy of activity, rescue crews in yellow slickers hauling equipment and shouting commands. Coast Guard vehicles lined the pier, their red and blue lights flashing in rapid, disorienting bursts that painted the dark, angry sky in chaotic streaks of colour.

"Alice!" he shouted, his voice hoarse and desperate. It was swallowed by the wind, carried off before it could reach anyone's ears. He stumbled forward, his shoes slipping on the wet pavement as he made his way toward the commotion. Every fibre of his being screamed at him to move faster, to find her before it was too late.

A uniformed officer spotted him and stepped into his path, holding up a hand. "Sir, you can't be here—"

"Where is she?" Aiden cut him off, his voice a low growl. "My wife—Alice Chandler—where is she? Is she out there?" He gestured wildly toward the roiling ocean, his panic boiling over.

The officer hesitated, his expression softening slightly as he recognised Aiden.

"She's out there. Do something! Send a boat, a helicopter—anything!"

"Sir, we've already coordinated rescue efforts," the officer said firmly. "But if she's not already in distress, we risk putting more lives in danger by sending anyone out there."

Aiden's chest heaved as he stared at the man, his words barely registering. His mind was a cacophony of fear and regret. He should have stopped her. He should have listened more closely, seen the signs, done something—anything—to prevent this.

His phone buzzed in his pocket, startling him. He fumbled to retrieve it, his wet fingers struggling against the fabric. The screen glowed dimly in the rain, a single message flashing on the screen: David: *We're in trouble. Weather worse than expected. Boat unstable.*

Aiden's blood ran cold. His vision narrowed, the world around him reduced to the glowing screen and the weight of the words it carried. Boat unstable. The phrase echoed in his mind, a death knell that threatened to drown him.

"Sir?" The officer's voice broke through his haze, but Aiden barely heard it. He pushed past the man, heading toward the dock's edge, his shoes slipping dangerously close to the water.

"Alice!" he screamed, his voice raw.

Somewhere out there, Alice was fighting for her life—or worse, she wasn't. And Aiden, for all his power and wealth, was utterly helpless. The realisation hit him like a blow to the chest, leaving him gasping for air as the rain poured down, mingling with the tears he could no longer hold back.

The rain was relentless, a cold, biting force that blurred Aiden's vision as he sprinted toward the edge of the harbour. His shoes splashed through deep puddles, soaking his trousers, but he barely felt it. The storm roared around him, the wind tearing at his coat and sending stinging droplets against his face. He skidded to a stop on the slick pavement, his chest heaving as his eyes locked onto the distant lights of a boat emerging through the driving rain.

It wasn't just any boat. He recognized the red and white markings of the Coast Guard. The vessel bobbed precariously as it fought its way toward the harbour, each wave threatening to swallow it whole.

"No," Aiden muttered under his breath, his heart pounding in his chest.

He spotted an officer on the pier, a woman in a bright yellow rain slicker, her face shadowed under the brim of her hood. She was shouting orders to a group of crew members who were scrambling to prepare for the boat's arrival. Aiden made a beeline for her, the desperation surging inside him overtaking any sense of decorum.

"What's happening?" he shouted. "Why is the boat coming back?"

The officer turned to him, her face grim and wet with rain. "Sir, you need to stay back. It's not safe."

Aiden ignored her, stepping closer, his hands clenched into fists. "I need answers! My wife is out there! Why are they turning back? Did they find her?"

The officer hesitated, her lips pressing into a thin line. "It's worse than we first thought," she said finally, her voice steady but laced with frustration. "The conditions are too dangerous."

Aiden's stomach dropped. "You're giving up?" His voice cracked, raw with disbelief. "She's still out there, and you're giving up?"

"We're not giving up," the officer said firmly, meeting his wild gaze. "We're regrouping. The team's been out there for hours in impossible conditions. If we lose them, we lose everyone."

"That's not good enough!" Aiden shouted, the words ripping from him like a primal cry. "You can't just leave her out there to die! She's—she's out there, and you're just... turning back?"

The officer's expression hardened, though there was a flicker of something—pity, perhaps—in her eyes. "Sir, I understand how you're feeling, but this is unlike anything we've seen in months. If the boat stays out there, they won't make it back. We're doing everything we can to keep the search going, but we have to do it safely."

Aiden's jaw clenched. He turned back toward the water, his eyes straining to see through the rain. The Coast Guard boat was still far from the dock, its running lights flickering like fragile beacons against the chaos of the waves. Each time it dipped into a trough, he feared it wouldn't rise again.

He turned back to the officer, stepping closer, his voice low and trembling with desperation. "You don't understand. She's all I have. If she doesn't come back..." He broke off, unable to finish the thought, the words choking him.

The officer placed a firm hand on his arm, her grip grounding but unyielding. "We're not stopping, sir. We're going to keep looking. But you need to let us handle this."

Aiden jerked his arm away, pacing the slick dock like a caged animal. His mind raced, images flashing before him of Alice, her voice calling his name one last time. He pressed his hands to his face, trying to block the thoughts, but they wouldn't stop.

Another voice broke through the chaos—a Coast Guard crew member running up from the shoreline. "The radio's back up!" he shouted, his voice strained. "They've reported a potential sighting just before they turned back."

Aiden froze, his hands dropping from his face. He spun to the officer. "A sighting? Of what? The boat? Did they find it? Did they find her?"

The officer didn't respond immediately, turning to the crew member for clarification. "What kind of sighting?"

The crew member hesitated, glancing nervously at Aiden before answering. "They didn't say. Just that the weather forced them to retreat before they could confirm."

Aiden felt a surge of anger rise in his chest. "So you're telling me they might have found her, and they just left?"

"It wasn't safe!" the officer snapped, her patience fraying. "Do you think we want to leave anyone out there? Do you think we're not doing everything we can?"

Aiden opened his mouth to argue but stopped, his shoulders slumping as the weight of her words hit him. The rain continued to pelt down, cold and unrelenting, as the Coast Guard boat drew closer to the dock. Aiden watched, gripped by a mix of dread and hope as the vessel neared and the crew aboard moved with weary efficiency, their faces etched with exhaustion. Aiden stepped forward again, his voice shaking as he called out, "Did you find her? Did you find Alice?"

No one answered immediately, and the silence that stretched

between his question and their reply was deafening. Aiden's knees felt weak, and the air suddenly seemed quieter, the howling wind muffled by the pounding of his heart.

The officer touched his arm again, more gently this time. "We'll go back out," she said, her voice softer. "As soon as it's safe."

Aiden shook his head, his voice barely a whisper. "I can't lose her."

The officer didn't respond. Aiden turned back to the water, his hands trembling as he watched the boat come in. All he could do now was wait, hope, and pray that Alice was still out there, somewhere, alive.

44

Aiden watched in breathless anticipation as the rescue workers disembarked first, their faces weary and grim as they helped the crew unload equipment.

And then he saw her.

Alice appeared at the edge of the gangway; her frame draped in a heavy blanket that hung loosely around her shoulders. Her soaked hair clung to her face, and her pale skin seemed almost translucent in the harsh glare of the dock lights. She moved stiffly, her steps uncertain.

Aiden broke into a run, his feet splashing through cold puddles as he closed the distance between them. "Alice!" he shouted, his voice cracking with desperation.

She looked up slowly, her eyes dull and unfocused. Her expression was eerily calm, her movements mechanical as if she were moving through a dream—or a nightmare. When Aiden reached her, he stopped short, unsure of how to approach her. He wanted to grab her, to pull her into his arms and feel the warmth of her presence, to confirm that she was truly alive. But something about her stillness stopped him.

"You're safe," he said at last, his voice trembling with relief. "Thank God, you're safe."

Alice's lips parted, but the words seemed to come from somewhere far away. "They pulled us out just in time," she murmured. "The boat... it was taking on water. We had to abandon it."

Aiden frowned, his relief quickly giving way to unease. "What did you find?"

Alice's eyes flicked to his, dark and hollow, and for a moment, she said nothing. Then, with an almost imperceptible nod, she answered, "We found it. The yacht. It was down there, just like I thought."

His breath hitched. "Then... then it's over."

Alice's lips curled into a faint, bitter smile. "Is it?" she said softly. "I'm not so sure."

Aiden's stomach sank. "What do you mean?"

Her gaze drifted past him, toward the churning sea. "She didn't want me to find it," Alice said, her voice barely above a whisper. "I felt her out there, Aiden. It was her. She was trying to pull me under, just like she did with the others.

Aiden blinked, stunned. "Alice, that's..." He hesitated, his words faltering. "That's just shock. You were scared. It's normal to—"

"No." Her voice cut through his protests, sharp and certain. She turned back to him, her eyes blazing now with an intensity that chilled him. "It was her. I know it sounds crazy, but I felt her, Aiden. She didn't want me to survive."

Aiden stared at her. His throat tight with disbelief. He reached for her arm, his fingers brushing against the damp fabric of her blanket. "Alice, you're exhausted. You've been through hell. Let's get you home, and we can talk about this."

But Alice shook her head, her expression hardening. "She

wanted me to join her, Aiden. She wanted me to drown, to disappear just like she did. But I didn't. I survived. And now..." She exhaled sharply, a shuddering breath that seemed to release some of the tension in her body. "Now, she can't hurt me anymore."

Aiden didn't know what to say. He wanted to tell her she was right, that it was over, that Lydia's spirit—or whatever shadow she'd cast—was gone. But he knew their ordeal was far from over.

Because something was waiting for them back at Evermere. Another victim of this nightmare.

The memory of Ian's lifeless body flashed in his mind, the blood pooling on the marble floor. The consequences of that decision were waiting for him.

"Aiden?" Alice's voice drew him back, her gaze searching his face. "What is it?"

He forced a smile. "Nothing," he lied. "I'm just... relieved you're okay."

She didn't look convinced, but before she could press further, David appeared at her side, his face lined with worry. "Alice," he said softly, his voice gentle but firm. "We need to get you checked out. The medics are waiting."

Alice hesitated, her eyes flicking between David and Aiden. Then, with a small nod, she allowed David to guide her toward the waiting ambulance.

Aiden watched her go, his chest tight with a mix of relief and dread. She was safe, for now. But the danger she had escaped at sea was nothing compared to what was waiting for them both back at home.

45

The soft hum of fluorescent lights filled the quiet hospital room as the first rays of dawn filtered through the blinds. Aiden sat slumped in a plastic chair by Alice's bedside, his head resting against the wall, his eyes half-closed. He hadn't left her side all night. The sterile smell of antiseptic lingered in the air, mingling with the faint rustle of nurses outside in the hallway.

Alice stirred in the bed. The thin blanket tangled around her legs. She blinked against the pale morning light, her eyes finding Aiden. He straightened when he saw her awake, leaning forward with an anxious expression.

"How are you feeling?" he asked, his voice low, as though afraid to disturb the fragile calm of the moment.

"Tired," she murmured, her throat dry. "But okay."

Aiden reached for the water cup on the side table, handing it to her.

"You didn't have to stay all night," Alice said softly, though a part of her was glad he had.

Aiden shook his head. "I wasn't going anywhere. Not after..." He trailed off.

Alice didn't press him, but the unspoken weight of

everything they had been through settled on her chest like a stone. She pushed herself up into a sitting position, wincing as her stiff muscles protested. "What time is it?"

"Just after seven," Aiden replied, glancing at his watch. "The doctor said you could leave this morning. I've already signed the paperwork."

Alice nodded, swinging her legs over the side of the bed. She hesitated, her feet dangling just above the cold floor. Aiden stood immediately, stepping closer to help her, but she held up a hand. "I can do it."

He stepped back reluctantly, watching as she planted her feet and stood unsteadily. She swayed slightly, and his hand shot out instinctively, steadying her by the arm. She didn't pull away this time.

"I'll grab your things," Aiden said, his voice softer now. He retrieved her coat and shoes from the chair, setting them down in front of her.

Alice dressed slowly, the simple act feeling oddly significant. When she was ready, Aiden opened the door for her, and they stepped out into the corridor.

The hospital was quiet in the early hours, the muffled sounds of distant conversations and the soft beeping of monitors creating a subdued backdrop. They walked side by side toward the exit, neither speaking.

When they reached the revolving doors, the crisp morning air hit Alice like a shock. It was a stark contrast to the clinical atmosphere of the hospital, and for a moment, she simply stood there, breathing it in.

Aiden had parked the car nearby, the sleek black Lamborghini glinting in the early sunlight. He moved ahead to open the passenger door, his movements careful, as though afraid to break whatever fragile equilibrium they had found.

“Ready?” he asked, looking at her with a mixture of concern and hope.

Alice nodded, sliding into the seat without a word. As Aiden walked around to the driver’s side, she stared out the window, watching the world slowly come to life. The normalcy of it all felt almost alien after everything that had happened and what was wating for them at home.

When Aiden got in and started the engine, the familiar low growl filled the air. He pulled out of the lot smoothly, and for a while, neither of them spoke, the quiet stretching between them like the open road ahead.

Finally, it was Alice who broke the silence. "I’ve been thinking," she began, her voice measured. "About Lydia. About that day."

Aiden’s hands tightened on the wheel; his gaze fixed on the road. "You don’t have to—"

"No," Alice interrupted, her tone firm but not unkind. "I need to say this. I’ve spent so much time trying to understand her. Trying to piece together what happened, why she was the way she was. And after everything—after finding her yacht, I think I finally see it."

Aiden glanced at her briefly, his expression wary. "See what?"

"How manipulative and cruel she was," Alice said quietly, staring out the window. “I thought I could handle it. I thought I was immune to it. But I wasn’t. She got to me, too, even when she wasn’t here."

Aiden didn’t respond as he navigated a sharp turn. When he finally spoke, his voice was soft. "She wasn’t always like that, you know. At least, I don’t think she was. But by the time I realised what she’d become, it was too late. I was in too deep."

Alice turned to look at him, her gaze steady. "I believe you. And I understand now. I see how much you’ve been trying to make up for it—for everything. And I know you love me, Aiden. I see that, too."

His grip on the wheel loosened slightly, and he exhaled, a small but noticeable release of tension. "I do," he said simply. "More than anything."

They drove in silence for a few moments, through the quiet streets. The Evermere estate was still a way off, but the thought of returning to it—its grandeur, its ghosts—loomed in the distance like a thunder cloud.

"I want us to start again," Alice said finally, her voice cutting through the quiet. "No more lies, no more secrets. Whatever was left of Lydia, I've laid it to rest. I don't want her shadow hanging over us anymore."

Aiden glanced at her; his brow furrowed. "After everything—"

"I'm sure," she said, cutting him off gently. "I survived, Aiden. I survived her. And now, I want us to move on. To build something real. Together."

Her words hung in the air, fragile but full of hope. Aiden nodded slowly; his hands steady on the wheel. "I want that, too," he said.

The car drove through the rolling countryside, the rhythmic sound of the tyres on the wet road the only thing breaking the silence between them. Aiden kept glancing at Alice, her gaze remained fixed out of the window, distant and unreadable.

Finally, Aiden couldn't take it any longer. "Alice," he began, his voice tentative. "Are you going to tell me what happened out there?"

Her eyes flicked toward him briefly before returning to the blur of passing fields. For a moment, she said nothing, and Aiden wondered if she was even going to answer. But then she exhaled, a long, slow breath, and turned to face him.

"I saw her," she said, her voice barely above a whisper.

Aiden's heart stuttered. His hands tightened on the wheel. "What do you mean?" he asked, his voice trembling slightly. "Saw who?"

"Lydia," Alice replied, her tone flat, emotionless. "Or what's left of her."

Aiden's chest tightened, and he swallowed hard. "Alice, I don't—"

"She's gone, Aiden," Alice interrupted, her voice gaining a sharp edge. "Truly gone. There's no doubt anymore. I saw her skeleton. The camera feed—it showed the remains. She was still on the yacht, lying there in the wreckage, surrounded by the sea. It's over. She's... over."

The words hit Aiden like a punch to the gut. He kept his eyes on the road as he tried to steady his breathing.

Alice shook her head, a bitter laugh escaping her lips. "The way she was lying there... the way the sea had claimed her. It was her. Lydia is dead, and now I've seen it with my own eyes."

Aiden didn't know what to say. His mind raced with questions, with the haunting images her words conjured. "The others... David, Eloise—did they see it too?"

Alice hesitated, then nodded. "They did. But no one said anything. Not out loud, anyway. We all knew what we were looking at, though."

The air in the car felt heavy. Aiden's throat tightened as he tried to form a response, but nothing felt adequate. "I don't know if this gives you the closure you were looking for," he said finally, his voice barely above a whisper. "But... I'm sorry you had to see that."

Alice turned back to the window, her fingers gripping the edge of her coat. "It does," she said after a moment. "In a way. I always thought that finding her, knowing for sure, would help me let her go. And maybe it will, eventually. But right now..." She trailed off, shaking her head.

"Right now?" Aiden prompted gently.

"Right now, all I feel is exhaustion," Alice admitted, her voice breaking slightly. "She's been a spectre between us for so long, haunting every corner of my life. It's like I've been fighting this battle for so long, I don't know how to stop."

Aiden's chest ached at her words. He reached over, his hand resting lightly on hers. "You don't have to do anything right now," he said softly. "Just breathe. Take it one step at a time."

Alice didn't pull her hand away, but she didn't acknowledge his touch, either. She simply stared out the window, her expression unreadable. "Do you think she hated me?" she asked suddenly, her voice small.

Aiden blinked, startled by the question. "What? No, Alice. Why would you think that?"

"She fought so hard to keep me out of your life," Alice said, her voice trembling. "Even in death, it felt like she was trying to push me away. I can't help but wonder if..."

Aiden shook his head vehemently. "Lydia wasn't capable of love, Alice. Not for me, not for anyone."

Alice turned to him, her eyes searching his face for answers. "And what about you, Aiden? Are you?"

Aiden's hand tightened on hers. "You have me," he said firmly. "You always have."

For a long moment, Alice held his gaze, her emotions flickering just beneath the surface. Then she pulled her hand away, folding her arms tightly across her chest as if to shield herself. "I need time," she said quietly. "To process all of this."

Aiden nodded, his heart sinking as he watched her retreat back into herself. "Take all the time you need," he said hoping she would come back to him soon.

The rest of the drive passed in silence, the weight of Lydia's final resting place lingering between them like a spectre. Aiden couldn't shake the image Alice had painted in his mind—a skeleton lying forgotten on the ocean floor, the last remnants of a woman who had once dominated his life. And now, even in death, she continued to cast a shadow over everything he held dear.

Alice smiled faintly, leaning her head back against the seat. For the first time in what felt like forever, the weight she'd been carrying eased, just a little.

But for Aiden, the nightmare was only beginning.

Aiden's grip on the wheel tightened, his knuckles going white. His heart raced, a cold sweat breaking out along his spine. Inside the walls of Evermere, Ian's body lay sprawled across the marble floor. The fight replayed in his mind—Ian's sneering threats, the surge of rage that had overtaken him, the sickening finality of it all.

He glanced at Alice, who was gazing out of the car window, oblivious to what was waiting for them. She believed they were free now, that they could start over. But the truth was a rotting weight in his chest, heavy and inescapable.

They came to a traffic light, and Aiden drove forward, his movements mechanical. He was dreading the moment the house would come into view, its imposing facade.

There was no way out of this—not now, not ever. He was resigned to the fact Ian, and Lydia, had won.

"Aiden?" Alice's voice broke through his thoughts. She turned to him, her brow furrowing. "Are you okay?"

He forced a smile, though it felt like his face might crack under the effort. "Yeah," he lied. "I'm fine."

But he wasn't fine. Everything was about to fall apart, and he had no idea how to hold it together. The past wasn't just behind them—it was waiting for them, inside that house, ready to destroy everything all over again.

46

The Lamborghini glided along the rain-slicked road, the faint hum of the engine filling the silence between Aiden and Alice. The storm had passed and beside him, Alice seemed at peace, her face calm as she gazed out the window, the weight of the past few days seemingly lifted from her shoulders.

Aiden, however, was far from calm. Every mile that brought them closer to the Chandler estate felt like a noose tightening around his neck. And yet, it wasn't Ian's death that truly haunted him now. It was Lydia's. The memory came unbidden, sharp and vivid despite his efforts to suppress it. The day they fought was etched into his soul, as inescapable as the estate itself.

Beside him, Alice sat motionless, her head leaning against the window as she gazed at the passing trees. She didn't know. Not the whole truth. And now, after everything, he wasn't sure how much longer he could keep it from her.

The memory crept in, slow and insistent, until it consumed him entirely.

. . .

It had started as so many of their fights had—with Lydia's voice, sharp and cutting, slicing through the fragile calm of the house. Aiden had been in his study, poring over paperwork for a deal that was already teetering on the edge of disaster. When Lydia stormed in, he had barely looked up.

"I'm leaving," she announced, her tone devoid of emotion, as if she were discussing the weather.

He'd blinked, his pen pausing mid-signature. "Excuse me?"

"I'm leaving, Aiden," Lydia repeated, stepping closer. Her eyes gleamed with something he couldn't place—triumph, maybe, or cruelty. "I've had enough of this charade. Enough of you."

Aiden had set the pen down, his chest tightening. "Don't be ridiculous, Lydia. You're not going anywhere. What about the baby?"

Her laugh was cold, a sound that cut through him like a knife. "You don't control me. Not anymore. And the baby, well" she examined her perfectly manicured hand.

She had thrown a stack of papers onto his desk, the force scattering them across the polished wood. "You think I didn't know?" she hissed, leaning closer. "The deals you've made, the corners you've cut—I know everything, Aiden. And when I leave, I'll make sure everyone else knows too. You'll never be a part of this child's life."

He'd felt the blood drain from his face as he scanned the papers. Emails. Contracts. Evidence of deals he had buried so deeply he thought they'd never surface. "Where did you get these?" he demanded, his voice low and dangerous.

Lydia smirked. "Does it matter? You should've been more careful. All you need to do is let me go and all this goes away."

The fight that followed was a blur of shouting and accusations, each word sharper than the last. She goaded him, pushed him further than she ever had before. And then she said it.

"Ian's better in every way," she had spat, her voice venomous. "He's smarter, stronger—and he doesn't flinch when I tell him the truth."

Aiden had frozen, his vision tunnelling as her words sank in. "What truth?" he demanded, his voice trembling with barely restrained rage.

Lydia's smile widened, a cruel, deliberate thing. "You're not the father, Aiden."

He didn't remember lunging for her. Didn't remember his hand striking her cheek or the sickening sound of her head hitting the edge of the desk as she fell. But the sight of her lying there, blood spreading beneath her head, was etched into his mind with terrifying clarity.

For a moment, he had stood frozen, his breath coming in ragged gasps as he stared at her motionless body. Panic clawed at his chest. He dropped to his knees beside her, his hands shaking as he touched her shoulder.

"Lydia," he whispered, his voice cracking. "Lydia, wake up."

But she didn't move. Her face was pale, her chest still. He had backed away, his hands slick with blood.

The sound of Alice's voice pulled him back to the present.

"Aiden?" she said softly, her brow furrowing as she turned to look at him. "Are you okay? You're gripping the wheel so hard."

He forced himself to relax, loosening his grip and flexing his fingers. "I'm fine," he lied, his voice tight. "Just tired."

Alice nodded, seemingly satisfied, and turned her gaze back to the road. But Aiden's heart was pounding, his chest tight with the weight of his secret.

Ian's death felt like an echo of Lydia's—a grim reminder that no matter how far he tried to run from his past, it always caught up to him. He had told himself her death was an accident, that he hadn't meant for it to happen. But now, with Ian's body lying in the estate, he couldn't shake the feeling that this was his punishment.

The universe, or fate, or whatever cruel force governed his life, was finally delivering its verdict. He had tried to start over. But the past had claws, and they were digging into him now, dragging him back into the darkness he had tried so hard to escape.

As the car raced along the coast road towards the estate, a cloud of smoke appeared on the horizon and as the turned the corner they saw it. The gates of Evermere came into view, Aiden felt a cold sweat break out along his spine. The mansion loomed ahead; its pristine facade being consumed by large angry flames.

47

The sky above Evermere was a smouldering canvas of orange and black, the fire raging with an intensity that seemed to consume not just the house but the very air around it. Smoke climbed in twisting plumes, choking the morning sky, and the roar of the flames was a deafening, relentless symphony. Each crackle, every crash of collapsing beams, reverberated in Aiden's chest like a drumbeat of doom.

He stood motionless at the edge of the driveway, his figure silhouetted against the chaos. His eyes, wide and unblinking, reflected the inferno as if the fire had burned its way into his soul. Beside him, Alice's trembling hand clutched at his arm, her soot-streaked face pale, her lips parted as though words were forming but couldn't quite escape.

"It's... gone," Alice whispered, her voice hollow. "Everything. All of it."

The words barely registered. Aiden's pulse roared in his ears, drowning out the world around him. His gaze was fixed on the crumbling mansion, the estate that had been the cornerstone of his identity. The empire he had built with Lydia, the legacy she had left behind, the lies he had buried within its walls—it was all disintegrating, swallowed by flames that danced higher with each passing second.

It should have felt like freedom. Like an absolution he didn't deserve but was somehow being granted. Yet the knot in his stomach tightened with every beam that fell, with every flicker of the fire's ravenous hunger. He wasn't free. Not yet.

Ian's body.

The thought struck him like a physical blow, and his breath hitched. He tried to push it aside, to let the fire be his saviour, but the pit of dread in his gut only deepened. His eyes darted involuntarily to where he knew the entryway had once stood. Beneath those flames, beneath the caved-in ceiling and the collapsing walls, Ian lay. And with him, the secrets that could tear Aiden's world apart.

He clenched his fists, the sweat on his palms mixing with soot and rain. The fire could erase so much—the bloodstains, the shattered glass, the echoes of their struggle—but it couldn't touch the bullet lodged in Ian's skull. That single, unyielding piece of evidence could undo everything. It would survive, impervious to the flames, waiting to be discovered.

The fire wasn't saving him. It was taunting him, consuming the facade he had worked so hard to maintain while leaving the truth intact.

"Aiden?" She turned to face him, her expression a mixture of shock and grief. "What happens now?"

He forced himself to meet her gaze, his heart pounding so loudly he was sure she could hear it. "We rebuild," he said, the words tasting like ash on his tongue. "This is just... a house. We'll rebuild."

Alice blinked, her brow furrowing as tears welled in her eyes.

He reached out, pulling her into his arms. "What matters is that we're safe," he murmured against her hair, the lie rolling off his tongue with practiced ease. "As long as we have each other, nothing else matters."

She nodded against his chest, her trust in him as unshaken as it had always been. But Aiden's mind was elsewhere, racing through a thousand possibilities, a thousand ways this could go wrong. The fire department would arrive soon—he could already hear the faint wail of sirens in the distance. They'd search the ruins, sift through the rubble. And they'd find him. Ian. Or what was left of him.

He pulled back slightly, his hands gripping Alice's shoulders as his eyes searched hers. "Listen to me," he said, his voice low but urgent. "No matter what happens, we'll get through this."

Alice nodded again, though the flicker of uncertainty in her gaze made his stomach twist. She didn't know. She couldn't know. And if he had any hope of keeping her, he had to make sure she never found out.

As the flames roared louder, the heat scorching even from a distance, Aiden watched his past evaporate like dust. His empire was gone, reduced to ash before his eyes. But it wasn't the house or the wealth that mattered now. It was the truth buried beneath it—and the lengths he'd have to go to keep it buried.

The sirens grew louder, the first flicker of red lights appearing on the horizon. Aiden's grip on Alice tightened as he turned her away from the inferno, shielding her from the destruction as though it would somehow protect her from the nightmare that was still to come.

Because the fire wasn't the end. It was just the beginning.

48

The flames lick higher into the sky, their orange glow turning the clouds into a bruised, fiery canvas. I stand at the edge of the woods, my breath visible in the cold night air, my hands trembling—but not from the chill. The heat from the fire washes over me even from here, its roar drowning out the distant sounds of sirens.

It's beautiful, in a way. Destruction always is. There's a kind of purity in it, in how it takes everything—truth, lies, regrets—and reduces them all to ash. Watching Evermere burn feels like writing the end of a chapter no one should ever read.

I can see them, standing together near the driveway, silhouettes against the raging fire. Aiden and Alice. So close, so unsuspecting. He doesn't know I'm here. He doesn't know I was *there*.

I heard everything.

I had come back to the house, my umbrella nearly torn from my grip as I made my way inside. The place was eerily quiet, the usual hum of the estate muted by the tempest raging outside. I'd come to confront Aiden, to ask him about the things I'd pieced together—the lies, the tension, the memories of Lydia that clung to him like a curse. But I hadn't expected to find *him*.

Ian.

He was pacing in the grand entryway, his voice sharp and venomous, echoing off the marble. I froze just inside the doorway, hidden by the shadows, as Aiden descended the stairs to meet him. Their argument started as most arguments do—with words, accusations hurled like daggers. The anger in Aiden's voice was the same as it was then. On the day he hit Lydia. On the day she disappeared.

"You're pathetic," Ian sneered, his voice carrying over the weather

outside. "You can't even keep your house in order. You've always been a fraud, Aiden. A fraud playing at being a man."

I removed my sodden shoes and crept forward, my footsteps silent.

"Get out," Aiden growled. "You've said your piece. Leave."

But Ian didn't leave. He stepped closer instead, his words dripping with venom. "Do you really think you can protect her? That little wife of yours? She's no better than Lydia was—grasping, desperate. And you? You'll ruin her, just like you ruined Lydia. It's who you are."

I heard the sound before I saw it—the crack of the gunshot echoing like a thunderclap inside the house. My breath caught in my throat, and I clutched the wall for support as I peeked around the corner.

Ian was on the floor, blood coming from his head, his lifeless eyes staring at the chandelier above. Aiden stood over him, the gun shaking in his hand, his chest heaving. For a moment, he looked like he might drop it, like he couldn't believe what he'd just done.

And then he moved. He knelt down, touched Ian's neck as if checking for a pulse—pointless, of course—and cursed under his breath. He staggered backward, his hands in his hair, muttering something I couldn't hear over the rain pounding against the windows.

I slipped away before he could see me, my heart racing, my mind spinning.

I could've called the police. I could've run. But I didn't. I protected him. Like I always have.

I made a choice.

I waited until Aiden left the house. I waited until the mansion was silent, ransacked the wine cellar of all its liquor, and I used it.

I didn't expect the fire to take so quickly, to spread like it had been waiting for someone to unleash it. But as the flames grew, licking hungrily at the wood and marble, I felt nothing but resolve.

Now, I watch the estate burn, my fingers tingling with the memory of the match I struck.

They'll call it an accident—weather damage, faulty wiring, something mundane.

I know better. I know where his body is now. And it will never be found. It's in the boot of his car. And soon, while eyes are focused on the fire, I will despose of both. Ian, like Lydia, will lie in a watery grave and this body will never give up its secrets.

I wonder if Aiden will ever realise I was the one who set the fire. Maybe he'll think fate intervened. Maybe he'll think it was Lydia's ghost. Maybe he'll think he just got lucky.

But I know the truth.

As I turn and walk back into the woods, the warmth of the fire fading with each step, I feel no regret. Sometimes, you have to burn everything down to start again. And is the chance I've given them. The chance to start again.

I just hope they make the most of it and don't let me down.

49

The California sun streamed through the expansive windows of their new mansion, casting a warm glow across the open living space. Aiden stood in the kitchen, sipping his morning coffee as he flipped through the stack of mail that had just been delivered. The aroma of freshly brewed beans mingled with the subtle scent of ocean air wafting in from the terrace.

Upstairs, Alice was humming softly to herself, her footsteps light as she moved about the soon-to-be nursery. Swatches of pastel fabrics draped over the furniture, and sample paint colours lined the windowsill. Her hands gently caressed her growing belly as she imagined the room filled with the laughter of their child.

"Aiden!" she called out, her voice laced with excitement. "What do you think about a woodland theme? Lots of cute animals?"

"Sounds perfect," he replied, a smile touching his lips.

He continued sorting through the mail—bills, a few housewarming cards, an invitation to a movie premier. Then his fingers paused on a simple postcard tucked between a glossy magazine and a utilities statement. It featured a serene beach at sunset, the colours vivid and inviting.

Frowning slightly, Aiden turned it over. His heart skipped a beat as he read the message written in neat, familiar handwriting:

"Enjoy your new life. Don't forget me. Don't forget what I did for you. I will always keep your secrets. I will always keep you safe." It was signed only with a K.

A chill ran down his spine. Karen. Karen who he'd let go after the fire at Evermere, who he'd paid off telling her to enjoy her retirement. Karen who had been by his side for years.

Memories of the fire surged back—the flames consuming the estate, erasing the evidence of Ian's death. He had suspected it was an accident, a tragic twist of fate that had saved him from ruin. But now it was clear: Karen had been there. She knew what he'd done, and she'd covered it up.

"Aiden?" Alice's voice floated down the staircase. "Could you come up here for a moment?"

He shoved the postcard into his pocket, forcing a calm expression onto his face. "Be right there!"

Quickly, he moved to the waste bin, hesitating for a fraction of a second before tearing the postcard into tiny pieces. He buried them beneath crumpled receipts and discarded envelopes. His mind raced as he headed toward his study, detouring to check the security system. The monitors displayed feeds from cameras strategically placed around the property—gates, driveways, perimeters—all appeared normal. No signs of intrusion.

But the unease persisted. The sanctuary of their new home now felt exposed, vulnerable.

"Aiden?" Alice called again, a hint of curiosity in her tone.

He took a deep breath, smoothing his features before making his way upstairs. He found her in the nursery, holding up two tiny onesies—one adorned with playful foxes, the other with smiling moons and stars.

"Which one do you like better?" she asked, her eyes sparkling with joy.

He managed a genuine smile. "They're both nice. But I think the foxes suit our little one."

She grinned. "I knew you'd pick that one." Placing the outfits on the crib, she approached him, wrapping her arms around his waist. "Everything okay? You seem a bit distracted."

Aiden looked into her eyes, the weight of his secrets pressing heavily upon him. "Just thinking about how lucky we are," he said softly. "How far we've come."

She rested her head on his chest. "We have a second chance at a real fresh start."

He held her close, wishing he could freeze this moment. "We do," he murmured. "And I want to make the most of it."

As they stood together, the sun bathed them in its warmth, but Aiden couldn't shake the cold dread settling in his stomach. Karen's message was clear—a reminder that she held the key to his darkest secret. The security he thought they'd found was an illusion, fragile and easily shattered.

"Why don't we take a walk on the beach later?" Alice suggested, pulling back to look at him. "Get some fresh air before the decorators arrive?"

"That sounds great," he agreed, forcing the anxiety from his voice.

She kissed him lightly on the cheek before turning back to her planning. "I'll just finish up here."

Aiden watched her for a moment, then slipped out of the room. His mind raced with possibilities. Could he confront Karen? Persuade her to stay silent? The uncertainty ate away at him.

Back in his study, he sat at his desk and stared blankly at the computer screen. The cursor blinked rhythmically, waiting for input. Instead, he reached into his pocket, fingers closing around the phantom weight of the postcard that was no longer there.

Aiden glanced out of the window toward the horizon, where the sea met the sky in a seamless blend. The future had seemed as boundless as that view, but now unease lurked at the edges.

He squared his shoulders, determination hardening his features. Whatever came next, he would face it. For Alice. For their unborn child. He would do anything to keep them safe.

But as he reached over to double-check the security system once more, a lingering doubt settled in his mind. Somewhere out there, Karen waited—a silent guardian or a ticking time bomb. Only time would tell.

50

Karen adjusted the wide-brimmed hat on her head, its soft grey fabric casting a shadow over her face. Her dark hair, usually straight and glossy, now cascaded in loose, unkempt waves, dyed a reddish hue that made her almost unrecognisable. A pair of oversized sunglasses shielded her eyes as she stood in the bustling shopping centre, blending seamlessly into the crowd.

From her vantage point near a café, she could see Alice walking leisurely between the stores, her hand resting protectively on her protruding belly. Her face was radiant, her smile soft as she browsed racks of baby clothes and nursery decorations. Karen noted the way Alice's other hand occasionally drifted to her stomach, a gesture that spoke of excitement and affection for the life growing within her.

Karen sipped her coffee, the bitter liquid grounding her as her gaze followed Alice's every move. She had always been good at watching, at staying unnoticed. It was a skill she'd honed over years—years of being the invisible helper, the silent protector. And now, it continued to serve her well.

Alice stopped in front of a window display featuring cribs and mobiles, her face lighting up as she stepped inside.

Karen's grip tightened on her cup, the thin cardboard crinkling slightly under the pressure. She rose from her seat, discarding the cup in a nearby bin before trailing Alice into the store.

The shop smelled of wood polish, the soft hum of music playing overhead. Karen kept her distance, lingering near a shelf of plush toys as Alice moved through the aisles, selecting items and placing them gently into her cart.

"A woodland theme," Alice said aloud to herself, smiling as she picked up a framed print of a fox nestled among trees. "Perfect."

She stepped closer, her movements careful, unhurried. Alice was examining a tiny pair of shoes now, her expression soft as she ran her fingers over the delicate fabric. Karen hesitated, her hand hovering near a row of blankets.

For a moment, she imagined speaking to Alice, letting her know she was there. Perhaps even congratulating her, as though they were old friends running into each other by chance. But she quickly dismissed the thought. It wasn't the right time—not yet. But she was close enough to smell the familiar scent of Alice's heady perfume. She breathed it in before she turned and moved toward the exit, slipping back into the flow of shoppers. Outside, the world felt brighter, harsher, the sun glinting off the glass storefronts. Karen adjusted her sunglasses, her mind racing as she walked to her car, parked strategically near the exit.

As she slid into the driver's seat, she allowed herself one last glance toward the shopping centre. Alice was still inside, oblivious to her presence, to the invisible threads that bound them together. Karen traced a finger along the steering wheel, her lips curling into a faint smile.

She had done so much for them. The fire, the secrets, the lies she'd buried to protect Aiden, to give him and Alice the life they so desperately wanted. She had erased the past for them, ensured they could start fresh.

Then her thoughts turned to Lydia. Aiden thought *he* was the one who had killed her, and Karen had allowed him to believe it. After all, that guilt had made him manageable, made him desperate to move forward. But Karen knew the truth, the truth she'd carried with her since that night.

It wasn't planned, not exactly. She had returned to the estate late that evening to deliver some documents Lydia had demanded. Karen had always been at Lydia's beck and call—her silent shadow, picking up the pieces of Lydia's manipulations and lies. But that night, the house felt different. The air was charged, thick with tension. As she walked inside, she heard the argument—Aiden and Lydia's voices cutting through the silence like knives.

Karen had stayed hidden, not out of fear but curiosity. She had known Lydia well enough to predict her manipulative tendencies, and she had wanted to see if Aiden would finally stand up to her. When he did, she felt something almost like relief.

Then came the crash. The sickening crack of Lydia's head hitting the table. Karen had waited, breathless, as Aiden froze in shock. When he stumbled out of the room moments later, Karen knew this was her moment.

She approached Lydia, who was still alive but barely. Her eyes fluttered open, her lips moving in a weak attempt to speak. Karen crouched beside her, leaning in close.

"Always the queen," Karen whispered, her voice low and trembling with years of suppressed anger. "Always the one in control. But not anymore."

Lydia's eyes widened, her hand twitching weakly, and for the first time, Karen saw fear in them. It was intoxicating.

She pressed her hands against Lydia's throat, her grip steady, ignoring the feeble attempts to struggle. It didn't take long. Lydia's body went limp, her last breath slipping away as Karen released her hold and sat back, her own breath shuddering.

When Aiden returned, panic written across his face, Karen had already cleared the area. She was the one who dragged Lydia's body to her car and then the yacht, and she was the one who took the boat out to sea and ensured it would sink. She was the one who had returned to shore under the cover of nightfall, in the small dingy. She was the one who let him believe the guilt was his alone.

The weather covered her tracks. Her loyalty had been absolute—her secret gift to him, though she knew he'd never know it.

Now, Karen pulled out of the parking lot, her eyes lingering on her reflection in the rearview mirror. The disguise suited her. It reminded her that she didn't need wealth or recognition to be powerful.

She had burned Evermere to the ground to protect Aiden from the evidence, just as she had dealt with Lydia to ensure her manipulations ended. She had saved him twice now, ensuring he could build the life he wanted with Alice.

But she hadn't done it for him entirely. She had done it for herself. And for Alice. For the daughter she never had. For the family she always wanted but had sacrificed in order to serve the Chandlers.

She had no choice but to put an end to the chaos Lydia had wrought. To ensure her own place in the story, even if it was hidden in the margins.

As she merged into the steady stream of traffic, Karen smiled. They thought they were free, that they had escaped the past. But she was still here, still watching, still ensuring the world didn't crumble beneath their feet.

Aiden and Alice didn't know it yet, but Karen had no intention of ever letting them forget. Because one day, they would need her again. And when that day came, she would be ready.

For now, she let the car blend into the steady stream of traffic, fading into the city as effortlessly as she had arrived. Caretakers never truly disappear—they linger, waiting for the moment they're needed.

And Karen had all the time in the world.

THE END

A NOTE FROM THE PUBLISHER

Thank you for reading! We hope you enjoyed this book. If it left an impression, we'd love for you to share your thoughts in a review on Amazon—your feedback helps other readers discover it too.

At **Black Swan Digital**, we're redefining storytelling with fresh, exciting releases at unbeatable prices. Plus, our community gets **exclusive discounts and early access** to new books. Want in? Join our mailing list here and never miss a great read!

Printed in Great Britain
by Amazon

60427974R00180